D0763443

Vienna Triangle

Other books by Brenda Webster:

Fiction:

The Beheading Game

Sins of the Mothers

Paradise Farm

Memoir:

The Last Good Freudian

Translation:

Lettera alla Madre, by Edith Bruck

Critical Studies:

Yeats: A Psychoanalytic Study

Blake's Prophetic Psychology

Edited:

Hungry for Light: The Journal of Ethel Schwabacher

VIENNA TRIANGLE

A Novel

Brenda Webster

San Antonio, Texas
2009

Cover art: "The Kiss" by Gustav Klimpt (permission applied for)

First Edition

ISBN-10: 0-916727-50-5
ISBN-13: 978-0-916727-50-5

Wings Press
627 E. Guenther
San Antonio, Texas 78210
Phone/fax: (210) 271-7805

On-line catalogue and ordering:
www.wingspress.com
All Wings Press titles are distributed to the trade by
Independent Publishers Group
www.ipgbook.com

Library of Congress Cataloging-in-Publication Data:

Webster, Brenda.
Vienna triangle : a novel / Brenda Webster. -- 1st ed.
p. cm.
ISBN-13: 978-0-916727-50-5 (alk. paper)
ISBN-10: 0-916727-50-5
1. Women college students--Fiction. 2. Freud, Sigmund, 1856-1939--Fiction. 3. Deutsch, Helene, 1884-1982--Fiction. 4. Andreas-Salomé, Lou, 1861-1937--Fiction. 5. Tausk, Victor, 1879-1919--Fiction. 6. Suicide--Fiction. 7. Psychoanalysis--History--20th century--Fiction. 8. Psychoanalysts--Fiction. I. Title.
PS3573.E255V54 2009
813'.54--dc22

2008012028

For my grandchildren,
Guillermo, Emmet, Rose,
Julian and Lucia.

Contents

Author's Note

This is a work of fiction, not of history. Nevertheless, it is based on the lives and relationships of real people: Viktor Tausk, Sigmund Freud, Lou Andreas-Salomé and Helene Deutsch. I have attempted not to violate the known facts, but have invented diaries, dialogues, and secondary characters in order to bring the actors, their ideas and passions to full imaginative life.

Vienna Triangle

Chapter One

Helene could not help but notice the attractive middle-aged woman with her large shopping bag. She was wearing white socks with expensive-looking sandals and an equally unusual array of colors: red with orange and purple. Somehow she had managed to pull it all together – an artist, probably thought Helene. After a lifetime analyzing patients Helene could not break her habit of lightning appraisals. She prided herself on being able to reconstruct a person's history from something as seemingly inconsequential as a watch fob or a piece of jewelry. As if to confirm Helene's assumption, the woman put up her hand and touched one of her gold earrings as though to reassure herself that it was still there. The gesture reminded Helene of an artist she had treated during her early days with Freud in Vienna.

The woman continued along the sand-blown Provincetown street at a steady pace, her colorful dress whipping in the breeze. At 84, Helene could, though somewhat short of breath, still keep up with this woman who was probably only in her early fifties. The thought gave her a certain amount of self-satisfaction, which she immediately suppressed as unprofessional. She had given up all but a few special patients in 1963, five years ago, but old habits died hard.

The woman stopped in front of the steps of the gray shingled house right next to the vacation cottage Helene had rented for a few weeks that summer. It had been relaxing to be away from Cambridge for a while, to be someplace where she wasn't regarded as an institution. She had hoped her son or one of her grandsons would come and join her, but that hadn't happened. Something about the slightly melancholy expression of the woman's face made Helene surmise that she wasn't going home to a family, either.

She was wondering whether the eccentrically dressed lady would prove to be an interesting neighbor when the woman tripped, spilling the contents of her bag – some pieces of colored fabric, two oranges and a jar of instant coffee – across the weathered steps. Helene hurried over and crouched next to her. She was groaning and holding her leg.

"I think something's broken," she said, biting her lip. "Oh my god, it hurts." Her leg seemed bent in an unnatural position.

"You'll be all right," Helene assured her, in her light Polish accent. "Stay just as you are. Don't move and I'll call an ambulance."

"Please stay with me."

"I'm just going to the next house, there." She pointed at the green-shuttered house next door with the blue hydrangea blooming wildly in front of it. Then she gently removed the woman's hand from her arm. "I'll be right back. I promise."

Ignoring her own arthritic joints, she straightened and a few minutes later was back with a cup of water and the news that an ambulance was on the way. Meanwhile, the woman had edged into a half-sitting position and was leaning on one elbow, looking dazed.

"Would you like a drink?" Helene asked sitting down next to her. The woman nodded and held the cup carefully to her mouth. The early morning fog had blown off and the day was bright and warm; soon it would be hot, and the woman sipped it gratefully.

"Are you feeling any better?" Helene asked, after a moment.

"The water helped. I don't feel so faint now but it hurts like hell."

"It shouldn't be long now," Helene said, glancing at her watch.

"I don't know what happened. Clumsy of me," the woman said. Then, wincing at the pain, she added, "My daughter will be angry. She didn't want me to come down here alone. I probably should have stayed in New York. I should have listened."

"Please, don't distress yourself. Try to breathe more slowly. I'm sure she'll understand." But the woman had covered her eyes with her hands. "I know, I know how children can be," Helene went on. "Breathe in now," she said, touching the woman's arm. "Breathe out."

She herself had perhaps erred in the opposite direction, Helene thought, as she illustrated the slow rhythm with her own breathing – too much neglect, and to her sorrow, her son was still resentful about it. It was so hard to get it right. Patients often supposed their doctors had all the answers, but in fact they were often as much in the dark as the people they were supposed to be helping. Helene stroked the woman's hair, consoling her for her broken bone and whatever other sorrows life had dealt her.

The ambulance came to a stop, tires squealing – there wasn't enough traffic for them to put on the siren. It was a jaunty blue Cadillac with red crosses front and side. Helene could see places where the paint was chipped and black showed through. Lots of the ambulances nowadays were repainted hearses. She hoped the woman wouldn't notice. Two orderlies in crisp blue trousers and matching blue caps jumped out with a stretcher, and after taking the woman's relevant information – Helene learned her name was Emily Berg – plunged the stretcher into the dark interior.

A week or so later, Helene was out walking again and saw Emily Berg on crutches maneuvering slowly along the sidewalk a few feet from her house, accompanied by a tall, slim, young woman with a mass of black curly hair, and an intriguing birthmark on her cheek next to her mouth. Like a beauty spot, Helene thought, but instead of being round it was in the shape of a tiny triangle the size of a finger nail.

"Oh, Mrs. Berg . . . Emily," Helene said, bending down to her. "How good to see you back. I've been thinking about you, wondering how you were. That was a nasty fall." She caught a whiff of an exotic perfume, heady with a touch of spice. Helene smiled approvingly. Obviously, Emily wasn't giving an inch to her injury. Right now she was wearing a flowing, richly colored African print dress which mostly covered the cast on her right leg. The young woman was severely dressed in black jeans and T shirt with "We Shall Overcome" written across her chest in white block letters.

"It wasn't the worst kind of fracture, apparently," Emily said. "Though I have to be in this cast for six weeks at least. The doctor said I musn't let the muscles in the other leg atrophy – so here I am. A bit stoned on opiates."

The young woman looked pained. "Mom, you're hardly stoned. You took a little codeine that's all."

"My daughter doesn't like it when I use slang. Or is it my abysmal ignorance of the drug scene you're objecting to?"

Her daughter didn't answer, just sighed and put a hand on her mother's shoulder with a mix of tenderness and irritation that Helene was well acquainted with. Emily, balancing her crutch against her body, reached up and patted the hand.

"I'm Kate," her daughter said pleasantly. "I have a lot to thank you for," she proffered her free hand, "but I'm afraid I don't know your name?" Her hand was warm and firm, a good grip.

"Helene, Helene Rosenbach," Helene said. She tended to use her maiden name on vacations. She was famous enough to have people fuss over her, something she hated. "I didn't do anything more than any passer-by would have done. Your mother's fortunate to have you here now to help."

"I hated to drag Kate away from her busy life, but she insisted. She's getting a graduate degree in psychology," Emily added proudly.

Kate frowned. She withdrew her hand from under her mother's. Emily's fingers lingered a minute at the place on her shoulder where the hand had been withdrawn.

"Perhaps I should come spend some time with you another day," Helene said.

"No, please stay," Kate murmured. "I'm sorry."

"Nothing to be sorry for." Helene smiled, "I'd like nothing better than to stay and stroll with your mother. You probably have a great deal to do," she added gently. Kate's eagerness to be elsewhere was palpable. She kept moving slightly ahead and had to stop repeatedly, shifting her weight from one foot to another in place like a colt confined to a stall.

The young woman smiled gratefully. "There are some things I need to take care of. I have to get a new aide to help out. Mom didn't like my first pick."

"Poor Mrs. Jenkins," Emily said. "Even the color of her hair was depressing. She was in worse shape than I am. I could get by very well with help going up the stairs a couple of times a day from a nice, cheerful college student – one of those adorable boys, for instance." She nodded her head at a small herd of young men trotting by engrossed in a vigorous exchange of "You knows" and "whatevers."

Kate gave her mother a quick act–your-age look and with a slight bow of her head strode back towards the house.

"You'll have to excuse me, " Emily said, leap-frogging over a sandy patch. "The drugs make me silly."

"You have a sense of humor," Helene said, nonetheless beginning to see how a somewhat oversensitive child might be embarrassed by Emily.

"Sometimes it's the only way to deal with one's children," Helene said, thinking that her daughter's disapproval had clearly wounded Emily, "and you're very brave. Even with the codeine you must be in pain." She had noticed Emily wincing every time she swung forward. "Is it manageable?"

"It does hurt," Emily said, with defiant cheerfulness. "But they threatened me with an early demise if I didn't walk until I couldn't stand it anymore. I'd really rather sit out with my watercolors and see if I could duplicate that blue." She pointed at a newly opened hydrangea leaning against a remarkable piece of driftwood, weathered gray with patches of golden brown, then smiled at her companion. "It's very nice of you to volunteer to be my minder. I'm afraid Kate finds this unbearably tedious. She was a gymnast when she was little. Always in motion. Twirls, flips. I think she believed if she just practiced enough she could conquer gravity." She bit her lip with the effort of moving forward, one slow foot at a time. "Do you have daughters?"

"Just a son."

"That must be easier."

"Freud once said that the only truly uncomplicated love relationship was between a mother and her son."

"Did he? Well, I haven't much use for psychiatrists generally, but I've always thought a boy would have been more forgiving . . . not pick up on every little fault."

Helene fingered the letter in the pocket of her green slacks that said her son wasn't coming next weekend after all. She had hoped her daughter-in-law, Melinda, would have been able to persuade him.

"Not necessarily," she responded. "My work took me away a lot when my son was young. He resented it." She didn't think he'd forgiven her yet.

"Well, Kate doesn't have that to blame me for. I was only too much around. I used to think that if I'd had more of a career, she would have respected me more. Though maybe not. My mother was a concert pianist. The piano was like part of her body, like a hard black shell. If I wanted anything as a child, I'd have to howl like a banshee outside her studio door, and then I'd usually get a scolding for my pains."

A young man was coming towards them, followed by a little boy. He walked ahead of the boy and every few minutes would turn and throw him a football. The child was clearly having trouble reacting in time to catch it. "Pay attention, Tommy," the man said.

"What about your father?" Helene asked as the boy went past them, his forehead wrinkled with concentration.

"I never knew him. He left my mother before I was born," Emily paused, "before we came to this country. From your accent I'd guess you're from Austria or Germany yourself."

"I'm actually Polish – but you speak English perfectly, I don't hear any accent."

"That's because I was only a child when we came here. Mother stopped speaking German to me at home after we came. I guess she just wanted to forget everything connected with my father – he'd hurt her so terribly. I didn't understand. I only knew I missed my friends and my house and my language."

Helene nodded in sympathy. "People think it's easy for children because they learn so quickly, but it isn't."

"Kate won't believe that I know so little about my father, only that he was a brilliant, handsome man who kept changing professions and women – and came to a bad end." Emily stopped and rubbed her palm over her cheek, brushed back her hair. "Even if I knew more, I'm not sure I'd tell her. What good would it do her to pry into the past? I never wanted it to weigh on Kate the way it had on me as a girl – always thinking that maybe my father left because of me, because he didn't want a child. And now all Kate seems to want to do is bring back his ghost."

"It's hard to get things right," Helene said. "In fact, it's almost impossible. Luckily, unless we do everything wrong, our children manage to grow up somehow. I wish now I'd had a daughter. Though when I was pregnant I have to admit I was terrified that I'd have a daughter who would hate me the way I hated my mother."

Emily looked at her with interest. "Most people wouldn't admit that." Sweat was beginning to bead on her forehead under her straw hat.

"Especially to a stranger," Helene laughed, "but you don't feel like a stranger. And I guess hearing a lot about people's intimate lives in my work, it's hard to shock me. I'm so old now, if I want to say something, I do. I've dealt with enough rebellious teenage girls in my day to be sorry for my mother, poor lady. But there was a time when even the starch she put in our petticoats enraged me. I was sure she meant to embalm us all."

"Are you an analyst, then?" Emily asked.

Helene nodded. "Indeed. One of the first."

"What an odd coincidence."

"Because you don't have much use for us?" Helene laughed.

"It's more complicated than that. . . ." Emily straightened and glanced at her wristwatch.

Helene noticed that she seemed suddenly abstracted like a snail pulling in her horns, and after a few more minutes of near silence Emily said she thought she'd better turn around. They had gone so far towards intimacy in such a short time, maybe too fast for comfort. Helene wasn't offended . . . she was accustomed to the fact that lots of people had no use for her profession. Finding you had been talking unguardedly to a mind doctor could be jarring. She helped Emily maneuver the walker around and they headed towards the house.

"I think I forgot my red pill," Emily said softly, "it's such a bore." Her own advancing age seemed a safe subject, so Helene made some light remarks about how maintaining her body was becoming more tedious than maintaining her old Peugeot. Every morning she checked her body parts to see how they were functioning. And the pills one had to take, some with food, some with water, not with calcium, not with iron – it would take a mental giant to keep up with it all.

Emily's preoccupied look had softened by the time they got back to the house. At the top of her stairs, helped back up by her daughter – who, revived by her brief freedom, was offering to massage her mother's feet and shoulders – Emily turned and waved. It was a gallant wave. Helene liked her. Liked the daughter, too.

Helene fully intended to visit again and inquire how things were going, but a summer cough turned into a bad bronchitis, keeping her bedridden for several days and her Armenian housekeeper adamantly refused to let her out until all her symptoms were completely clear. Helene distracted herself by imagining the conversations going on in Emily's house. Despite Kate's irritability Helene thought she had observed strong affection, too. There had been no such mixture in Helene's feeling for her own strong, big-bosomed, handsome mother. But of course it wasn't so simple, really. By now she could imagine what it must have been like for her straitlaced mother to be faced with her defiant-sixteen-year old self – that perfect luminous flesh and those moist lips, as dangerous in their instinctual innocence as a tiger escaped from its cage.

Now, as she checked herself over in her hand mirror, she observed matter-of-factly that her eyes were one of her best remaining features. Luminous, green, they might still surprise with their beauty. Her high clear forehead – under silvery hair brushed dramatically back – still gave the impression of intellect. But the once fine nose had thickened and there were deep furrows alongside the slim lips. The magic of her heart-shaped face was gone. She put the mirror down on her bedside table. It had traveled everywhere with her, from Chemesh, her small town in Poland, to Vienna, Berlin and finally the States.

Her first lover, Lieberman, had given the mirror to her and told her to think of him every time she looked in it – and Freud said only women were narcissistic. She brushed her short hair vigorously, sighed and put the mirror down. The loss of her beauty, the absence of men's stares when she walked down the street or into a room, had bothered her a lot at first. But she could honestly say she had gotten used to it. In a way, her invisibility gave her more freedom as an observer. And according to her doctor, her chemistry was intact and her mind still sharp. Her biggest problem, she thought wryly, was that she lacked a situation to observe. More than that, she lacked the stimulation provided by intimate contact with another person. Whatever their problems, she and Felix had kept up a lively dialogue for over fifty years. Now she had only her past to commune with.

Chapter Two

Kate, sitting by the window while her mother napped, replayed her conference with Professor Downes, her advisor at Columbia, wondering if she could have done anything to mollify her. The woman was impossible. Brilliant, yes – Kate had loved her course on experimental psychology – but then she hadn't realized how rigid she could be, how insistent on facts.

"Speculation," she spluttered when Kate first told her she wanted to see how women's lives influenced their theory. "Pure speculation." It was even worse when she'd sold her article to *The Atlantic Monthly* and Rachel, a young agent from the Rivington literary agency, had expressed some interest. Kate had expected her advisor to be pleased, that somehow it would help to validate her, but Downes was cold as ice. She thought it was wrong to publish in the popular press before you'd done seasoned research. "That's journalism," the advisor had said, "not scholarship, not professional."

Downes had been against her dissertation project from the beginning.

"Why women analysts," she'd asked, "when there are so many other things needing investigation? Gender isn't really pertinent. And why their lives?" What mattered was theoretical meaning and accomplishments. "You know people will say you're not able to do research, they'll say it's because you're a woman."

Kate had wanted to believe Downes was just probing her weak spots, trying to help her make the best case. She'd been so convinced that it would be good to work with a woman. It had taken her a while to realize that Downes didn't think of herself as a woman; she considered herself an honorary male, and Kate was rocking the boat. Kate's independence actually offended her. Kate tried to make up for what Downes considered her wrongheaded approach by stressing the facts – later, she thought, when she turned the thesis into a book, she could do what she wanted, but for now Downes had the power to make her miserable.

Kate picked up the phone and dialed Keith again. No answer. Where was he when she needed him? When she'd called him earlier and couldn't reach him, she'd told herself he was at the library or at a meeting, but by the third time she was wondering whether, bored and restless, he was with some other woman at a café or bar in the Village. He had a weakness for women who shared his ideas about the war. Of course, it helped if they had long legs and firm, high breasts. Just because he had the softest brown eyes imaginable didn't mean he wouldn't betray her. On the contrary.

The degree of her passion scared her. Even hearing his voice in another room made her melt. She'd had a few other lovers, but she'd always managed to keep a certain degree of distance, never letting herself get fully engaged, intersecting with others only at carefully controlled moments like the lines in a Mondrian painting. She supposed she was so scared because of the bad examples of her mother and her grandmother. Not only had her grandfather deserted her grandmother and done something so terrible that her mother refused to talk about it, but her own father had left her mother when Kate was only a child. She had loved him passionately from the time she was an infant, crying to be taken by him, even when Emily was holding her.

"You were a Daddy's girl from the beginning," her mother would say.

When they divorced, her father told Kate all the usual things: that he still loved her, that he'd be seeing her every week. But his plans often changed at the last minute, and she still remembered sitting, looking out the window, waiting stubbornly even though Emily had already told her he wasn't coming.

And then there was a war and her father had been sent overseas. She was too young to understand what the war was about, anymore than she'd understood the divorce, only that he couldn't visit her any more for a while – he had to fight some bad men in a far-off place. She had to be a brave big girl and be patient. "I'm not a patient girl," she'd said, and he'd laughed and told her to work on it. He'd promised he'd be all right and be back soon.

He broke his promise and died in France.

The message, at its most benign, was be careful; at its worst, it was don't trust a man, because the more attractive he is, the more likely he'll abandon you.

Kate ordinarily found patterns soothing – her work, after all, consisted of making sense of them. But it certainly didn't soothe her to imagine some quirk of mind or gene in her family's women that made them find just the man who would undo them. She was engaged in spinning out this unpleasant possibility when she was shocked to see a familiar figure, backpack on his shoulders, walk up the front steps.

She opened the door and rushed to meet him. "Keith, what are you doing here?" she managed to gasp before he had her in his arms and was whirling her around.

"I came to see how you're getting along," he grinned.

"But what about your seminar?" she stammered.

"Don't worry, it's fine, I'm fine. I'll take a night flight tomorrow and get ready on the way." He searched her face. "You look tired but beautiful."

"You're a sweetheart," she said, kissing him. "Mother's been in a lot of pain but she'll be glad to see you. I'm afraid I'm not much good at nursing. I keep snapping at her."

"I don't believe it," he said. "You're so even-tempered."

She laughed. "I'm not even anything. I'm a Pisces, after all."

"Actually, I thought it might help to offer some distraction – take the heat off you for a day. Especially since I like your mother."

"If I were reading about her in a novel, I'd probably like her, too."

"Who is it?" Emily called from inside.

"It's me," Keith said, going to the door. He disengaged a couple of magnificent roses from the straps on top of his pack and presented them to her – he'd obviously picked them from a neighbor's yard with his usual disregard of private property.

"Lovely," her mother said, not questioning their origin. "Come sit by me, Keith. You're just what the doctor ordered. How's teaching? How are things going with the student protests?"

Standing on tiptoe to take down a blue glass vase from the cupboard, Kate could feel herself tense. Her mother wasn't doing anything wrong, but just the way she patted the sofa next to her, her proprietary tone, her asking about "school" almost as if Keith were a child, annoyed her. She gave herself a mental shake. Grow up, she told herself, you should be glad she likes him. Would you prefer that she hated him? A lot of mothers would have been worried about his anti-war activities, afraid they would get him in trouble, but she was all for them.

"It's a nasty war," Emily had agreed. "Probably not something we can win, either." Kate was against the war in Vietnam, too, but sometimes it seemed as if her mother was more in tune with Keith than she was. Hitler had been a bogeyman to Kate, but to her mother he was the madman who had killed off most of her own mother's family. Emily felt the horror of war in her gut, while to Kate, though she hesitated to admit it, this struggle going on in far-off jungles and rice paddies sometimes seemed less real than her investigations into the past.

Her mother's voice was notably buoyant, Kate observed, as she put together a light supper of cracked crab and salad. Luckily, she had picked out two big ones, minor gluttony being her way of coping with tension, and she had a round of crusty French bread. If Helene hadn't taken her mother for a walk, they'd probably be eating canned tuna.

At dinner Keith lamented the aggravating smugness of some of his students – Keith was teaching in the Sociology department at Columbia.

"I could hardly believe my ears when this kid repeated – without any irony, mind you – the official line that killing Vietcong in order to save them wasn't at all the same as killing Jews because they're Jews." Attacking a crab leg rather viciously with the steel nutcrackers Kate had provided, he wondered aloud what was wrong with his students.

"Haven't I succeeded in teaching them anything? At a major Ivy League school like Columbia, they don't have any excuse. Unless they were sent in by the right-wing student organization to disrupt my class. Of course, being a professor," he added, "I had to give them rational answers, keep repeating that it shouldn't be our mission to interfere in another people's efforts at self-determination, that a human being is a human being, whether Viet Cong or Jew, and in any case, violence is unacceptable."

Listening to him, Kate remembered the first time she had heard him speak. Her friend Monica had dragged her to an SDS meeting where he was guest speaker. Monica told her that she loved his class on the civil rights movement – he walked up and down the aisles of the huge classroom trying to wake them up and shake them, showing them electrifying movies of Southern brutality. Before Kate had even entered the room, she heard his magnetic crowd-rousing voice. It raised the little hairs on the back of her neck. Made her desire him before he'd even touched her.

"Being smart in the head doesn't mean they have emotional understanding," Kate said now, wanting to touch his arm but not wanting to do it in front of her mother who was already too avidly interested in her life. "I'm not sure people learn that way anyhow, en masse. If they're going to change, maybe it has to be from the inside, by facing their own demons."

"So we're all murderers under the skin?" he asked her.

"In some cold reptilian part of our brain, maybe we are," she said.

Her mother roused herself from what seemed to be a pleasant end–of-meal torpor. "In that case, it's hopeless?"

"I guess I believe in the individual approach. If everyone took care of their own neurosis, war might not seem so necessary." Kate had just read something like this in Anais Nin's diaries and was tempted to quote her but she knew it wouldn't impress Keith.

"Submit themselves to analysis? What nonsense," her mother pronounced with uncharacteristic bluntness. "I'd wager that the mind doctors are just as blind as anyone else and maybe more dangerous because they claim superior wisdom. I don't believe for a minute they don't have the same lust for power as everyone else." Keith gave a slight nod but said nothing. Kate was grateful for his restraint. She knew he thought of analysis as an authoritarian, closed system, or worse, a means of inducing adaptation to the status quo.

"I don't understand how you can be so sure," Kate said, wincing at the plaintive sound of her voice. "You've never tried it. You probably don't even know any analysts."

"Of course I do." Emily said. "They may not be close personal friends but I've seen enough to see that they ruin their lives as thoroughly as other people. Look at – his name has slipped my mind – but he's on his third wife. Married for thirty years, he went off with a younger woman, leaving his poor wife, Nora, in tatters. His idea of mental health was being brave enough to act on his impulses. Why would I want a person like that giving me suggestions about my inner life or my moral dilemmas?"

"Every profession has its failures. Some people die of heart attacks despite going to the best doctors," Kate continued.

"Every profession has its scoundrels, too. And I have a feeling that psychoanalysis has more than its share. Operating the way they do, behind closed doors with no one controlling what they do, God knows what might be going on."

"Why is it I always feel as if you have a personal grievance against therapy? Or would you dislike anything I tried to do on my own?"

"Easy," Keith said, putting a hand on her arm. "It's just an exchange of opinions. I'm sure your mom didn't mean any harm."

"Do me a favor, don't side with her, will you?" Kate hated herself when she reacted this way, but once her mother pushed her buttons, it only made it worse for Keith to intervene. And somewhere she knew she was right; her mother had some hidden reason for being antagonistic to talk therapy.

They managed to get through desert of ripe strawberries and cream without any further discussion, and after she washed the dishes they sat for a while all together working on a puzzle of tropical birds that her mother had found in a cabinet under the television. When her mother went off to bed, Kate took Keith for a walk on the beach. Though she knew her mother had no objections to her taking Keith to her bedroom – her mother prided herself on her sexual open-mindedness – she didn't want to make love in such close proximity. Her mother had been her confidante all through her adolescence, sharing in her fledgling adventures, but gradually Kate was pulling away. And Keith, especially, she didn't want to share.

The night was warm with a soft breeze blowing from the sea. She took Keith's hand and swung it gently to and fro as they went down the back steps to the beach. There was a full moon that made the water over the flats gleam invitingly. Quite far out a sailboat was moored at the edge of a patch of sand. They looked at each other.

Kate took off her sandals – Keith had left his at the house and was draped in a blanket like a poncho – and they walked out towards the boat through the shimmering water, feeling the moist sand caress their feet. She had rolled up her jeans a little, though in most places the water was only a silky skin over the sand.

When they reached the sailboat, Keith whipped the blanket from his shoulders and with a gallant flourish laid it in the hull, then, telling her to watch the boom, he helped her clamber in, drew her down beside him and wrapped the blanket around them. The bottom of the boat was hard but Kate thought it was probably better than wet sand and certainly more private. Keith whispered in her ear that he wanted to kiss her all over slowly until she was crazy for him, but that's not what she wanted tonight. She reached down to tug open his fly.

"Wait," he said. "Aren't you going to let me take off my clothes? I want to feel your skin against mine." He managed to slip out of his jeans and threw them outside the blanket. Then he tried to take off hers but when they got down below her knees she stopped him.

"Oh," he said, amused. "That's how it is, is it. You bad girl. I want romance and you just want a quickie. Tell me, tell me that you just want a quick fuck. Say it."

She wouldn't say it – she had a strange inhibition about putting things into words – but she pulled her T-shirt up and put his hands on her breasts. Her feeling that this was a bit sluttish, like some girl taken against a wall outside a bar, only made the sensations more intense.

When she opened her eyes again, the silver moon was partially veiled by a soft mist that seemed to pour out of the darkness above it. Stars throbbed in the black sky. She could feel a comfortable heat radiating from his body, warming her. They nuzzled, talking for awhile, and then when the wind turned cold and a fog started to roll in, they got dressed and walked back hand-in-hand to the cottage.

Her mother had gone to bed. She'd left the porch light on for them, and a lamp in the tiny living room. "How about a snack?" Keith asked. "And a cup of coffee."

"It'll keep you awake."

"You should know by now that it doesn't – even a double espresso doesn't have the slightest effect." He gave her a light slap on the bottom, designed, she thought, to send her in the direction of the kitchen.

"You know where the kitchen is," she said. "Why is it always me? Why can't you fix me something once in a while? It would be a radical new experience."

"Still mad because I sided with your mother at dinner?"

"I was just kidding," she said, disingenuously. The joke was a tiny escape valve for her irritation. It hadn't really occurred to her that he would make coffee. The one time she'd called out to him from the bedroom to put the kettle on, he'd asked where it was, how much water, how much coffee, which burner. She'd answered cheerfully until she realized he was putting her on. When she finally went into the kitchen, he burst out laughing. Even in the SDS meetings where radical ideas were flung out like rice at a wedding, the women still made the coffee and sandwiches.

"But sometimes I feel that you don't take my work seriously . . . it hurts my feelings." She walked off into the kitchen, head down.

"Oh, baby," he followed her, puffing out his lips, obviously frustrated by the turn the conversation was taking.

"It's bad enough that I have an unsympathetic advisor," Kate said as she filled the kettle with water and turned to face him. "My mother hates what I'm doing. I really wish you were more supportive."

"I try, but . . ."

"What?"

"Well, frankly what goes on in the minds of a few rich people isn't. . . ." He started again. "Psychoanalysis is beside the point – at least right now. Every day bombs are being dropped on innocent women and children, bodies horribly burnt, endless killing – you know it as well as I. You've seen the pictures, read the news. People should be spending their energy on finding ways to stop this brutal war, period."

"There's more than one important issue in the world, Keith. The whole of life doesn't have to shut down just because there's a war. Scientific discovery, art, music, these things still have meaning . . . maybe even more meaning when they're threatened."

She rummaged in the fridge and brought out a piece of chocolate cake, set it on the table with a fork, and motioned him to sit down.

"Aren't you having anything?" Keith asked. She shook her head.

"You know, we have such different backgrounds, you can't expect us to agree on everything," Keith said, appeasingly. "My father ran a grocery store. He kept his store open late just to make a few extra dollars. I worked there every day after school . . . your grandmother played the piano, your mother paints, you. . . ."

"I'm just playing?"

"Hey, I never said that. I know you're a serious scholar. If anything, you're pushing yourself too hard. Making artificial deadlines for yourself."

"But what if I'm right?" she asked, pouring him a cup of coffee. "Maybe we could solve the big problems if we understood what's going on in our minds – what pushes our buttons."

"That can't be the solution for masses of people, even if they could afford it. Besides, the analyses of behavior I've seen tend to be so simplistic. Like that asshole who said that most of the student activists came from broken families and our idea of a beloved community was just a surrogate tit. You can't tell me that explains anything real. I, for one, don't need analysis of my unconscious motives," he added more lightly. "The best thing Freud did as far as I'm concerned was to point out the importance of sex." Keith put his arm around her. "Isn't that something we can agree on?" He started kissing her neck, but it wasn't any good. The mood was spoiled.

Later that night, she was awakened by a scream from her mother's room. Pulling on her robe, she ran in and found her mother half sitting in bed, her eyes tight shut, seemingly still asleep. Her Chinese-silk nightgown flowed in a sinuous line over her breasts, covering them with yellow peonies, and she looked almost beautiful.

"Mom," Kate said softly, not wanting to startle her. "It's just a dream. Wake up."

"No, no," her mother cried in a small child's voice. "You don't want me. You never wanted me."

"Mom? What is it?" Kate asked, wondering if she should sneak back to her room, if this was something too private, something her mother wouldn't want her to know. It was pretty obvious that Emily was pleading with her own mother, Grandma Hilde.

Ordinarily, Emily treated the whole story of her illegitimate birth with a sort of fey humor. Once Kate had heard Emily telling her best friend about it in the kitchen over coffee, laughing: "It can't have been easy for my poor mother in the middle of her piano tour to start throwing up and realize she had an unwelcome visitor." At the time, Kate, only eight or nine, hadn't understood her mother's talk about surviving hunched inside her mother like a tenacious gnome as Hilde jumped off the table and scalded herself in baths so hot they made her faint. In retrospect, Kate thought, it must have been awful for her mother to think of herself as a despised dwarf whose hostess was desperate to get rid of her.

"Are you sorry you had me?" Emily whimpered, falling back against the pillows.

"I'm not Hilde, Momma, I'm Kate. I'm your daughter," she said, but her mother, eyes still clamped shut, ignored her correction.

"Are you sorry? I need to know," Emily insisted, plaintively.

"Of course I'm not sorry," Kate said, not sure whether her voice could enter her mother's dream but willing to try. Subject to nightmares herself, Keith had often calmed her that way. "I grew to love you. You were so pretty and had such winning ways."

Her mother's eyes opened but seemed to look right through her, obviously still not clear who she was. The pull of the dream was so strong. "I didn't know you thought that," she said hesitantly. "Remember the china cup with the willow pattern? I was bringing you your tea and I stumbled. You said I was a clumsy girl. . . ."

"I know you were only trying to please me," Kate said. "It was an accident." She found herself in tears.

Her mother reached up shyly and touched her tearstained cheek, then put out her arms in such a trusting way that Kate couldn't do anything except push the covers aside so she could slip in beside her and take her in her arms. At first she was almost frightened, felt slightly suffocated by the warm flesh, the faint musty sweetness, the soft skin that could have been that of a much younger woman. She hadn't been so close to her mother in years.

Poor mother, it had been painful to hear her speak that way in that tiny child's voice. For an instant she remembered her mother bending over her to kiss her goodnight as a child, shadowy and white-limbed, talking to her in a singsong voice, long ringed fingers smoothing back her hair. Kate made a vow to be nicer to her, not to get so irritated when she said outrageous things. Her mother hadn't had the sort of beginning that would give her self-confidence. She probably needed to exaggerate a little just to convince herself that she was worthy of being born.

"Go to sleep, now," Kate said. "Everything's all right."

Her mother clung to her, her eyes open now, trying to make out her daughter's face. "No, it's not. I made you angry at dinner," she whispered, her voice still slurred. "I'm sorry. I must have seemed unreasonable."

"Mmm," murmured Kate, wearily, not wanting to renew their quarrel. Especially not at this hour, when she needed to disentangle herself from her mother's embrace and return to Keith.

"If I tell you something will you promise not to ask me anything else?"

"I don't know if I can . . . I'll try," Kate offered, tentatively.

"My father was hurt by that therapy you're so interested in writing about," she said. "Hurt very badly . . . so you see . . . it frightens me when you . . . I don't want you to get too involved. . . ."

"I'm not involved, Mom, not like that, not to worry," she responded, trying to keep her voice low and soothing. "Are you sure this isn't just part of your dream . . . you were having a nightmare, you know."

"It isn't a dream, Mother told me. . . ."

"But how was he "hurt"? Was he a patient, was it a friend? What did your mother say exactly?"

"I love you, Kate."

"I know, I know," Kate shook her mother's shoulder gently. "But it's not going to hurt me to hear more..really, please..if you would just tell me grandfather's name, I could find out more myself . . . can't you even tell me his name?" But it was no use, her mother had fallen into a deep sleep.

She slipped out of her mother's arms, and stopping to take a drink of milk from the fridge, went back to bed and slid in beside Keith. Her mind was spinning with wild speculations.

Perhaps her grandfather was a patient whose analysis had failed – wrong interpretations had been made like those in the famous case of Emma, whose bleeding nose turned out to be caused by gauze Freud's colleague Fliess had left in during an operation, not by a passion for her doctor.

Or perhaps this was the wrong track entirely. Could he have been one of the early analysts? She went over the names of some of them in her mind – Abraham, Sachs – but there was no way of guessing who it might be. Perhaps her grandfather had gotten into a quarrel with one of them – there was so much contentiousness in the early days of analysis. It could have been a quarrel with Freud himself over interpretations perhaps, or the future of the movement.

Or maybe it was rivalry with a colleague over a woman. Kate's imagination ran riot. Duels were still fought in the early 1900's; perhaps her grandmother had another lover who was outraged over her pregnancy and confronted her grandfather – maybe even killed him.

She tossed and turned, dying to wake Keith up but knowing he wouldn't like it. Well, it would just have to wait till morning.

If her mother was keeping a secret to protect her, it must involve something shameful or violent, something her mother was afraid might be passed on like the hideous taint of madness in Poe's story of the House of Usher. Kate's mother had had a breakdown after Kate's father left. Kate had been too overwhelmed by her own sorrow to remember much, but she kept a dim recollection of her mother wandering around the house in robe and slippers, her hair untidy and the dishes piled up in the sink, and herself tugging at her mother's skirt asking for something.

It was better somehow when her father was sent to France. She had learned to read by then. Perhaps being far away and in danger had made him miss her; she heard from him more regularly than when he was in New York only a half-hour away. She still had his collection of V-Mails in a box on her closet shelf. The small rectangles with her name and address outlined in red and "V-Mail" across the top. Inside were stick cartoons of himself in his uniform peeling potatoes or getting her letter. Sometimes he sent little stories about a buddy – "Kugelhead" – who was always getting in trouble: he couldn't seem to pull tight the hospital corners on his bunk, or remember that his jacket button needed sewing. I know you'd do better, princess, her father would say. You see the picture of the plane on the envelope? That's carrying you oodles and oodles of love and baskets of kisses.

When she wrote him – dictating her letter to Emily – about their victory garden and how much she loved to see the little green shoots come up, her father told her he had heard of a place called Paradise Island where it was all green with every kind of beautiful flower. All the animals there were friends with each other. Children who lived there could have twelve pets. And best of all, there were no rules. When he came back, he said, he was going to take her there for a visit .

And then one day her mother told her he had been wounded and was in a field hospital. It was incomprehensible to Kate that he could be hurt; he seemed so solid, so strong . . . but before she had time to fully absorb that news, Emily got a telegram and a few weeks later, Kate was told to put on her black velvet party dress, for a funeral. With childish illogic Kate blamed her mother for letting her father die – just as she had blamed her for the tension before he left them that had exploded nightly into angry voices behind the bedroom door.

For years afterwards, Kate played games in which her father did heroic deeds, was hurt by bad soldiers or monsters and then found and revived. It always ended that way, with her finding him. Even when she had buried him under stacks of pillows or under the sofa, she – or her doll Lola – would triumphantly uncover him and bring him home – where she, not her mother, would care for him. But after awhile it was hard even to remember what he looked like.

She didn't have even a blurry image of her mysteriously lost grandfather. Only the fear that he might have done something terrible. She had a strong urge not only to find him but to find him blameless, though of course she told herself that she would be objective. What she knew, she mused now more calmly, all she knew, was that her grandmother was in Vienna after World War 1 – so whoever her grandfather was, he had to have been there then. Probably before the war too, if he was involved with any of the early analysts, but certainly by 1918, because that's when – she'd figured backwards from her mother's age – Grandma Hilde got pregnant.

A week later, Helene, finally cough-free, resolutely climbed the stairs to Emily's house carrying a chicken dumpling casserole made by her housekeeper. Kate answered the door after the first ring.

"I thought you might enjoy this," the older woman said. "I meant to visit again sooner but I've been sick myself, and then I thought the last thing in the world your mother needed was to come down with something. I hope you're not a vegetarian."

"No, I'm a throwback, a real carnivore." Kate smiled faintly and took the proffered casserole. "I know Mother would have loved to talk to you but she's out taking a walk with the aide. I finally got someone she liked enough to walk with once a day." She gave a slightly conspiratorial smile. "I was just going to stop for a coffee break. Please come in and let me give you something."

"I'd like that, but . . ." Helene looked over Kate's shoulder at the rather messy room – bottles of medicine, clothes not hung up. Kate clearly wasn't keen on housekeeping. "I think you have much to do," she said. "Isn't there any way I could help? Perhaps you would like to borrow my housekeeper for a day. She's not young, she has been with me for thirty years, but she's still a paragon of order."

"How kind," Kate said graciously. "Thank you, but we're managing. Mom isn't a neatness fanatic and I . . . well, you see." She shrugged her slim shoulders apologetically. Helene noticed the feminine gesture of hapless charm. The small birthmark on the left side of the young woman's face was actually quite fetching; it added a piquant touch to her regular features, the slim nose and firmly chiseled jaw. If Kate had been a patient, they would have talked for hours about the symbolism of the triangle, coming to rest finally on the tangled Oedipal relations between father and son, mother and daughter.

Kate was similarly studying her visitor. "You know, I have the oddest feeling that I know you from somewhere, you look extremely familiar," she said.

"I gather you are interested in psychology. Perhaps you saw a photo – one came out in an article about me recently in the *Psychoanalytic Quarterly,* though it wasn't very flattering. Or maybe you heard me speak at a conference. I was at the meetings in New York last year."

"I don't recall," Kate said, embarrassed at the thought that Helene was someone she ought to recognize. "Perhaps I haven't got your name right, with everything that was going on with mother. Was it Rosenbach?"

"Usually I go by my married name," she said. "Deutsch, Helene Deutsch."

Kate gasped. "Dr. Deutsch! Oh. . . ." She felt confused, slightly dizzy. Of course, now she realized why the name Rosenbach had sounded familiar – she had thought at the time it was because Rosenbach was a fairly common Jewish name.

"I can't believe it," Kate said. "Mother's neighbor turns out to be just the person I wanted to talk to. And bringing food, no less," she added wryly. It was almost too perfect.

Dr. Deustch looked baffled. "I don't understand."

Kate struggled for a minute with the wish just to avail herself of the comforting presence and gift of food – not to remind Helene about Kate's letter asking for help. But it wasn't professional to take advantage . . . and certainly she would be tempted to get Dr. Deutsch to talk about things she might not have revealed to someone who was apt to publish them.

"Actually," she stammered, "this is a quite a coincidence. I hope you don't mind, but I wrote you a letter last month, asking for an interview. I'm writing a thesis on the early women analysts. You were just going away. When we met earlier, I had no idea it was you. . . ." She blushed, suddenly aware of her unwashed hair. She'd been so preoccupied with helping her mother and snatching time to do a little work that she hadn't looked in a mirror in days.

"That is a coincidence! But of course, Kate Berg. I should have made the connection, but we've never met, of course, and I certainly wasn't expecting you down here." Helene paused. "After I answered your letter, I saw your article in *The Atlantic Monthly.* You have an energetic prose style. Not at all in keeping with the name of an Edith Wharton heroine."

"I hope there was some substance, too," Kate said, standing awkwardly with the casserole in her hands.

"What you said about the problems in Freud's approach to women was very interesting. I think by now we have to admit there are some problems, and you were quite eloquent in pointing out the places where more work needs to be done. It will make people think, no doubt about it."

Unsure of what Helene really thought and slightly at a loss for words, Kate led the way to the small kitchen with its linoleum floor and squeezed the casserole into the fridge between a basket of strawberries and some left-over soup.

Her hands freed, Kate began rapidly collecting the books and newspapers scattered on the small table and piling them on a chair. A Pyrex pot sat jauntily on a colorful woven mat. Behind it, a portable Olivetti exhibited what looked like a perfectly blank sheet of paper. Kate pushed it to one side.

"I don't mind. I'm not a neatness fanatic myself," Helene said with a smile. "My husband was always the more orderly one in our family. Felix always knew where everything was. He sometimes even packed for me."

Her women's group would approve of that, Kate thought, relaxing slightly as she poured the French Roast into blue ceramic mugs. Still, this wasn't at all her idea of how their first meeting would go. She had pictured herself walking through Dr. Deutsch's house, allowed to look at her things – photographs of her with Sigmund Freud and other members of his inner circle, perhaps a group photo at one of the early analytic congresses in Vienna or Berlin; there'd be other mementoes too, precious things brought across the ocean with her, late in life – faded mezzotints of her beginnings in a small Polish castle town.

Dr. Deutsch seemed to have done everything. She'd had a dazzling career, a husband, a child, and Kate was eager to hear how she'd done it. She hoped that she could get beyond the icon to the woman herself. It seemed so paradoxical that such a powerful woman would agree with Freud and insist that women were inherently masochistic. It had alienated some of the young feminists and kept her from being taken seriously, but Kate had seen signs in

Dr. Deutsch's case histories of subtle revisionist thinking and hoped to clarify her impressions and provide a fresh view of Deutsch's work.

Kate's hand was trembling in her excitement. She spilled some of her coffee onto the saucer and she carefully poured it back. "There are so many things I wanted to ask you about," Kate said. "Your route to Freud, what it felt like being there at just that moment – especially as a woman. Did being a woman influence your theory or your practice? Were there differences in the way Freud reacted to his female disciples?"

"All good questions," Helene said, "but so many of them!" She held up her hands in mock dismay.

"Sorry. It's rude of me. I invited you for just a coffee, not a seminar. And I didn't even offer any cake. I actually have some, too." She went over to the counter and came back with a boxed Sara Lee. "Coffee Crumble . . . not bad, really. Will you have some?"

Helene nodded and Kate cut her a piece. She would have to slow down, Kate thought, not let her excitement show too much. "Is there any chance that you might let me come and talk to you?" she asked.

"I was hoping to have a complete vacation from work, but there are special circumstances." Helene smiled and took a bite of cake.

"You were kind enough to ask what you could do to help," Kate said, emboldened by the smile. "Really, the thing that would help me most right now would be to get back to work at least for part of the day."

"I certainly appreciate the value of work, though some of these new women act as if I wanted to keep them perpetually on their knees scrubbing kitchen floors. I suppose you're a feminist." Helene had been working off and on at her memoir since Felix died but lately she'd lost momentum. She missed his habitual interrogating voice.

"Not a militant one," Kate said, "and after studying your cases carefully, I'd say you were one too."

Helene suddenly had the same slight stirring of anxiety as when she was with a patient whose underlying ambivalence warned her of some hidden motive, but the girl seemed sincere – maybe her antennae weren't as sharp as they used to be. She drained the last drops of coffee from her cup, tasting the sugar on her tongue, and stood up.

"Who knows? Maybe we could help each other. Will you let me have a day to decide?"

When she left, Kate watched the small figure with the crisp white hair go briskly down the stairs where just two weeks ago Emily had tripped and fallen. It seemed ironic that her mother should be the link to a specter from the family past that Emily had tried so hard to forget, falling almost literally into the lady doctor's arms.

Chapter Three

Helene walked along the beach with a new energy. Well, so, she'd done it. She had agreed to talk to the young woman. She made a mental note to keep up with Emily, too. Emily might not be too happy about their plan – perhaps a bit jealous, Helene thought. She hoped it wouldn't be a problem.

She could feel her mind limbering up, preparing to exercise. It was almost like having an interesting new patient, she thought with a wry smile. Except the one trying to make sense of it all would be on the other side of the couch. What she had gotten in their brief exchange was a pleasant sense that Kate had read her work with an open mind, not automatically condemning her as a reactionary – the fashion among the new feminists. They thought of her as a strict Freudian who believed in women's penis envy and innate masochism and blamed her – quite unfairly, she thought – for promoting the doctrine of female subjugation.

So often it seemed that the young, bombarded as they were by daily facts and messages, were less and less interested in knowing the truth about the past and seeing things in context. Helene wondered, for instance, how many high school students knew who fought in World War I. Surely only a tiny fraction would have any sense of the dying Hapsburg Empire and the rich ferment of Freud's pre-war Vienna.

As a young woman, Helene had been prepared by her revolutionary lover, Lieberman, for the intense discussions of politics that took place in cafés all over the city, each clique, including Freud's, with its own meeting spot. What she hadn't been prepared for was Vienna itself, the confident breadth of the new public spaces, the magnificent Ringstrasse, with the University and the galleries filled with imaginatively daring new art. She had walked the wide boulevards those first days in a state of high excitement.

Her youthful interviewer would be used to the thrust of city skyscrapers against the sky but probably unaccustomed to passionate discussion. Americans were a practical people, Helene thought; they tended to live in the day to day. Even the psychoanalysts, who back then were often brilliant but always quirky, were becoming bland technicians of the spirit.

But of course, she knew that the old idealize their past. She smiled to herself, scenting the salt in the air. She didn't want to be like her friend Maggie who made her house into a mausoleum filled with photographs of old Vienna and sketches by Klimt and Egon Schiele. No. Helene still had a hunger for life. She didn't want to cut herself adrift from the young and what they were thinking or not thinking. This young woman, for instance. Just being young was exciting, having smooth skin, electric hair, a lithe body. Having your whole life still open to choices.

How oddly elusive were actual moments of decision. Sometimes she hadn't known when she'd made a choice. It was as though an express train suddenly shifted tracks. Its forward motion seemed the same, it continued gliding along, but the passenger's course was irretrievably changed. Once, for instance, Helene had reached a "station" knowing with painful certainty that she must leave Lieberman. But the train had switched tracks long before: that afternoon bathed in late summer twilight when she had told him she was pregnant and he'd looked aghast instead of tender. Such moments of not-yet-conscious choice fascinated her. The difficulty of capturing them was one reason she had temporarily put her memoir aside.

Today the sky was a soft blue overhead and a glowing white lower down at the horizon. Luminous water lay stretched under it, merging almost imperceptibly with the sky. It was low tide and two couples were already far out – appearing like light-blue pencil strokes in the magical white light.

Helene would have liked to walk out, too, and sit on one of the raised sand islands feeling the soft air on her face and watching the tide come in around her, but she'd left her suit in the cottage, and Kate was coming soon.

Her thought drifted off to the river in her village, where she had gone swimming as a girl, her strong arms and legs propelling her swiftly through the brown water full with spring rains. Then she caught herself. That was what kept happening to her. Memory was always drawing her back to the days before Vienna and her choice of career, to Poland.

After Felix died three years ago, it had seemed natural to seek sanctuary in her childhood memories. She'd started the memoir to soothe herself, and as a psychoanalyst, of course she thought beginnings were crucial. But she bogged down there, unable to confront . . . what exactly? She dreamed repeatedly of a clock tower where, when the faded wooden doors opened, Death marched stiffly out with his scythe.

For a few moments in the girl's presence she felt a lightening of her feelings. She had always followed her intuitions – sometimes contrary to Professor Freud's suggestion. Now she turned back across the waterscoured sand, anticipating the girl's eager questions as much as if she were preparing to stretch out in her bathing costume under a warming sun.

Kate arrived at Helene's house dressed casually in black jeans, sandals and T-shirt, carrying her necessary coffee in a chipped mug.

"You must think I am very inhospitable, that I wouldn't even provide a cup of coffee," Helene said, motioning her to a comfortable overstuffed chair and seating herself carefully in the New England rocker that was so good for her back.

Kate seemed nonplussed for a moment. "Not at all. I didn't want to bother you. Besides, I'm used to doing for myself."

Kate settled herself in the chair, balancing her coffee cup on the chair arm for a moment while she took out her tape recorder. "Is it okay if I use this?" she asked.

"As long as I can declare some things off the record," Helene said, with the trace of a smile.

"That's understood in all my interviews. And I'd be glad to let you go over the transcript, and to see anything I write before I publish it."

"Thank you. Now tell me how I can help you."

Kate turned on her recorder. "Well, as I said, I'm interested in women in the early days of the movement. Their effect – as women. How they influenced Freud's perceptions of femininity. For instance, Ruth Mack Brunswick and Marie Bonaparte put a new emphasis on the importance of early mothering – the pre-oedipal phase – something which Freud ignored. I'm also interested in exploring the connection between the women's lives and their theory.

Most of the people I've been able to interview," Kate went on, "like Phyllis Greenacre and Muriel Gardiner, are from the second wave of women analysts. I need someone from the earliest days. You were in the inner circle from the beginning, and so much of your life has been spent writing about female psychology. You were an obvious choice."

"And I have the advantage of being one of the few still alive and not senile," Helene said cheerfully, knocking three times on the wooden arm of her rocker.

Kate frowned. Her mother was an almost compulsive knocker on wood. "I wouldn't have thought you'd be superstitious."

"When I was your age, I wasn't. I thought things could be explained. I thought I had found a method that would unravel the mind's tangle like a ball of yarn and take me right to the heart of what it meant to be a human being."

"And now?"

"Let's say I'm much more aware of the mysteries, and the older I get, the less I think I know, really know." Helene was on the verge of telling her that she thought it was very probable that psychoanalysis wouldn't last the century. It took too long and was too expensive. She rocked back and forth, easing the ache in her sacrum. She wasn't being quite fair, she thought, substituting this skeptical self for her earlier impassioned one – most probably the one Kate was interested in.

"So," she said, "you want to know whether my being a woman mattered. Whether I, we, had any influence on the direction psychoanalysis took. Certainly, you know Freud thought of women as the dark continent and asked his female disciples to help him explore it?"

Kate nodded. "But I'd like to have your first-hand view, the way you experienced his ideas in relation to your own life. When you joined, there was only one other woman. Freud kept repeating that he didn't know what women wanted. What did you want, Dr. Deutsch?"

"Not an easy question to answer, is it? Certainly, even as a child I wanted to matter, to have an effect, you might say. I was a lively, questioning sort of girl, not one whom my mother found easy to handle."

"I can relate to that," Kate said with a smile.

"From what I've seen of your mother – and it isn't very much I admit – mine was a very different type. Very moralistic. Rather like an abbess, I imagine. I was always being beaten for some infraction or what my mother called my attitude. I was desperate to find something to take me away from the family and give me a place of my own. Now you take that sort of thing for granted, but at the time it was very difficult. There weren't many avenues of escape." She saw Kate make a note on the small, lined pad she kept next to her tape recorder. "One of them was the stage. My family often went to the theater together. I loved Shakespeare, and for a while I dreamed of being an actress."

"Really?' It was hard to imagine this stocky, almost squarish woman, her silver hair cut short, dressed in brown corduroy trousers slightly reminiscent of German hiking gear Kate had seen in the Alps, playing Ophelia or Juliet. But when she looked at her face carefully she could see that her features were fine, remnants of a lost beauty. And Helene's green eyes were startling.

Helene seemed to read her thoughts. "I had pretty plumage once," she said, quoting Yeats. At one time she had read widely in the English poets. "I was also a Romantic – like many adolescent girls."

She thought of her purple notebook with the thick creamy paper that drank up her ink.

"When I was around eighteen, after a particularly bad fight with my mother, I started to imagine an alternate life for myself as a young girl named Madi. She was much more compliant than I could ever be and got along a lot better with her parents. I kept a journal describing the balls she went to, the books she read. I thought of it as a novel and was quite proud of it."

"I should think most people would write about their dark sides in their journals," Kate said, "hidden desires, that sort of thing." She'd never kept a diary – her mother had been the repository of so much of her inner life until her brother died, and Emily's increased scrutiny made Kate pull away.

"I'm afraid I was living them," Helene said, not sounding at all repentant but not enlarging on it either. She sighed. At eighteen she was already scandalizing her neighbors by her affair with Lieberman, who was not only a highly public figure, but a much older married man. That affair with its tumultuous ups and downs had consumed the best of her energies for years.

"I'd always been ambitious, but for a time when I was about your age – perhaps a little younger – I was in danger of losing sight of my goal of going to university," she said slowly. "Just then, a friend took me to a socialist conference where Rosa Luxemburg was speaking."

The irony was that it had been Lieberman who'd insisted she accompany him. "Rosa was an astounding woman, a socialist leader. Talk about effect. I had never seen a woman holding the stage like that, authority in every gesture. It inspired me."

"But not to a career in politics?" asked Kate, somewhat embarrassed at her lack of clear ideas about Rosa Luxemburg and Eastern European female socialists. She made a vow to research the subject to better understand the context. In the meantime, she thought she'd ask Keith. She was sure he'd know.

"No, not then. I'd thought about politics a lot, most people of any interest did. As a girl, I participated in rallies. Once at a demonstration, I was prepared to throw myself in front of the hooves of the mounted police if they charged us."

Again Kate looked surprised.

"Protest wasn't a recent invention, you know, any more than sex," Helene said tartly. "Though no one ever seems to learn much from what went before."

"People like to think they can avoid their parents' mistakes. It goes without saying that I'm determined to do that myself." Kate smiled and ruffled her hair with one slim hand, making light of it. Then she looked down at her notepad. "You said it was difficult to strike out on your own then. Did your parents make it hard for you to have a career?"

"We were a bourgeois assimilated Jewish family in Poland, but, still, expectations were different in those days. My mother assumed I'd marry and live nearby the way my sister did. And my poor father couldn't really grasp the idea that such a feminine young girl would want to do the things boys do. But he loved me very much and eventually he came around. Father had always singled me out from my brother and my sister. When I was a child, he would let me sit under his desk and listen to him talk with his legal clients, hearing their secrets. Learning how to ferret out relevant information."

Kate felt the pang she often felt when people mentioned their fathers in that loving tone. Helene clearly adored hers. Kate had a vision of herself sitting pathetically chewing on a strand of her hair while she fantasized that the army had made a mistake, that her father wasn't really dead and one day the doorbell would ring and there he'd be. He'd lift her up in his arms and twirl her around, hugging her so hard she'd think her ribs would crack.

She brought herself sharply back to attention – to Helene's crouching under her father's desk trying to read the boundaries of her world.

"I thought about being a lawyer for a long time," Helene was saying. "But the University law faculties weren't opened to women yet."

Analysts didn't often get the pleasure of talking about themselves unless they went for refresher analyses, and Helene hadn't done that since the early years of her marriage. Now she retreated shamelessly to her father's dark wood office, shelves packed with books on legal theory. One of her father's visitors had such a beautiful voice, she told Kate, that she was sure he was tall and handsome with a face like the prince in her illustrated book, but when she peeked out from under the desk she saw he was small, almost a dwarf.

"My fascination with the variety of human nature stems from those early days with my father," she said.

She caught a flicker of impatience on Kate's face." But I'm boring you."

"Not at all . . . it all sounds so cozy, so close. And you see, my father left us when I was small, so . . ." she hesitated.

"So it's hard to hear about someone else's . . ."

"It makes me a little sad, that's all. My father wrote me such wonderful letters when he was sent overseas, telling me about all of the things we'd do together when he got back. Roller skating, picnics, going to the zoo, to the Planetarium, the latest Mickey Mouse film. I would read bits of his letters before I went to sleep. I just wish he'd lived long enough to do some of those things."

"Of course . . . it's only natural to be sad. But sometimes not having a father can be an advantage," Helene said kindly. "It leaves you freer to invent yourself. To seek out your own ways of making sense of things."

Helene sighed. She would have liked to tell Kate about her romantic trips with her father into the villages in winter wrapped in a fur-lined sack, but she stopped herself.

"Anyway, I was lucky," she went on briskly. "Though my father never understood my wanting to do graduate work, he never tried to stop me. In those days you needed a certificate, the Arbitur, to be admitted. I'd only a patchwork education, and the two places in Poland that offered an entrance examination were for men. I had to get special permission. It was hard, but I did it. In the fall of 1907 I came to Vienna to the university to get my medical degree."

Kate drew a deep breath. Dr. Deutsch was in Vienna very early then, earlier than she'd realized.

"And it was then that you met Freud? Did you go to the Wednesday meetings? Sorry, they started a little later didn't they, in 1909." It occurred to Kate that if her grandfather had been a patient of one of them, Dr. Deutsch might have known. If there had been another sort of scandal, she might know that too. The circle of analysts was quite small. But who knows if they spoke of their patients to one another? Probably they did. They weren't supposed to but they still did: Kate heard analysts talking at the gym.

"No. I didn't meet Freud, not yet, though of course I knew about him. My husband Felix went to some of his seminars and wrote me about them when we were engaged a few years later." Helene glanced at the birdfeeder outside the window where a brilliant red bird was pecking at the few remaining seeds. Dear Professor Freud. It was strange to think of him as part of history, neatly shelved. She herself perhaps serving as a trim end-piece.

"I wasn't allowed to begin clinical studies until I had passed my first set of examinations, and then I wasn't in Vienna at all. I spent a year in Munich studying and working at Professor Kraeplin's psychiatric clinic."

"Why did you leave Vienna?" Kate asked, leaning forward attentively. "Was there anything particular?"

Helene hesitated. A little too intrusive, this young woman. But then, she had offered herself as an object of scrutiny; it was her own doing. And she was planning to talk about Lieberman in her memoir. Not by name and not everything, of course, but. . . .

"I had been involved with someone for many years," she said dryly, "an older married man, a socialist revolutionary. I couldn't bring myself to make a clean break, so I did the only thing I could manage, moved away for a year."

Kate nodded her head. She found herself liking Helene.

"And did it work?" she asked with a smile.

"Yes, as a matter of fact. I met my husband, Felix, that year . . . we got engaged almost immediately."

For a moment the age difference didn't matter. Kate had been an escape artist for years, easily breaking with an assortment of lovers, always keeping some part of herself aloof. But then she'd fallen in love with Keith and was alternately thrilled and terrified by her own feelings. She caught herself wishing that Dr. Deutsch was still just the kind neighbor who had helped her mother. Then Kate could have asked her the sort of questions they bandied about in her women's group. She could have asked which was the better lover, though she thought she could already answer this: the one she left, the socialist revolutionary. He must have been quite something to have gotten a young girl, one as strong and willful as Helene had obviously been, to defy her family and stay with him for so many years.

She was curious about the husband, too. It happened awfully quickly – on the rebound. Did she love the husband as much as the lover? Did he help her stalled career take off – or was it just released from the drag of loving someone who wasn't supportive? Well, she couldn't ask. At least, not yet. But maybe if they got to be friends. Kate had never had a friend who was so much older. She tended, perhaps unfairly, to agree with Keith that most of the older generation were wrong-headed. But this woman seemed as revolutionary in her way – certainly in her sexual freedom – as any 60's radical.

"So you went to Munich in 1910-1911," Kate looked down at her pad, "in order to break off from this man. That must have been difficult after so long."

"Let's say, it was not a fruitful year for me, personally," Helene said wryly – certainly an understatement. She cast her mind back. The images she retrieved had the grainy quality of an old black and white movie. It was as though they came from an alternative universe. "I had lost a child," she said simply.

"Oh," Kate exclaimed. "And you wanted it? I mean . . ." she stammered, wondering.

"Yes, I did . . . ."

"But your studies? How would you have managed?"

"I might have found a way," Helene answered, suspecting even as she said it that she was being sentimental. "My sister might have helped me – taken care of the child until I was able to afford to care for it. I sometimes think I would have had a more satisfying life if I'd had that baby . . . though of course, it might have ruined everything. But this isn't what you came for, is it? You are interested in my relation to Freud – the birth of a new science!"

Kate was about to remind her that she was interested in both the woman and the science, but it was too late, she had gone on.

"That year, difficult as it was for me, was also when I first read Freud's *Interpretation of Dreams.* I had always been fascinated by puzzles. Following the sequences of associations Freud laid out was as exciting as watching fireworks burst in widening rings." She threw out her arm in a vigorous circle.

Kate smiled. Dream symbols had become something of a cliché by now. But Helene's face shone with her discovery. For years Kate had recorded her own dreams in beautifully bound notebooks, but they were like vivid short stories. She never could get them to lead to an "Ah ha" moment. She supposed Dr. Deutsch had had better luck.

"I still remember the moment when I got the book. How thick and heavy it was. Joseph Reinhold, the neurologist friend who gave it to me, joked that if I grew tired of reading, I could use it as a weight to improve my muscles. It had a creamy cover with black lettering. He'd turned down pages and marked them; there were exclamations sprinkled everywhere. Ah Joseph, he's been dead for many years now. He was a good friend to me. A fellow Pole."

Helene had spent evenings sitting by the little heater in Joseph's attic room curled in his single armchair picking at the stuffing emerging from the tatty velvet and trying to make up her mind. "You've got to leave Lieberman," Reinhold had insisted. "He's dragging you down, destroying your reputation . . . you've already decided, you just don't know it."

"Joseph knew I was miserable because I used to complain to him. Not very loyal, but I couldn't help it. He had been interested in Freud's theories for some time, and he hoped the dream book would distract me. He was right.

"At the time, I was supervising a hysteria patient at the hospital clinic. This young girl had recently undergone a tonsillectomy and woke up after a terrible dream with an excruciating headache and legs that buckled when she tried to walk. I made the usual charts, keeping records of her bodily functions, her stool, what she ate, her massage therapy and warm baths – the prescribed treatments at the time for mental illness. But after I read Freud's book, it was as if an electric light turned on in my head.

"Before her legs failed, the girl had dreamed that a monstrous animal was biting off her leg. Her symptoms had seemed chaotic and senseless to me. My neurology professors explained them as random events of an organically malfunctioning brain, some sort of lesion, but I wondered if they made psychological sense.

"I started to question her about her family. I didn't have long enough to test out the possibility that her unconscious mind had interpreted the operation as a punishment for sexual impulses, but I talked to her enough to find out that her very strict mother was forever warning her of the dangers of pregnancy. Just a week before the operation, this mother had observed my patient kissing her boyfriend goodnight and lectured her severely. Unfortunately, I couldn't follow through on this case, though her headaches lessened – her parents withdrew her from the hospital after a week."

"It's hard to imagine a time when what was going on in a mental patient's family wasn't important," Kate said. "It must have been a great help to you to see so many patients in a hospital setting. Freud never got to see patients that way, did he? And the ones he saw weren't as sick. Would you say that was a difference between you ?"

Helene shrugged. "He made use of others' observations when he needed them."

Kate saw that she didn't want to continue this line of thought. At least for now.

"You said this work – using Freud's theories – distracted you from your sadness at breaking up with your lover and losing your baby," Kate said with some hesitation. "I realize the baby would have been illegitimate and that makes a huge difference, but I wondered what the orthodox analysts in Freud's circle thought about motherhood and work."

"I don't recall anyone discussing it. And I didn't know any of them intimately. Except maybe Viktor Tausk because we'd worked together at Hochwart's clinic. He made sly jokes about my secretly planning to bring my baby in to nurse when I saw patients so as to save time for my writing. I think he was a bit misogynistic. His wife, Martha, was an ardent, highly committed socialist, and he was jealous of her activities. But he was also attracted to women of intellect and power. He had an affair with the most famous woman intellectual of her generation, Lou Salome. . . ."

"I've heard about her affairs with Rilke and Nietzsche, but I don't recognize Tausk's name."

"You wouldn't have heard of him . . . Jones only mentions him tangentially in his Freud biography, but he was perhaps the most brilliant of the disciples – an excellent clinician." Helene paused, needing to be fair, though not yet needing to have this girl know how important Viktor had once been to her. "And a good friend of mine. There weren't many of us working clinically with psychotics. We often discussed cases and gossiped about things going on in the hospital. Who was in favor, who was harsh, who wasn't – things like that, and he would relay what was going on in Freud's circle. In addition to being brilliant, he was a very humane, progressive man."

"How so?" Kate prompted, curious.

"He served as a psychological consultant during the 1914 war. As you can imagine, it was a stressful and exhausting position. Officers were expected to have the proper patriotic attitudes, and deserters were judged very harshly. Tausk thought that the men were being condemned or released indiscriminately. He felt that it was tragic for the courts to decide on the fate of men forced to participate in the destruction of other human beings. He felt it was particularly unfair for illiterate peasants who had no idea of what they were fighting for and would sneak back to their homes to tend their crops without any sense of wrongdoing."

"A war protester !" Kate said. From what she'd read, there weren't too many of them in Austria – at least in the early days of the war. "My boyfriend would love to hear that. He's been very active against this dreadful war of ours in Vietnam."

"And you?"

"I haven't been as active as Keith would like." She continued piously, "I certainly believe that war is almost never the right solution to conflict. Except maybe when you're dealing with a madman like Hitler."

For the first time Kate found she was able to visualize one of Freud's circle as a living, breathing man . . . could imagine him speaking eloquently against the cruelties of war. The way they were doing now at Berkeley and Columbia. She wanted to find out more about him to tell Keith. He thought her investigations were irrelevant to life in the present. He had a rather ahistorical mind, she thought, with a mixture of affection and irritation, but the right values. He couldn't seem to see that the past was important to society as well as to the individual.

"Did Tausk protest the war actively?" Kate asked.

Helene raised her eyebrows. "He would have been court-martialed and probably shot – there was a war on, you know. He knew the laws couldn't be changed in a wartime atmosphere – people were hysterical with patriotism – but he clearly hoped it would happen some time in the future. He thought the laws lagged behind our social values. The penal code was early nineteenth century, and badly needed to be updated."

She stopped, not wanting to talk about what had happened to him after the war. After all these years, she still had a nagging feeling of failure associated with him. She tended to push down unwanted thoughts and turn her mind to something fruitful and positive. That had always been her way after the final break with Lieberman. Be active, productive. It wasn't like her to brood.

There was a glow in Dr. Deutsch's still beautiful eyes. She was obviously stirred by her memories. Kate realized she must have been exquisite when her skin was fresh.

"I'd like to hear more about him," Kate said, imagining offering the stories to Keith as a gesture of goodwill after their quarrel.

"Well, maybe I'm wrong to say he didn't protest actively. Certainly he acted on his conviction – often against his own interests. There was the case of a young man who was being court- martialed because he was unwilling to shoot some captured enemy soldiers. Tausk convinced his commanding officers that having been brought up in a highly civilized environment, the boy would not have been able to execute men in cold blood. He saved the boy's life. He confessed that his dislike of judging others was related to his love of children. He had two boys."

"Oh," Kate said, feeling faintly disappointed that he had no girl, "and a socialist wife."

"They were divorced actually, though he stayed in close contact with her because of the boys. She was pregnant when he married her and he wasn't ready. They were very young. He felt tied down, forced to a career prematurely. He practiced law for a while but hated it – hated the judgmental aspect of it." Helene looked out the window. The sun was high in the sky, casting a clear merciless light on everything. Not a time, she thought, to be indoors remembering *der arme* Tausk, poor Tausk, as Freud called him.

Kate noticed that Helene suddenly seemed tired. "I've kept you too long," she said, giving a guilty glance at her watch. "Do you want to rest?"

"No – this may sound odd, but I'd like to go for a swim. It's perhaps a little imprudent for me to go alone at my age, but I love the water. I was hoping I could persuade you to go with me. Please don't be afraid to tell me no, if you don't feel in the mood or need to get back to your mother . . . we could continue to talk, if you like."

"I'd like to swim very much. I just have to run back to the house and change into my suit, then I'll come back to get you."

"It may take me a little longer to get ready," Helene said.

"That's okay. I'm not in a rush." Kate picked up her coffee cup and tucked her pad back in her pocket. She had an impulse to offer a hand to help Helene to her feet; the chair was deep and made it look as if standing up might be a difficult task, but she guessed the older woman wouldn't like that. At any rate, she wasn't moving and was clearly waiting until Kate left to start trying. Feeling slightly awkward, Kate picked up her coffee cup and recorder, and ducking her head in a gesture of goodbye, went out the door.

Emily wasn't back from her walk yet, so Kate wrote a note saying she was going for a swim before lunch and changed into her suit, pulling a light chemise over it. Contrary to her expectation, Helene was ready for her, waiting eagerly on the porch, when she got back. When they were just about to set out, the front door was thrown open and a stout middle-aged woman with large dark eyes and hair drawn back into a bun, rushed out of the house with a paper bag clutched in her hands.

"Doctor, you forgot your pastries," she said, reprovingly, "and I've put in something to drink. The sun is hot, you'll be thirsty. I'm sure the young lady will carry it for you."

"Gladly," Kate said, taking the proffered bag.

"This is my housekeeper, Mrs. Dubrovsky," Helene said. "She thinks I neglect myself. I'm lucky I have her watching over me."

Mrs. Dubrovsky bobbed her dark head in acknowledgment of the compliment and made a dignified exit.

Helene and Kate went down the steps lined with rose hips, at the back of the cottage, through a patch of compass grass bent over by its weight, the tips sweeping in wide circles over the sand. The tide had come in and small, choppy waves covered the flats where she and Keith had walked the week before. In the distance, gaily colored sailboats skimmed over the water.

"My housekeeper won't let me go anywhere without provisions," Helene explained with a laugh as they walked along. "She acts as if we're under siege and might not get another chance to eat for weeks."

Kate was walking slowly, enjoying the varying colors of the sand, from deep ochre to rusty orange.

"Maybe she had family who suffered from hunger in the war," Kate said idly, just to make conversation. "I had a friend with an aunt like that. She was always hiding provisions away in odd places." Her friend had explained it as a sort of shtetl mentality.

Helene's expression darkened as she thought of her own family. All the provisions in the world wouldn't have helped them.

"Oh, I'm sorry," Kate said, noticing her expression. "That was a thoughtless thing to say. Did you . . . did you have . . . you must have had people there too. Or did your family emigrate when you did?"

"No. My father died but my mother stayed in Poland, in our family home. Perhaps I didn't do enough to convince them to leave – who knows if they could have gotten out, but . . . my sister lost her sons and my mother . . .," she hesitated, "chose not to wait for Hitler's armies to find her."

"She . . ."

"She felt she was too old to flee her home."

"I'm sorry," Kate stammered again. By mistake she had blundered into the midst of a tragedy.

"I don't often speak of it," Helene said as a cluster of gulls flew screaming overhead. "Or think of it, for that matter. There are so many situations where I can be of help. Why dwell on the one where I could do nothing . . . nothing at all."

They walked along silently for a few minutes, moving away from the little knot of bathers that was clustered under a blue umbrella. The far end of the beach was practically deserted, except for a few people walking their dogs.

"You look shocked. What happened to my mother is shocking, is terrible. I've always liked to think I had some control over events. We all like to think so. And the loss of that sense of control is as terrible as anything. Certainly, I tolerate it badly. I admit it." She put her bag down on the stony remains of an old wharf, and kicked off her sandals.

"But why use your mind to make yourself miserable?"

Why indeed, if you could help it? Certainly as an analyst, Dr. Deutsch must have pushed patients to face their own denials of weakness. But then, even the greatest analyst was human – something hard to remember, especially when one was as famous as Helene Deutsch. Kate remembered reading somewhere that whereas outsiders often wrote hysterical prose about atrocities, real concentration camp victims spoke of their sufferings in rather flat, seemingly affectless voices. It had been too much to take in emotionally.

Helene was stripping down now to her suit. She'd seemed sturdy, stocky when dressed. It was strange how different she looked without her voluminous beach shirt. Kate took in the softened vulnerable flesh on arms and legs, the wrinkled skin and distended belly – an old woman's body – and felt a sudden strange protectiveness. She kicked off her own sandals, pulled off her shorts.

"What a pretty bikini," Helene said. "Blue becomes you, or is that lavender? How I wish I could wear those little bits of cloth, though really, I'd prefer going naked."

Kate laughed. "You're amazing. I don't know what to make of you," she said as they stood at the water's edge, accustoming their feet to the cold before going in.

"I used to swim all the time in my village. We had a wonderful brown river, and in the spring I loved to battle the current to see how far I could get before I was exhausted."

Helene bent and splashed a handful of water lightly against Kate. "Come, let's go."

Kate plunged in after her, marveling at how after wading part way in somewhat painfully, Helene had thrown herself forward and was swimming strongly. "Isn't it glorious," she said when Kate came up alongside her. "The water gives me back my body." Her face was shining with pleasure. "No pain anywhere."

Kate, so accustomed to the smooth functioning of her limbs, had to think for a moment before she understood that the weightlessness must free Helene's joints.

"I feel almost like a girl again." Helene turned on her back and paddled looking up at the sky. Kate was just about to suggest that they had gone out far enough – with the tide beginning to move out again – it would be harder going back, when Helene suddenly gasped. "I have a cramp in my foot." She turned, dolphin-like, reached down and started to massage her foot. The position was awkward and without thinking, Kate swam behind her and held her. "Ach," she gasped. "I can't get it to stop."

"Don't worry, I've got you." Helene couldn't let go of her leg and towing her in her present pretzel shape was difficult, but Kate was a strong swimmer, and adrenalin was pumping into her system.

"I'm having trouble keeping your head above water. It's getting choppier. Can you let go of your leg?"

"I don't think so . . . ," Helene stammered.

"I'm going to try a different grip. Hold your breath if I dunk you."

Helene's cramp must have relented, because she was able to stretch out into a plank position that made it easier for Kate to keep going until, with a last effort, she reached shallow water. Small purple and brown shells rolled around them as Kate helped Helene to her feet and they waded back to the narrow beach.

"Well, I guess I'm not as young as I thought I was . . . and I was certainly lucky to have you there. . . . Thank you. I'm much in your debt."

"I'm glad I was with you," Kate said simply. "But are you sure you're all right? There is some blood on your leg."

Helene brushed it off. "It's nothing, I must have scratched myself when I was trying to massage the cramp. But I do feel tired," she said walking slowly back to her things while leaning on Kate's arm. Kate, feeling the pressure, felt a surge of something like pride.

Helene asked if Kate would mind postponing their picnic, and she answered graciously that of course she didn't mind. "I'm not really hungry yet anyway," she said. Reaching their things, Kate held Helene's shirt for her to slip into. Then she offered her arm again with a little parodic bow as if she were a court nobleman, and they picked their way over the sand back to the path. Just before they reached Helene's house, Helene asked her if she would come to lunch the next day, Sunday.

"Oh, don't feel you have to," Kate said.

"Giving you a nice meal is the least I can do, I think – and besides, I'd enjoy it. Really . . . no reason we can't combine it with our talk."

As Helene was climbing her steps, Kate realized she'd forgotten something. "Oh gosh, I think I left my earrings back at the beach."

"No, they're here," Helene said, turning around, "in the pocket of my bag. Don't you remember you put them there for safe-keeping? And here they are." She produced them with a flourish and Kate ran up the steps to retrieve them.

"If you were in analysis," Helene said, smiling, "I'd say that meant you were reluctant to leave."

Kate smiled back. "Luckily, I'll be seeing you soon."

Kate usually ate almost nothing at midday, sometimes skipping lunch entirely when she was working, so she was aghast next Sunday when she saw Mrs. Dubrovsky bringing in a huge plate of sauerbraten and cabbage, yogurt and fresh bread.

"What a feast," Kate said, wondering how she'd ever manage to eat all this, but at the same time, she was touched. Mrs. Dubrovsky gave her a regal smile.

"Tell me a little about yourself," Helene said as Kate worked valiantly at her sauerbraten. "You have a boyfriend who protests the war, you are interested in psychoanalysis. How did you get this interest, I wonder?"

"I wanted to be a writer at first," Kate said. "My mother pretty much had painting sewn up – and I guess I thought I didn't have the talent." She compressed her cabbage into the smallest possible space.

"Not room in the world for both of you?" Helene asked, bemused. "So word-painting instead. Did you try to write?"

"I wrote a few essays about my brother. He was a few years older than I was – I was rather obsessed with him."

"Oh, I didn't realize you had a brother." Helene wondered if that might explain some of Kate's annoyance at her mother. Where was this sibling when there was trouble?

"He had a boating accident when he was eighteen," Kate said, lowering her eyes. "He drowned."

"That must have been a terrible shock for you." And for your mother, Helene thought, reflecting on the two women walled in with their losses.

"He was a daredevil; he thought there was nothing he couldn't do. I admired him tremendously." But sometimes she had hated him too – for lording it over her, for her own desire to follow him around like a puppy, always begging: Will you teach me how? Can I do it, too? Won't you tell me the secret, I promise I won't tell? Hated him for being so compellingly charming and handsome with his perfect sun-bronzed skin and wide eyes, the forelock that fell over them.

She pushed a dark curl back from her face. Sometimes she suspected that she had dared him to do it, even though a storm was coming up – but she knew that wasn't true, that in fact he'd been desperate over his girlfriend, a tall blond girl with a bright red mouth and white teeth. Kate had disliked her phony smile, and had tried to tell him she was no good. But he was older, he never paid the slightest attention – until the day he found his girl with his best friend.

Kate had come into his room to ask for help with her homework and found him crying. At first she couldn't believe it, it was so unlike him – and he muttered darkly about making someone sorry. There was no way, Kate had decided years later, she could even have conceived of what he meant. That he'd been lying there planning his funeral.

"After he drowned, my mother watched me like a hawk. She was always terrified that something would happen to me. Whenever I was in a bad mood, she'd hover over me, asking me every ten minutes how I felt. At the same time she'd get more and more cheery, reminding me that I'd had a great birthday party or done well on my algebra test. None of it made me feel any better."

"I can imagine . . . you knew she wasn't really cheerful inside . . . and how could she be?"

"She had our horoscopes done by an astrologer who told her that the star conjunctions at my birth were worrisome – the sun and Venus, or was it Mars? What rubbish." Kate heard a scornful tone come into her voice and stopped. This wasn't the way she wanted to see her mother. "I know people have different ways of coping," she finished. "I can't really blame her."

Obviously, she did though, Helene thought. "Writing is perhaps a more productive way of dealing with grief. What happened to your essays?"

"Nothing. No one wanted to publish them." Kate laid her fork down unable to eat another bite. "One editor said he was shocked that I was so angry at Josh. And I was. If he hadn't succeeded in killing himself, I think I would have strangled him. I mean how could he have done that? I think the editor would have preferred I idealize him – poor dead angel, that sort of thing. But Josh was anything but an angel." She could still imagine him grinning down at her. "Cm'on brat, you can be badder than that . . . think big, think wicked."

"Maybe you gave up too easily. Psychology and writing have a lot in common," Helene said. "Analysts also have to deal with the contradictions of a real life."

"And I guess you get in trouble for it sometimes, too," Kate said. "People hate hearing nasty things about their heroes."

"But they're often true. A person may discover a new law of physics, or write an exquisite poem and still behave badly in his private life. It's all in the balance as far as I'm concerned. Just because someone acts badly, it doesn't diminish their contribution."

"I guess I think therapists should be a little better than other people."

"You mean like the Jews?" Helene asked, with a touch of irony. "Always held to a higher standard."

"If you are going to tell other people how to live, it seems fair to ask you to face your own neuroses. . . ."

"Isn't any human being subject to the same frailties?" Helene asked, seemingly annoyed. "We disagree, that's all," she added more kindly, noting Kate's discomfort. "There's nothing wrong with that." Then after a moment's pause, during which she rearranged her expression to that of a considerate hostess, she continued, "Why don't we go into town for dessert and coffee? I think we need a little break – at least I do. A walk will be good for digestion and I need to get a book for a friend's granddaughter."

The Provincetown bookstore was a neat white clapboard structure with a blue door, standing on a sand-blown corner. Inside the small space, shelves crammed with books went from floor to ceiling. The place had a pleasant musty smell and was guarded by a middle-aged man with spectacles and a British accent. Two tables in the center were covered with brightly covered children's books. Helene thumbed through Sendak's *In the Night Kitchen* and laughed out loud at the illustration of the stark naked dreaming boy falling into a vat of milk. "This is wonderful," she said, "but I'm afraid it's for a younger child."

"Why don't you get *The Wizard of Oz,*" Kate suggested, drawing the book out of the pile. She handed it to Helene. "It's a magical book – even though the wizard turns out to be a fake. And Dorothy is such a fearless, sturdy little girl. When something scared me as a child, I used to think of what Dorothy would have done."

"Sounds just right."

While Helene was paying for the book and the clerk was wrapping it, Kate skimmed the pop psychology shelf and noticed Betty Friedan's *Feminine Mystique* – which she'd read avidly when it first came out – next to a newer book on abusive relationships and how to fight free of them. The topic interested her, but when she opened the book, it looked as slick as the glossy cover, and she quickly put it back.

"At the risk of offending you, may I ask you about something that bothers me?" Kate asked Helene when they were outside. They were in front of a pottery store that had a display of potbellied jugs and vases, glazed a deep ruby red.

"I saw you looking at that book on women in abusive relationships," Helene answered. "I imagine you want to ask me whether I still think women are naturally masochistic." Kate nodded and Helene went on: "Nine times out of ten female masochism is the concept that most offends modern women. They like to think of themselves as sprung fully armed from their mother's wombs, leaving female vulnerabilities behind. But if we're going to talk about masochism I have to sit down."

Kate laughed and followed Helene to the Café Blasé, where they sat down at a little white table outside in the sun. A tanned young man, probably a student there for the summer, took their order. He was back in a few minutes with decaf for Kate and coffee and cake for Helene. The cake was large and filled with layers of whipped cream and chocolate. Helene insisted that Kate – whom she'd observed eyeing it covetously – share it with her.

"I've seen the troubles my mother had, her bad choice of a husband, the way she's suffered," Kate said, offering up her mother to Helene's scrutiny. "But to say a woman wants to be in pain, or that she likes it, just doesn't seem right to me."

Helene noted a certain shrillness in Kate's voice. Certainly this wasn't a neutral subject for her. "I'm not advocating masochism," she said reassuringly. "I'm defending against it. Building firewalls. When a patient tells me that she spends her time kneeling on the floor scrubbing while her husband takes another woman to bed, do I commend her for exhibiting female masochism? Is that what you think I do?"

Kate shook her head.

Helene extracted a spoonful of the whipped cream and put it into her coffee. *Kaffee mit schlag* had always been a favorite of hers. If this young woman hadn't been so determined to quiz her, she would have liked to simply sit there in the sun and sip the hot coffee through the cool cream.

"On the contrary," Helene went on, "I encourage her to get off her knees and get angry. He should be the one on the floor immersed in dirty water. Then, if it is possible and she has the capacity, I encourage her to find some gratifying work. But I saw other much more compelling cases of masochism. Early in my career, I worked with teenage prostitutes who kept returning to the men who beat them. One particularly lovely girl, I thought I'd helped: she broke away from her pimp, met a kind man who loved her, married him and had a baby. But when her pimp got out of jail and called her, she left everything to run to him. What other word describes that behavior so well?"

"Maybe she was deadly bored and craved excitement," Kate offered. "Maybe she truly loved the man, maybe she'd been brought up to think that a man only loves you when he beats you . . . whatever her reasons, I can't believe that it was pain that attracted her any more than I believe masochism is what characterizes a woman, that it's a necessary part of being female."

Helene sighed. Telling a woman she was masochistic was a little like telling her she had cancer – instead of looking for a cure, patients often used every ounce of their force in denial. "Forget the term for a moment. You said the ex-prostitute may have craved excitement. I'd agree. What is irresistible is her desire to submit totally to a man. It gives her a sexual thrill that she doesn't get from her considerate husband. I think it is a temptation for many women."

Kate's head rebelled at this idea, but at the same time she remembered how her heart had raced when she first saw Marlon Brando on his motorcycle in *The Wild Ones.* "But men can be tempted too, can't they?" Kate asked after a moment, savoring the way the cream and chocolate were mixing on her tongue. "Look at Proust's Swann or the old man in *The Blue Angel.*"

"I never said men couldn't be masochists. Of course they can get pleasure from submitting too – to a woman or a stronger man."

"And maybe it's a result of social conditioning that there seem to be more women masochists than men," Kate added.

"That could very well be . . . time will tell. What concerned me most when I began working was the harm masochistic behavior inflicted on individual women, an effect I've always tried to counteract because I know how pernicious it can be. I myself was sorely tempted during that first long love affair I mentioned before to give myself over to my lover. My highest aspiration was to be a foot-soldier in his revolution. I took care of his things, waited for him for hours in cafes, never complained . . . and it was all hopeless. His wife was sick, and he kept saying that after she died we would be together. I knew enough medicine to know she wasn't going to die, and he was never going to leave her. I knew it, but I couldn't stop loving him."

"Until you heard Rosa Luxemburg speak," Kate said, imagining a young Helene at the edge of the crowd, standing close to a dashing man, suddenly becoming aware of her own strength and taking one small step aside so that she no longer felt the heat of his body drawing her.

"Yes." Helene was pleased that Kate remembered. "And she showed so clearly what a woman could do, how powerful she could be, that she made me ashamed of what I'd become." She ate another mouthful of cake, glad she didn't have to worry about losing her figure. It was one of the prerogatives of age. Kate, on the other hand, had pushed away her plate half-finished – eaten like a bird at lunch, too.

"Thank you for telling me this," Kate said, gratefully. "It makes me understand much better how you thought what you did. But what about Freud? He really did think that masochism and passivity weren't just tendencies to be combatted. He thought they characterized women. I guess," she pursed her lips, "I'm wondering why you didn't break with him."

"I didn't have to break with him to do my work well. I truly believe he was stating what he observed."

"In his limited clientele."

"And what I observed too, in my patients and in my life – and you know, sometimes an urge to give oneself totally wasn't a bad thing – if a woman was very motherly, if she found a good man and could put herself entirely into running her home. Of course, it could be a disaster if the woman chose wrong – as you say your mother did. As my young prostitutes did. And I'm certainly not saying it could never change. Perhaps now with all the awareness, with this movement of women, women will be more aware, are already more aware of the dangers of being too submissive and they are trying to change things, to pull each other up. Are you in one of those new consciousness-raising groups I've heard about? They interest me."

"Yes, I am."

"And is it helpful?"

"I think so. They point things out, things I'm not aware of. I have a tendency to put myself down."

"Not noticeable by me," Helene said, smiling as she scraped the last crumbs of cake from the plate with the back of her fork.

"Oh, well . . . sometimes I get confused about simple things like directions and make people think I'm not too bright. It helps that they catch me. It makes it harder for me to do."

"Perhaps if my young prostitute had had a band of sisters to go to who would have all told her not to go back to her pimp, and would have argued with her, maybe she wouldn't have gone."

"But you . . . you say you talked with her . . . and it had no effect."

"I used to believe that if someone understood the deep motives of her behavior, she would change it – almost automatically. But frankly, over the years I believe in 'insight' less and less. People have to have the will to change, and my young woman didn't. I've come to think social pressure, real hands-on, multiple encouragement, might have a better effect."

Just then the tanned young waiter came up with the bill. Kate had her money ready on her lap and she paid before Helene could react, though the older woman insisted on leaving the tip. Then she went inside and Helene bought a couple of Danish for her breakfast and they started back slowly.

As they walked along, stopping occasionally to look at a seascape or the window of an antique shop, Kate realized she was disappointed in Helene for not feeling it necessary to break with Freud. Breaking was in the air now: with politicians, with authority of all kinds, taking to the road with one's own impulses, expressing oneself, forming new alliances – like her women's group. Helene's experience had to have been different. It was hard to remember how Freud's theories had struck Vienna like an electric storm. Learned neurologists had called him a pervert and a danger to family values. For Helene to have left her family, gone to University, and taken up with Freud's radical new doctrines was already a great deal.

Though they hadn't yet talked about Helene's relationship to him specifically, it was evident from her tone when she mentioned his name that she not only esteemed him but had deep affection for him. Would she be willing, Kate thought now, to accept his shortcomings? She wondered suddenly if any of them had affected Dr. Deutsch personally. The atmosphere around Freud must have been remarkably volatile. She'd have to ask Helene more next time.

She looked at her wrinkled face with the bright green eyes and felt a surge of admiration. This woman had endured. She didn't deserve the scorn of feminists like Kate Millet, a fellow graduate student at Columbia, who blamed Deutsch for following Freud to the letter and sending women back to the stone age but never saw what she actually did in her practice – how in many ways she was as good a feminist as anyone.

Chapter Four

After dropping off Helene, Kate went home so full of stimulating thoughts that her nerves were tingling as if she'd drunk four or five cups of strong coffee instead of a mild decaf. These interviews were going to provide a wealth of material for her thesis on the early female analysts and the book she hoped would come out of it. Dr. Deutsch's views were even more subtle than she had thought at first and clearly merited a fresh look. She also determined, inspired by Helene's story of finding her strength, to find a way to confront her own mother more forcefully, and tell her that she deserved to know about her grandfather. If only so she could put whatever it was behind her. How terrible her grandfather's story must be if her mother wouldn't reveal it.

Kate waited until they had finished dinner and the dishes were washed and put away and her mother was resting on the sofa.

"Mother, I need you to tell me Grandpa's name. It's bad enough having a history like Grandma's behind me, but I'd feel much more in control if I knew the details."

"Sometimes it's better not to know," her mother said, crossing her arms over her breasts.

"That's just not true. It makes me incredibly anxious. I can't understand why you won't tell me at least his name."

"I promised my mother . . . ," Emily said, her lips closed to a tight, pink gash.

"Your mother has been dead for years. Certainly you don't believe she's watching you from heaven? Sorry, I didn't mean to be sarcastic but this is infuriating. You make me think he was a criminal. Well, was he? What did he do? Embezzle money, cheat his employers, cook the books . . . ," she paused. Her acquaintance with crimes was purely literary and she had no idea what profession he'd been in. Her grandmother was a pianist; perhaps he too had been in the music business. "Plagiarize? Steal someone's ideas and pass them off as his own?"

She watched her mother's face closely. A look she couldn't interpret passed over it.

"Am I getting close?"

"Don't be ridiculous, Kate, we're not playing twenty questions. This isn't a game, and, no, you're not close to anything."

"You had a strange look on your face."

"My leg hurts." She re-arranged herself on the couch, giving a groan as she did so. "Quite badly."

Kate felt a flush of shame. "I'm sorry," she stammered. "I thought you were feeling better."

"Well, I'm not, and on top of that, the doctor's office called – it seems there are some problems with the insurance, and of course I don't have any of the papers down here."

"I'll go into the city and get them for you," Kate said quickly, atoning for her outburst. "It's no big deal. I could see Keith, go to the library." She'd have to make sure the aide could sleep over.

"Thank you," her mother said. "Now I'm going in to take a nap. And Kate?"

"Yes?"

"Take my advice. Believe me, it's for your own good. Pretend he never existed." Her lips locked in that stubborn way she had and she pulled herself up on her crutches and lurched into the bedroom, closing the door firmly behind her.

"How are you?" Helene asked when Kate came over the next day. "You look tired."

"I'm all right, just frustrated. I have to go into the city to get some insurance papers for my mom. I don't mind that, but I'm just so annoyed with my mother. I've been trying to get her to tell me about my grandfather. Apparently, he got my grandmother pregnant and then walked out on her. Admittedly not nice. But my mother has made a big mystery of it. She hints that there is something too terrible to discuss, even refuses to tell me his name. In fact, she absolutely refuses to give me the slightest bit of information. It's so ridiculous. I've tried everything I could think of."

Helene knew she couldn't ask why it was so important. Kate wasn't her patient, after all. But she hazarded a guess that it was because Kate was beginning to think about marrying this young man of hers and having a family.

"Perhaps it would be easier if you assured her you wouldn't do anything if you found out."

"What do you mean, do anything?"

"Well, it occurs to me it might involve something that your mother feels would be harmful to you or distract you from your own life."

Kate was startled. "I hadn't thought of that."

"It's only a guess."

"It's particularly upsetting because last week when she was just waking up from a nightmare, she let slip that he had something to do with analysis. Perhaps he was a patient?"

The idea piqued Helene's interest. Being a patient back then was quite different from what it was now. An adventure into new territory for both patient and doctor. "Maybe, given your interest in the field, your mother was afraid you'd write about something she doesn't want discussed."

"She's not so wrong there. I'm an inveterate teller of secrets," Kate said. "I think that's why my research fascinates me. I love digging things up . . . getting at the truth. I suppose that's naïve."

"Still, perhaps it's better not to force things," Helene said mildly, "You remember the story of Bluebeard and his curious wife."

Kate shuddered. The story had terrified her as a child.

"I doubt I'm going to find a room of corpses," she said with more confidence than she felt, "but I can't just give it up, and, actually I wanted to ask you a favor." She hesitated, not sure how to put it. "If anything comes to mind . . . some scandal or crime involving a patient or even perhaps another analyst . . . would you tell me?"

"Of course, my communications with a patient would be private," Helene said.

"Though Freud wrote about his patients didn't he?"

"Well, let's just say if I can help you, I will. When are you leaving? Should we re-schedule?"

"No need. I'm not going until tomorrow."

"Would you mind if we talked at the beach? There are always treasures to be found at low tide."

"I'm a scavenger too," Kate said. "I saw a show in New York recently. There was a little sculpture made out of driftwood I particularly liked – it looked like a gull, with a string coming from its beak tied to a fragment of bone."

"It's not a new idea, you know," Helene said, taking a small bag and her straw hat from a hook near the door. "Leonardo used to crinkle up pieces of paper and throw them on the floor and let them suggest forms to him. I'm not looking for anything special; just the right piece of driftwood for my mantle."

They set out slowly, giving Helene's legs a chance to warm up. At the beach they both took off their shoes so they could walk near the water's edge. Kate put hers in her backpack. The waves had retreated, leaving a long stretch of moist darkened sand. It was cool and hard, and their shallow prints vanished behind them as they walked. In front of them a flock of sandpipers on ridiculously long legs was scurrying backward and forward at the water line, pecking at small crabs. Several young children were busy with buckets while their mothers sat nearby, soaking up the sun.

Helene bent to retrieve a piece of driftwood and stood examining it. Kate thought that maybe it had been a mistake to come out where there were so many distractions. She took the tape recorder from her pack and turned it on with a flourish.

"So," Helene said, reluctantly, jettisoning the wood, which though it had a nice shape was too small. "What will it be today?"

"Well, after you mentioned Salome, I checked in Jones's biography and saw that he described her as Freud's closest confidante after World War 1. Quite a privileged position. I was wondering how well you knew her and whether she was involved in the early struggles?"

Kate had once seen a photo of Lou Salome standing over Nietzsche and Rilke brandishing a whip with great verve. It had been in Switzerland, on a student walking tour, in the little mountain village of Sils, where Nietzsche lived in the summer. Lou had high cheek bones and a mane of blond hair. Kate remembered being quite taken with her, wondering where she got her power.

"Involved is perhaps too strong a word, but she certainly was in Vienna at a critical time. Adler had already broken with Freud over his doctrine of the inferiority complex, and Jung, his chosen heir, had been drawing away for some time. Lou was very clever and manipulative and played all camps. Right from the beginning, she saw that the struggle was partly a question of personalities. Adler disliked Freud personally, and she thought Adler was subtly malicious. She went from one faction to the other. Adler's meetings on Thursdays, Freud's on Wednesdays."

"Did Freud admit her as a member?" Kate asked. If he had, she would have been the first woman, even before Helene.

"I believe he did. Freud's Society had just voted, seven to three, to allow women to join. Lou sat in on the meetings quietly, insisting she was there to learn, but she dazzled them nonetheless – an enormously charismatic woman. Striking even at fifty when she joined the Society." Helene stooped to recover a curiously shaped nugget of blue glass which she slipped into her little bag. "I always thought that Lou, with her penchant for great men, wanted to have Freud as a lover. When she saw that was impossible, she turned to Freud's most brilliant disciple, *der arme* Tausk."

"Why 'poor?'" Kate asked, scuffing the sand with her toes, hoping for another piece of glass.

"Oh, people sometimes referred to him that way, and there was a certain fierce ruthlessness to Lou. She sailed in like some rare bird, perched, looked around, and took him." She paused, winced. While Lou was seducing yet another lover, Helene had just married Felix and settled into domesticity. Staying up late not making love but studying for her final medical exams. She frowned, remembering what a disappointing lover Felix had been after Lieberman. She'd thought naively that it was inexperience, that she could teach him, but Felix had only felt criticized, and despite his deep love for her, sex became a test of his masculinity. The truth was that what had drawn her to him wasn't sexual passion but his undemanding love and his total support for her ambitions.

Kate was intrigued that this Tausk had been the lover of a woman who had had two geniuses kneeling at her feet. "I imagine he wasn't completely passive," she said, laughing.

"You're right. He was a Romantic as well as a dedicated scientist – it's not an easy combination."

"A little like your own?"

Helene settled herself on a bleached driftwood log next to a partially finished sandcastle. "Do you see me that way? Maybe I've given you that impression by talking about Lieberman, but that was my girlhood. No, by then, my passion was for psychiatry."

"You made one choice, apparently she made another," Kate said casually. She squatted on her haunches at Helene's feet, and started idly building up the castle's main turret, enjoying the rounded shape.

"You said Lou kept quiet in the meetings. Was her lover, Tausk, involved in the disputes?"

"On the contrary, he was Freud's strongest defender. He tore Adler down whenever he got a chance – Lou thought he might even be harming himself by going too far in his criticisms – and Tausk was the only one teaching Freudian theory. Lou took his course and I was planning to take it. No one could have tried harder to win the master's favor." Helene sighed. "But, alas, it didn't work well. Tausk made Freud nervous. Freud had a physical dislike of being near him. Lou once told me that sometimes at the international meetings, when Tausk would move close to him to share a comment or joke, she could see Freud flinch."

Kate was intrigued by this suggestion of what seemed an irrational dislike. And why did Lou take it on herself to intercede with Freud? "How strange," she said, building her turret higher. "I wonder why?"

"Chemistry, I suppose," Helene offered, disingenuously. "Lou told me she tried to talk to Freud about it, but it was like trying to persuade a man to eat oysters when the sight of them makes him queasy."

"It sounds so strong . . . ."

"Freud was under a great strain then," Helene explained. That was an understatement. Freud had been infuriated by the defections and crushing in his disdain of his erstwhile favorites. "And perhaps he was more irritable." Helene trailed off, noting with some irony her loyalty alive after all these years. Eventually, she knew, everything – every word Freud had said – would be scrutinized and written about.

Helene slipped off the log and sat down next to Kate contemplating her work.

"Kate, I see you have no experience with sandcastles. The outside wall must be higher to resist the tide." Helene took up big handfuls of sand and patted them around the inadequate fortifications, working doggedly until weak spots were filled in and the wall was higher than before. When she finished, she took the chunk of blue glass and set it on one of the turrets, where it caught the light and blinked gravely.

Chapter Five

The day after her talk with Helene, Kate set off in her battered old Buick – a hand-me-down from her mother – for New York. She liked driving – it soothed her – and though the gentle rain obscured the views along the coast and slowed traffic, it cut the glare. About half way, after two and a half hours, she stopped at Mystic, a small fishing port, and had a chowder and a coffee on Main Street to fortify her for the slog on to the City. She was very tired when, more than two hours later, she finally squeezed the Buick into a parking space a block from her mother's apartment.

Emily lived in a rent-controlled building on the Upper West Side by the river. It was small but perfectly adequate for her needs. Kate had a rather seedy place on Broadway above Ninety-sixth.

Kate's mother told her she remembered putting the insurance papers in her desk – she'd find the key in her jewelry box. Once Kate got to the apartment, she went immediately to the closet where her mother kept the box on a shelf behind an old hatbox – she always put it there when she went out of town. She was sure, she told Kate once, that this would throw any casual thief off the scent, and anyway she didn't have much of value – she'd passed much of it on to Kate already. Thinking of that gave Kate a pang of guilt as she rummaged in the tangle of beads – amber and garnet – and lacy antique silver brooches and bangles bequeathed by Grandma Hilde.

The key was there, just as her mother remembered it. The desk was an American colonial with a top that opened outward, becoming a writing platform with a deep drawer beneath. Kate opened the top with the key and found the insurance papers under a heap of old bills, unfilled prescriptions and postcards from friends.

She was just about to shut it when she saw a gold key peeking out from one of the desk's many cubbyholes. She pulled it out and examined it, wondering what it was for. There was a small locked drawer under the cubbyholes, but when she tried the key, it was too big. That only piqued her interest, and Kate studied the desk more carefully. Snooping wasn't something she generally approved of. When she was a teenager and her mother had gone through her things searching for pot, Kate had been furious.

She sat, turning the key over in her hand, wondering if she should just put it back. But she wasn't looking for anything in particular, she told herself, she was just curious. She gave a tentative pull to the knobs on the desk's beautifully inlaid lower drawer. It stayed firmly shut, and after debating with herself another minute, she couldn't resist trying the key. It fit perfectly into the keyhole and Kate pulled the drawer open.

The drawer stuck a little because it was full to the brim with papers. The first ones she saw were bills, and she imagined Keith teasing her about the meager results of her nosiness, but then she saw some pen and ink sketches of what looked like a large private estate with open lawns and big trees, under which men strolled or sat. There were only a few women in the scenes, and they seemed to be dressed with aprons and starched caps as nurses. The sketches showed considerable talent, and alongside them were some poems and what seemed to be a play and clippings in German. She put them neatly on top of the desk and kept digging down.

At the very bottom was a small brown leather diary with the year 1908 stamped on the cover in gold. She opened it and sat down in her mother's chair to look. Inside was a photograph in mezzotint of an extremely handsome man in uniform: blond close-cropped hair slightly receding at the temples, a moustache over sweetly curving lips, wide-set eyes, a high forehead and a fine straight nose.

There was an inscription at the bottom: "to my beloved Hilde from her Viktor."

Facing the photo on the diary's first page was the name Viktor Tausk in black ink with a beautifully curved script. It took her a moment to realize what she was seeing. This handsome young man – whom Helene had been telling her about only a few days before – must be her grandfather.

She felt stunned, dismayed after all these years of her mother's inexplicable refusal to speak his name. It didn't seem possible . . . it was surreal, confusing. Just a day ago, she thought, her head spinning, she hadn't even heard of him.

But along with her confusion she felt exhilarated, even exuberant. Helene had referred to Viktor Tausk as the brightest of Freud's disciples. He had humane, progressive views, and on top of it all, he'd been the lover of Lou Salome. What could her mother have objected to about this man – except of course that he had declined to marry Hilde? Maybe she was just punishing him for that, determined that even posthumously he wouldn't have the affection of his granddaughter.

Then she made out in smaller letters in German: *Notes from the Asylum of Ahrweiler am Rein.* Oh my god, Grandpa was crazy. It took her a moment to recall that an asylum in those days wasn't for the insane – but a place to rest and regroup. She turned the page and saw the date written in the same beautiful hand, *September 26, 1908.* Her college German somehow began to come back to her as she slowly worked her way down the page.

Today I had my initial medical examination. The doctor was young and very attentive. Palpated me everywhere, examined me for tremors, checked my heart, which he said was nervous – I suppose he meant an irregular beat – and my lungs, which he found weak, then he asked me about the last years.

Kate stopped and took a deep breath; then she got up and carried the journal to her mother's armchair near the window, thinking it would be more comfortable for reading. Before she sat down again, she took down her mother's German dictionary from the nearby shelf, and wiped her hands carefully with a Kleenex to protect the journal's seemingly fragile paper. On closer inspection, she saw that only the edges of the yellowing paper were crumbling slightly; in fact, the journal was written on thick, sturdy stock. She'd just have to be careful turning the pages. She went on.

I told the doctor about my agonized decision not only to leave my wife but to give up the law – he knew about my separation already and gave me a sympathetic look. Martha had obviously been to see him and asked about me. He was surprised to hear that she was an excellent mother and loyal wife. Her carelessness about her appearance and the fact that she is obviously an intellectual and no beauty probably put him off. But he was baffled by my decision to give up the law.

So her grandfather had been married to a homely intellectual before he fell in love with Hilde, whose photos showed her to have been extremely beautiful. Not only that, he'd given up a law career.

Kate had wondered so much about her grandfather's profession. Now it seemed he'd had two: law and psychoanalysis. What would have made him give up a promising career for a completely different one? The doctor seemed to ask the same question.

My career seemed to him to be so full of possibilities. My love of art, my poetry, my writing for the theatre, none of that seemed to interest him very much. I gave him a copy of my last story, my best so far, I think, my gypsy tale of homelessness and murder, but he put it aside with only a perfunctory look. Perking up only when I mentioned that it was based on a real law case in which a man was tragically murdered by his own father. In his opinion, I couldn't experiment with an artistic life while trying to support my family by odd assignments as a journalist. It was clear he felt that to put my family first was the only possible solution and my duty. His diagnosis, when he finished with me, was mental and physical exhaustion.

In any case, he seemed to think that after rest and the proper treatment – which seems to consist mostly of warm milk, long walks and baths for my insomnia – I'd see the light and go back to making money. Though the doctor is so young, he manages to sound much like my father. Urging me to a career of law to "make money quickly." Certainly money and some success would do me good, but my nature rebels against making it by defending thieves or petty criminals. I told him my mother was melancholic for as long as I could remember. That gave him a moment's pause because he suspected an hereditary taint, an inclination, as he put it, towards psychopathology, but then he rallied and told me he didn't want me even to think of reading – nothing to over-stimulate the brain, just long walks in the countryside and plenty of fresh milk. I'm lucky he didn't take away my diary, which is small enough for me to secrete in my linen. Tomorrow, if I have the strength, I'll write a note to my poor boy – Martha tells me he is feeling my absence terribly.

Tausk had a son, then! Her mother had a half-brother. Kate shut the book and went to her mother's bathroom to pee. While she washed her hands with her mother's French soap, she thought about the fact that she had a half-uncle. Tausk sounded concerned about him – though Kate didn't want to read too much into a single line – and clearly torn by the conflict between developing his creativity and doing what seemed best for the child.

September 27

Got up today and had the warm milk that they think is so necessary to my condition, a terrific migraine nonetheless. Just to get up and brush my teeth was an effort. The warm milk was given me by a very pretty nurse, who said it came straight from the countryside, which is full of dairy farms and incredibly beautiful. I have to realize how sick I am by the fact that she didn't arouse the slightest desire except perhaps to lie against her bosom and have her stroke my hair while I was drinking. But after the milk – I drink a liter and a half a day – and a short walk in the fresh air, I was able to read my mail from Martha and even to write to my boys – Marius and little Emil. And then Martha.

Kate gave a start. So there were two boys. Her family had suddenly doubled in size! Kate looked to see if he said more about them but he had switched to his wife.

The fact that she has remained a faithful correspondent, never blaming me, only makes my guilt seem greater.

The truth is I love only people who are independent of me – which Martha, especially after the children, couldn't be . . . . Her being dependent on me made me depend on her, and I can't abide that. It makes me strike out at her even without wanting to . . . to take revenge for needing her. Then of course I feel like a beast . . . truthfully, I think I am doing the best thing I can for someone of my temperament. Or will be doing once I get out of here. I must find some work which truly satisfies my nature and live on my own with no one depending on me – not a slave because not a master.

Kate had taken in almost as much information as she could in one sitting, so she skimmed the next entries, noting that his condition got much worse before it improved. At one point he described the doctors as having intelligent faces but the patients looking like poisoned rats and mules, their faces destroyed. She jumped to the last entry, a month later, which had his "weight improving, color good, catarrh cleared," preparing to leave the hospital. Kate shut the book with a feeling of triumph.

Whatever his flaws, Kate thought, he was a complex, interesting human being. Her mother may have been frightened by the fact that he had had a minor breakdown, but though he was undoubtedly suffering, he wasn't cut off from reality – far from it. Even when he was most despairing, he tried to grasp his mental state and put it into words. Besides, she found herself empathizing strongly with much of what he said. Emily had never pushed her toward money-making – if anything, she was disappointed that Kate hadn't taken to painting – but she certainly had friends whose parents had pressured them to give up ballet or architecture or novel-writing and go into business. Keith's parents weren't all that happy with his decision to be a professor instead of a businessman like his father.

Other parts of Tausk's diary entry had also resonated in an almost uncanny way. His fear of people becoming dependent on him or him on them. Wasn't she experiencing something of that with Keith right now? Though certainly there was a downside to Tausk's predicament: he seemed to be in flight from what would have done him the most good. As he himself said, he needed the help (here Kate read "love") of some wise and good human being, a way of life that gets richer because you daily practice the duties of love. . . .

She went to the window of her mother's bedroom and looked toward the fringe of trees that barred her view of the river. Children were running and playing with a brightly colored ball; the air was muggy but blessedly, not overly hot, as it often was in early July. It struck her with a shock that her mother's half-brothers might well be alive somewhere. She checked back to the page with the names of Tausk's sons – Marius and Emil.

As she was putting the book down it slipped from her hand and two scraps of paper fluttered out. It was a program of the psychoanalytic meetings in New York a year before. She eyed it curiously. What was her mother, who professed no interest in psychoanalysis – in fact, an aversion – doing with a program? She ran her eye down the list of presenters and a name jumped out at her: Marius Tausk, 2:00 PM, Green Room, a paper on the precursors of Freud's death instinct.

So her brand-new uncle was an analyst too, like his father. Could her mother have been in touch with him? Or was she just interested in what he was doing? Perhaps she had been tracking him and his brother for years without ever trying to get in touch. That seemed more likely, given her wish to keep Kate in the dark.

She turned the program over and saw a lightly penciled number, a phone number. 831-4514. Next to it, almost illegible but there nonetheless, the initials MT. Without giving herself time to think of reasons to delay, she dialed the number. A man answered.

"Dr. Tausk please," she said, her voice quavering.

"Speaking," answered a soft, accented voice. "What can I do for you?"

"My name is Kate Berg," Kate said. "Perhaps my mother has been in touch with you? You're my mother's half-brother and I guess that makes me a sort of niece."

"No one has gotten in touch with me claiming a family connection," the doctor said rather suspiciously. "What's more, I have no sister of any kind. I think you must have made an error."

"My grandmother was Hilde Loewi," she explained, "the pianist Hilde Loewi. She and your father were sweethearts. They were supposed to get married but he abandoned her."

There was a short silence. "Abandoned her?" He seemed puzzled by the word.

"That's what my mother told me. It was after she got pregnant."

"I see . . . well . . . it's unfortunately true that they were sweethearts, but Hilde Loewi never had a child."

"Yes, she did. She had my mother. I have photos of Hilde nursing her. I have a photo of your father as a young man, too. He gave it to my grandmother. His resemblance to my mother is striking. I have –"

"These photos mean very little to me," he interrupted, suddenly harsh. "Your mother could still have been someone else's child. Did your – did she tell you to contact me? What does she want?"

Kate suddenly realized how bizarre this must have sounded, how he must think she was trying to get money or some other favor from him.

"No, no!" she said. "She doesn't want anything . . . this is all my own idea. You are an analyst. You can understand. There has always been a big hole at the center of my life, it seems to suck everything else into it. Unless I fill it I'll never know who I am. Mother would never tell me anything. Not even my grandfather's name."

"Then how are so sure of it now?" he asked dryly. "And how did you happen to have my number?"

"I found it in her drawer written on a program of the psychoanalytic meetings, along with a diary of my grandfather's, and other papers, sketches, poems. I think they must be his, too. I haven't gone through them all."

"A diary of my father's? Why didn't you tell me this first?" he said in a much more friendly manner. "What sort of a diary?"

"Look. It's very difficult to talk about this on the phone," she said, sensing both his lessened suspicion and his interest. "If you could spare the time, I'd like to meet you. I could bring the diary if you like."

"I'm very busy for the next few days, but I think I could make space for you on Tuesday afternoon around four. Why don't you come by, then, if that's convenient, and by all means bring the diary. I'd like to have a look at it." Again she noticed a catch of eagerness in his voice, though he was trying to sound unconcerned.

"I don't have your address."

"300 Central Park West. I'll let the doorman know you're coming. *Auf Wiedersehen* until Tuesday, then."

Kate felt frustrated. Two days felt like an eternity. She called her mother and told her that she had to stay in New York for a couple of days and was sending the insurance papers FedEx. After she hung up, it occurred to her that it would make sense for her to try and find out a little more about her grandfather before she saw Marius. Since Marius was a psychoanalyst, she decided to go to the Columbia library and see if she could find any of Tausk's analytic publications. She could come back to the poems and other things later.

It was a hot day and the summer students were out in droves in granny dresses and bright colored glasses. Kate found it pleasant to retreat into the coolness of Butler library. She rifled patiently through the card catalogue looking for Tausk's name but, to her disappointment, came up with only one journal article (translated from the German in 1933), "On The Influencing Machine in Schizophrenia." That sounded vaguely familiar; possibly she'd heard it mentioned in a course, but Kate wasn't sure. She checked out the journal and took it over to the long reading desk where she sat down, got her notepad and pen out of her knapsack and started to read.

She immediately felt the lucidity and strength of Tausk's mind. His words seemed to leap off the page. His presentation was balanced and clear. A footnote mentioned that the paper had been presented to the Psychoanalytic Society in January 1918 – after the war – and was discussed again at a further meeting. The two meetings suggested that the other analysts in Freud's group took Tausk seriously. It was rare in those days, Kate knew, for early analysts to investigate psychosis clinically, so he was ahead of his time. But it struck her again as odd that this obviously gifted analyst had dropped so completely out of sight.

She read slowly on. Making admirable use of his young psychotic patient's own words, Tausk described the patient's belief that her body was controlled by a machine in the shape of a coffin-lid, lined with red silk. How surreal! It made Kate think of a mummy case. The machine was being manipulated, the patient said, in such a way that everything that happened to it was reproduced in her body. Kate had read Bettelheim's famous case of a boy who thought he needed a machine in order to breathe, but this machine didn't function in a benign way; it produced slimy substances and bad smells, even manipulated the patient's genitals. It turned out that the young woman had previously rejected a suitor, a college professor. Hallucinatory voices explained that this man was using the machine to persecute her after it had failed to influence her in his favor. After several interviews, the young woman decided that Tausk was also being "influenced" and broke off their sessions.

Tausk explained with obvious excitement that he had been able to observe the formation of this young woman's delusions at an early stage, that she'd been able to tell him in her own words that the machine originally represented her body: "it is distinguished above all by its human form . . . [which] resembles the patient, and she senses all manipulations performed on the apparatus in the corresponding part of her own body . . . and apparently vice versa. When she loses genital sensation, her machine double loses its genitals. Eventually [it] loses all human characteristics . . . and becomes merely a typical unintelligible influencing machine" that mysteriously persecutes the patient by producing pictures, or manipulating thoughts, sensations, and even physical movements by various means, including rays and magnetism.

In other patients where this delusion had been observed so far, the machine had been unintelligible. So seeing it at an early stage was a real advance. Furthermore, Tausk was able to offer a reason for the projection. The patient was ambivalent about her suitor's proposal. As a result of her conscious negative feelings, she said no. But she had positive feelings as well. They were projected onto the body-machine, which then prompted her to change her mind.

The case was curious enough, but what struck Kate was the almost compulsive allusions to Freud. She made a list of them with her ballpoint on her yellow legal pad.

1. Tausk alludes to Freud's discussion of his paper, in which Freud suggests that the infant's feeling that others know his thoughts comes from the process of learning to speak. Having taken language from others, he has also received thoughts from them; thus, his idea that others have 'made' him the language and along with it, his thoughts . . . has some basis in reality. (A rather profound idea, Kate thought.)

2. Tausk reminds the reader that Freud discovered the mechanism by which the paranoid patient projects malevolent feelings outward and then imagines that they are really coming from others.

3. He notes that Freud, after hearing his "Influencing Machine" paper, proposed that ambivalence makes the projection possible. Once expressed, Tausk agrees that this thesis appears self-evident.

Here Kate paused and bit her pen, turning her bottom lip an inky blue. Wasn't that what Tausk had just shown so brilliantly? Whose ideas were whose? Tausk concludes that : "The present paper shows how, albeit unconsciously, I had been demonstrating Freud's formulation. (!)" Kate had had enough trouble with her thesis advisor at Columbia to know that a degree of kowtowing could be necessary. She wondered how it had been in Austria back then. "More or less ass-kissing????" she wrote in big letters. Or was this something peculiar to Tausk's relationship with Freud, a prime example of the desire to submit? She'd have to put it to Helene when she talked to her. She smiled to herself at the thought, and went on with her notes.

4. Tausk reminds his readers that Freud had already indicated in his paper on the psychotic Dr. Schreiber that the libido in schizophrenia is located at a stage even earlier than auto-eroticism. Tausk comments, "I arrived at this conclusion by a different route, and I take the liberty of presenting this fact as proof of the correctness of Freud's contentions." Modesty? Kate thought not. She thought she sensed a need for space to investigate on his own, "by a different route."

5. Tausk increases his protestations of innocence: "I am pleased to be able to refer to the many points of agreement between my con-

tentions and Freud's in his paper, of which I had no knowledge at the time." (He wants, Kate thought again, to be able to think freely without being accused of stealing.)

His final note – six – seemed more ominous, though she wasn't sure how much she should read into it.

6. He explains that melancholia is related to the phenomenon he is talking about. It is a persecution psychosis without projection, a renunciation of love for one's psychic self (which has lost its *raison d'etre*) and can lead to suicide. "While this paper was in proof," he adds, "Freud's article *'Trauer und Melancholie'* ('Mourning and Melancholia') appeared, to which I refer in this connection."

Kate finished her notes in a state of mixed excitement and puzzlement. Her first urge was to call Helene and tell her that she'd found out that Tausk was her grandfather. She wanted to ask about Tausk's defensive tone in relation to Freud, but after a few minutes' reflection, she decided to limit herself to talking about the paper. It had raised so many questions. As soon as she got back to her own apartment, she called her mother to see how she was doing in her absence.

"I'm afraid this new aide isn't working out," Emily said.

"She looked so nice."

"Well, she's not. She turns up the radio on inane daytime serials when I'm trying to paint in the other room. She's convinced I can't hear her, but of course I do."

"If she's nice otherwise, that doesn't seem like a reason to fire her. Just tell her again, Mom. Explain that it really interferes with your concentration. Be firm."

"I've tried, believe me. And when she isn't listening to the radio, she's lecturing me. She's always at me to take vitamins or meditate. . . . I keep telling her I'm not sick. I know perfectly well how to care for myself. I'm not sick or incompetent. I have a broken leg, that's all."

"She does sound unpleasant. What a nuisance. I suppose you could try the local paper or the bulletin board outside the grocery store in town. If that doesn't work. I'll try to help you get someone more suitable when I come back."

"Thank you, darling . . . are you coming back soon?"

"Pretty soon . . . I don't know exactly. Some things have come up with my thesis and I might have to stay a few days longer. Sorry, but I have to run now," she said, before Emily could think of any questions. "Good luck with the aide. Keep me posted." She threw two brisk kisses into the receiver.

After she'd said good bye and hung up, she called Helene. Apparently Helene had visited Emily for tea and agreed with her that the aide was overbearing.

"She acts as though your mother was a mentally deficient old lady." Helene said, "I don't blame her for being annoyed."

"Thank you. You really helped me out. Sometimes I'm not as empathetic as I should be."

"I've missed our talks," Helene said after a pause.

"Me too. Actually there's something I wanted to ask you about. Do you have a few minutes?"

Helene said that she did.

"Remember, you were telling me about Tausk and Lou Salome? I was intrigued, so I went to the library and looked him up."

"And what did you find?" Helene asked. She was fairly sure there was nothing much. Even now, none of the orthodox analytic journals were going to publish him.

"Not as much as I expected, but there was a fascinating paper on 'The Influencing Machine'," Kate said. "Do you know it?"

"I wrote a response to it. It was my very first publication, as a matter of fact."

"Was it . . . was it a positive response?"

"I was very impressed by his work. Everything he said was confirmed by my clinical material on the projection of impulses by a female psychotic." Helene remembered sitting – not much older than Kate – at the long table surrounded by serious, dark-suited analysts preparing to deliver her first paper.

"Tausk was really pushing out into new territory," she said. "Freud didn't deal with the psychoses – and with my clinical experience I was able to follow Tausk." She sighed.

"If you'd give me a copy, I'd like to read your paper," Kate said. "But I'm wondering, if Tausk's work was as innovative as you suggest, why does he keep giving credit to Freud? It's as if he were afraid at every moment of being accused of something. Was it the style then to be so deferential to a superior?"

Helene was a little taken aback – she had expected some question about method or theory.

"People were much more formal in those days," she began slowly, not sure where this was going. "Certainly, people were addressed by their titles. I was Frau Doktor, for instance. Freud was called 'the Professor' by his inner circle." She paused. It was clever of the girl to have picked up on the tension between Tausk and Freud, even in this article. "But I suppose you'd like something more specific," she added when Kate kept silent. "Well, I think I mentioned that Tausk made Freud nervous. I imagine Tausk was reacting to that, bending over backwards to reassure him."

"But why? I still don't understand. Why such nervousness on Freud's part?"

"I couldn't say, really. At that time, you know, Freud was threatened by defectors. He believed it was necessary for the survival of psychoanalysis to draw strict lines between friends and enemies. Once a member in good standing dared to suggest that Adler should be kept in the movement because his ideas weren't too different from Freud's. Freud was furious. He said Adler was dangerous to the future of psychoanalysis and had to go. Tausk was one of the few, perhaps the only, highly talented disciple left. Freud may have been watching him for signs of disloyalty."

"You'd think Freud would have cultivated him even more if he were so valuable," Kate said.

"People react differently."

Kate had been on the verge of telling her what she'd found out, but Helene's evasiveness here made Kate cautious. She had the distinct feeling that Helene was suddenly aware that she had portrayed Freud in an unflattering light and was clearly not eager to go on. Kate was glad she'd decided not to tell her immediately about Tausk. Having a close relation in Freud's inner circle might make Kate seem less neutral, might make Helene less, rather than more, willing to disclose certain things – especially things that might tarnish Freud's image.

As soon as Keith came in the door of Kate's apartment, Kate told him about her discoveries, starting with the photo of Tausk and Hilde that made her realize he was her grandfather. Even after they'd gotten into bed, she kept speculating about one or the other fascinating aspect of the thing: Marius's suspicion, Helene's evasiveness.

"It's as though Tausk and anything connected with him is somehow taboo. I can't figure out why. His paper was brilliant. The only thing that bothers me about him so far," she concluded, as Keith stifled a yawn, "is the way he treated his wife, Martha."

Keith had been about to switch off the light but he paused. "What's wrong with it?" he asked, "He sent her money for the kids, didn't he? Worked at a job he hated so that he could do it. That's the sort of over-responsibility that breeds resentment. He probably just got to the breaking-point and couldn't take it anymore."

"I don't know if he had far to go," Kate murmured. "He said in his journal that he hated having people depend on him."

"Did you recognize yourself a little bit?" Keith asked, laughing. "Weren't you the one who freaked out when I told you I needed you?"

"Stop." She pinched his arm lightly, not willing to admit how much that had frightened her.

"It sounds to me as though Tausk met his responsibilities. Maybe she didn't meet hers. You said she didn't take care of her looks. I'm all in favor of her fighting for socialism, but maybe she was too busy to be a good lover, or just couldn't relax in bed." Keith turned off the light, then reached over and hugged her, nuzzling his face into her neck.

"Now you're being silly," Kate said.

"No I'm not. I'm perfectly serious." He licked her neck. "Luckily, I have a beautiful woman who, working or not, is great in the sack." Kate felt herself getting aroused but she didn't want to succumb to it. It annoyed her that whenever they discussed anything having to do with sex roles, or even when they were speculating why friends had split up – whether it was his fault or hers – they ended up making love.

"Aren't you always busy with the Movement?" she asked. "Is that a reason for me to abandon you? Would you blame one of your activist students if his wife accused him of spending too much time and energy on protests? No, you wouldn't. You'd say she was a demanding bitch, that it's a great cause and she should be supportive, welcome him home with food and wine. Besides, Tausk doesn't say Martha's deficient in any way. Sexual or otherwise. He admits that she was a totally loyal, good wife . . . and that he feels terribly guilty. I wouldn't be surprised if he were having an affair with one of the nurses while he was writing Martha complaining letters – and she keeps answering them and talks to the hospital about his progress."

Now it was Keith's turn to be annoyed. He released her and lay looking at the ceiling. "I can't believe you're fighting with me over who was at fault in a marriage where both people have been dead for decades. If something is bothering you about us, just tell me straight." He waited a minute, but Kate was silent. "Lighten up," he said, turning his back and rolling away from her, and in another minute she heard him breathing slowly.

Marius's apartment was only a short taxi ride away in one of those luxurious old pre-war apartment buildings that lined Central Park. The uniformed doorman ushered her in without the usual call upstairs. The elevator was paneled in a beautiful wood and went up without Kate having to push the button. When it let her off at the eleventh floor, she turned left as the doorman had instructed her and found 11D at the end of the landing. Marius Tausk answered the door himself. He was an elderly man, tall and slightly hunched, with long arms, the wrists showing beneath the sleeves of his jacket. The man seemed at once stiff and almost painfully shy. He bowed slightly in the Germanic way, glancing at her surreptitiously from under his bushy eyebrows. A small golden brown spaniel came rushing out of a hallway, barking and jumping.

"Get down, Pujerli," he said, affectionately. "I hope you're not bothered by dogs, Miss Berg."

"Not at all." She scratched the spaniel behind his ears, and he promptly lay down and rolled onto his back, kicking his legs ecstatically. "I love them. I can't have one now because I'm out too much."

She noticed that as she rubbed the dog's stomach, Marius noticeably relaxed too. He smiled and led her through the large, light living room with its Chinese blue carpet and bronze head of Nephertiti into his study. The light abruptly dimmed. She felt as if she'd walked into a mezzotint from the early 1900s. Floor-to-ceiling bookcases loomed above her. A brown leather couch beckoned from one side, covered, like Freud's, with an oriental rug. And just like the pictures she'd seen of Freud's desk, Marius's was crammed full of antique statuettes and small bronzes – no photographs of children or grandchildren anywhere. Though there was one of a woman that Kate imagined was his wife.

Marius motioned her to sit in front of the desk and went around to sit behind it. Putting a safe distance between us, Kate thought, as she studied him. If he was a small child in 1907, she figured he must be in his late sixties. He had intelligent eyes behind thick rimless glasses, olive skin, iron-gray hair and thick sensual lips. "So you think we are related," he said looking at Kate. The golden spaniel had followed them into the room and was sniffing at her knee. She laid her hand on his head.

"It was a shock to me, too. . . ."

"I'm not shocked," he said, stiff again. She guessed he was one of those people who pride himself on self-control. Maybe with a father as passionate – and impulsive – as Viktor seemed to have been, that was a natural reaction.

Kate looked at the head of a bull on Marius's desk while she tried to think of what to say. It had a scornfully down-turned mouth and a regal set of horns. After a moment, she reached into her sack and brought out the diary.

"Here is the journal I mentioned to you," she said, proffering it to him, "and a few of his sketches. I haven't finished reading through the poems."

He took them from her and she thought she saw his hand trembling.

While he studied the sketches, Kate returned to her observation of the desk's statuettes. An enigmatic shape near the bull appeared to be the handle of a clay club – but on closer inspection she saw the "handle" was an erect phallus – a votive object of some sort. Thanking the gods for a healed prick. She had read Freud had something similar. Could Marius have copied Freud to the extent of duplicating pieces of Freud's famous antiquities collection?

"My father was a talented man," Marius was saying.

"I thought so too . . . and the poems were full of interesting conceits."

"But not a genius . . . ," Marius sighed.

"Well, how many people are?" she asked lightly.

"He wanted to be."

"He seems to have had talent in so many directions."

"Yes, he tried everything – he painted, played the violin, wrote poetry and plays, did journalism. In a way, being so talented made it harder, not easier, to accept his limitations."

"Well, he seems to have decided he could never become more than a proficient amateur. That is accepting a limit of a sort."

"But I fear he didn't accept his limitations as a theorist. Not with Freud." He sighed again. "But one can't compete with genius."

"No, I guess not," said Kate, somewhat at sea, "though I thought the way your father described his breakdown was impressive, and from reading one of his papers, I'd say he was extremely deferential to Freud."

"Deference can hide a great many things." He leaned towards her. "May I ask where you came on his paper? . . . so few are in print."

"Dr. Deutsch had talked about him to me," she said, "and when I found out he was my grandfather, I looked him up in the library."

"Ah, . . . are you friends, then?"

"I am doing some work on the early analysts, actually, the women. I have gotten to know her a little and I like her very much."

"What did she tell you about my father?"

"Nothing much. Just that he was a fine clinician. She told me about his war papers – though I couldn't find them – and she told me a little about Lou Salome."

Marius seemed suddenly agitated. "What did she tell you?"

"Only that they had an affair and that when Freud was annoyed at Tausk for some reason, Lou interceded."

"And?"

"That's all – except . . . I found your father . . . my grandfather . . . despite his distress, somehow immensely likeable."

"Many women found him so," Marius said, lowering his eyes so she couldn't read his expression. "My mother loved him until the day she died, and tried always to make us children see how important it was for Papa to realize his gifts."

"That must have been hard to understand."

He folded his hands primly and gave a barely perceptible nod. Then he took the diary in both hands and looked at it. "So this is Papa's journal of his days in the asylum. I didn't know about this breakdown, but I'm not surprised. He had enough conscience to be aghast at what he was doing to our family." She looked at him, surprised at the strange note almost of relief that she heard in his voice.

He glanced across his desk at her and, taking a cigar out of a drawer, asked her politely whether she minded. Kate thought to herself that he was aping Freud in yet another way, and she hated smoke – it always made her throat itch and her eyes water. Still, he was a bristly opaque man, and she wanted to make a better connection with him, so she shook her head to indicate that she didn't mind.

He smiled, pleased. "You've filled in a part of my father's life that I was unaware of," he said, drawing in the smoke, "and I'm grateful. But I wonder what I can do for you in return."

"You could tell me more about him. He doesn't seem to have been much as a husband. What was he like as a father?"

"Oh, he loved us well enough, I think. Even after he left, he wrote me and my brother Emil affectionate letters at least once a week. The letters were full of little stories – no doubt he had an inventive mind. There was one story that went on quite a long time – about two mice who come to the city to seek their fortune. They had an enemy cat who made a strong impression on me – a mangy tortoiseshell named Crac with a docked tail who spoke in a slangy way that seemed incredibly daring and lurked in wait for the hapless mice beside the choicest garbage can. Father drew sketches to illustrate him. I'd keep his letters with me sometimes when I went to bed."

Marius's face softened and for a moment Kate felt close to him. She remembered how before she went to sleep, she'd think about the treats her father promised when he came back. She could imagine Marius as a thin, intent child, carefully placing the letters under his pillow, hoping his father would visit him in his dreams.

"That was before I realized he'd left us for good," Marius went on, "that he wasn't just working in Berlin for awhile. Then I was very angry at him for leaving us. It made no sense at all to me. It only aggravated me further when my mother made excuses for him. She understood that he had to fulfill himself. Well, why couldn't he do that at home instead of in another city? As a child I felt the injustice of it. And though he sent us money when he could, we were always short. And the tragic thing is he could probably have made a good living as a journalist if he hadn't worn himself out by writing plays at night. Even when his plays were produced, he only earned a pittance. It's no wonder his health broke down."

Kate was getting a strong urge to defend her grandfather. "His breakdown seems to have been relatively short, judging from the diary, and then – whatever his problems – he pulled himself together and decided he wanted to be an analyst. That's not a small decision. It must have taken courage in those days, when analysis was considered a quirky little movement led by a sex-obsessed professor."

Marius looked at her over the top of his wire-rimmed spectacles. "Freud was exceedingly good to my father – sent him patients, even loaned him money to keep us afloat."

"Yes, but Dr. Deutsch, told me that your father made Freud uncomfortable in some way," Kate blurted out. "She said that Freud didn't like being around him. That seemed strange, given Tausk's complete devotion. I wondered about it. Perhaps you –" she didn't have a chance to finish her sentence.

"Dr. Deutsch, charming as she was and is, has some unanalyzed . . . some unanalyzed elements," he shot back with a vehemence that seemed quite surprising in him. "But I can assure you that if Freud was uncomfortable, as Dr. Deutsch put it, there must have been cause. And if the reason you came here was to get confirmation of some irrational dislike on Freud's part, I must tell you you've come to the wrong person."

Kate felt a certain perverse pleasure in rousing some emotion in this man, even if it was counterproductive, but what could he be so worried about?

"I didn't come to prove anything," she said soothingly. "Certainly not any impropriety. It never crossed my mind. I've told you what interests me, to find some missing parts of myself. I didn't mean to offend you, please. . . ."

He cocked his head to one side and studied her. "There are people who are always trying to stir up controversy. I'm glad you're not one of them . . . but I'm afraid," he looked at his watch, "I have to terminate our interview."

"Oh, really? I was hoping you could tell me something about his later life. I still have no idea why my mother kept him a secret from me."

"I'd have to know you better to discuss that with you," he said, not unkindly. "It sounds rather complicated. I'd be irresponsible if I rushed in with my speculations."

She was trying to think up objections to his caution when the phone rang. He picked it up. "I can't talk now, Emil," he said in German, using the familiar form. "I have a visitor. I'll call you back."

"I'm afraid I really do have to go now," he said. "Family business. I wonder whether you'd trust me with the diary for a couple of days. I'd photocopy it and get it back to you later this week."

"All right," Kate said. "Sure." She took a small piece of paper and a pen out of her purse, bent over the big desk and wrote her phone number and address.

Hour up, she thought to herself. Did he really have an appointment, or did he just want time to think how to handle her and her prying into things that, like her mother, he seemed to think were better left alone? She'd read that patients often delivered themselves of important information right at the close of the analytic hour when there was no time left to discuss it. Well, he was turning the tables on her, closing the door on her last question.

Kate walked over to her mother's apartment and called Keith, but he didn't answer. At first she was worried – she'd left before he woke up, and she hadn't known if he was still angry at her. Then she remembered he was at one of his interminable meetings.

She left a message that he should call her and turned back to the pile of Tausk papers on the desk. It was astonishing how much there was. Kate had tried sorting things roughly into categories – she made one for sketches, another for poems, there was even some music for the violin, his play manuscripts. There were four or five of them, most with the pages out of order. At first she attempted to collate them, but there were too many, and some of the pages from one play were confused with the others, so she put them all aside and looked through the letters. Most of them were drafts of letters to Martha, but one was a love letter to a woman named Berthe in Berlin, written during his asylum stay. So Kate's wild guess had been right. While her grandfather was complaining to Martha, he'd been carrying on some sort of affair. She couldn't find any other love letters, but in the same paper folder with the one she'd found was a short story. It was an odd little tale of crime and punishment about a Slavic gypsy with no close ties who becomes a murderer and is eventually killed by his own father! Strange, Kate thought. Maybe after the breakdown, Tausk was afraid he couldn't keep his own impulses under control. Yet the story itself was beautifully crafted, tight and controlled, and Kate was moved by it. Tausk had a strong talent here, too.

But she was puzzled that among drafts of psychoanalytic papers and notes on cases he'd treated during the war there were no examples of later work. Then suddenly she saw why everything seemed to end after the war. A small faded newspaper clipping from the *Wiener Zeitung* announced the death in 1919 by suicide of Dr. Viktor Tausk. Suicide! She felt as though she'd been punched in the stomach and sat doubled over, trying to get her breath back. Her eyes were shut, but she could still see the word "suicide" pulsing on the inside of her lids. Her grandfather had killed himself. Without wanting to, she imagined him putting the muzzle of a pistol into his mouth. The thought horrified her. She imagined herself coming in, convincing him to put down the gun or knife or whatever it was that was about to cut or burn. The thought was absurd, but it made her realize she'd been fantasizing that she'd find him still alive – she hadn't found her father but she'd find him. . . .

When she opened her eyes, for a moment she thought maybe the whole thing was a waking nightmare. She made herself look at the clipping again. Across the top, in what she imagined was Hilde's writing, were the words *VT Death Notice.* Just those colorless words, nothing more. Poor Hilde must have been numb with shock.

Kate suddenly understood why Hilde – not Martha – had these things: as his fiancée, she must have collected them from his apartment after his death.

Kate sat still, staring at the small piece of paper with an uncanny sense of familiarity. Suicide. Another image popped into her mind of herself, a year after her brother had turned his boat into the storm. A boy she had liked in high school had jilted her cruelly, showing to his friends the despairing love poems she'd written him. She had wanted to go somewhere alone to think and smoke a cigarette – something her mother didn't allow, so she told her mother she was going up to the roof to get some air. She remembered the look of terror on her mother's face. Afraid, no doubt, that Kate was going to clamber over the low wall and pitch herself down ten flights. Now she remembered something else. Whenever Emily read in the morning *Times* about a distraught wife, husband, or mother committing suicide, she would use it as a sort of lesson, an inoculation against possible infection.

"This is so selfish," she would say. "Didn't she think what it would do to her family, to the child who finds her mommy strung up from a beam? I don't care what the reasons are." She'd be almost panting in her agitation. "Even if I were sick with a terminal illness, I would never, never kill myself."

"Do we have to talk about this at breakfast?" Kate would ask, sullenly, pouring milk into her Wheaties.

What if Marius and Emil had been among the ones who found the body? Perhaps he had sent them out for a walk or to pick up some cigars for him at the corner kiosk. They'd be all washed and brushed and in their best suits, coming back and finding the apartment empty, calling "*Vati, Vati,* we're back," finding a note – the boys not quite understanding until they went into the study and saw him.

She'd heard a story once of two sisters who had seen their mother hang herself and had tried to hold her body and lift her up to give her air, but they were too small. When Kate's brother's body had been found, she wasn't allowed to see it. It had been too bloated and discolored, only recognizable by the clothes. Her mother had fainted when she was brought in to identify it. Kate had persisted in seeing him as he was when he set out, in his white shorts and a sailor cap she had given him for his birthday.

It was reported as an accident. They never talked about it between them after that. Her mother swallowed it deep into the depths of her body, back to where he'd grown as an infant. As if not talking would keep it from having happened.

Tausk's intent would have been unavoidable. Kate hadn't ever really cried for her brother; now she found herself sobbing. She sat, perfectly still, while rivulets streamed down her face. After half hour, the tears stopped as abruptly as they had begun. She got up and blew her nose hard before going into the bathroom to wash her face with cold water. Then, exhausted, she pulled the blinds, took off her shoes, lay down on her mother's bed, and fell into a deep sleep.

When she woke up, she called Marius told him she needed to talk to him. She said she'd found the notice of her grandfather's death in the *Zeitung*. Marius was immediately solicitous. Ten minutes later he was sitting awkwardly next to her on the beige sofa in her mother's living room while she nursed a scotch – he wouldn't join her, he said, he never drank in the morning. She almost laughed. She'd had some crazy idea that he would take her in his arms and comfort her. But he was as serious and stiff as he'd been in the morning.

"I'm so sorry," he said. "I wish I'd been with you." His dark eyes peered nearsightedly at her through his thick glasses. "It might have been better if I'd told you right away. But I didn't know for sure that it was in those papers of yours. And I didn't want to be the bearer of such terrible news. I'm sorry, but you see my predicament."

"Hmm," she felt the warmth of the scotch spreading in her chest. "Yes. Why did he do it?" she asked abruptly.

Marius looked pained. "These things are hard to understand even when you've known someone all your life. At the time, I didn't have any idea that he had any thought of such a thing. As it happens, I was visiting him the day before. I was quite young and rather preoccupied with my own problems. He gave me some advice. . . ."

"What sort of advice?"

"Rather strange advice for such a principled man. Not to be too rigid in my principles . . . ," he hesitated. Kate smiled faintly. Grandpa was certainly right-on there. "I thought later that if I'd been more aware, less preoccupied, I might have noticed that something was wrong."

"Perhaps he hadn't decided yet when he saw you?" Kate said. "You certainly shouldn't blame yourself."

"Freud was quite sure it was the strain of the war," Marius said. "He was an army psychiatrist in occupied Russia during World War 1, treating soldiers for shell shock. He wrote my mother that he worked from eight in the morning until seven at night. Still, he managed to write some of his best papers – God knows when."

"Where were you during the war?" she asked. "You must have suffered too."

"Nothing to speak of," he said, stoically. "My mother had trouble finding work, there were food shortages. Everyone experienced them, and my father was too worn down by his own situation to be able to help us much." Here a note of bitterness crept into his voice. "Eventually we moved in with my grandmother because the food situation was better there in Zagreb than in Bohemia."

I'm so spoiled. Kate thought, not for the first time. As a child during the last years of World War 11, she'd complained when they'd had to eat apple butter instead of butter, or when they couldn't have steak.

"Professor Freud wrote an eloquent obituary for my father," Marius was saying, producing another folder from his worn black briefcase. "I thought it would mean a lot to you so I had it copied along with the diary. Freud really gave him the highest praise." He handed her the envelope.

She opened it and read: *Among the sacrifices, fortunately few in number, claimed by the war from the ranks of psychoanalysis, we must count Dr. Viktor Tausk. This rarely gifted man, a Vienna specialist in nervous diseases, who had been for years one of Freud's inner circle, took his own life before peace was signed.*

Kate read slowly through the account of her grandfather's change of profession from lawyer-magistrate to journalist to physician and psychoanalyst – changes which Freud described as "great difficulties and sacrifices."

He had begun building up a considerable practice and had achieved some excellent results as well as a means of support; but he was all at once violently torn from them by the war. The stresses of many years in the field could not fail to exercise a severely damaging effect on so intensely conscientious a man. At the last Psychoanalytic Congress . . . in Budapest, Tausk was already showing signs of unusual nervous irritability. Soon afterwards in the late autumn of the year, he came to the end of his military service and returned to Vienna, where he was faced for the third time, in his state of nervous exhaustion, with the hard task of building a new existence. In addition . . . he was on the brink of contracting a new marriage . . ."

So he didn't abandon Hilde," Kate burst out. "He was planning to marry her . . . when?"

"The wedding was to have been that day," Marius said slowly, as though the words had been dragged out of him.

"How awful," Kate said, conjuring up an instant picture of the bride putting on her white dress surrounded by her friends, some fixing her hair, arranging the wreath of orange blossoms, others making adjustments to the gown – while in another part of the city her grandfather was fixing a noose to a beam. But of course this fantasy would have to be amended, because Hilde must already have been quite pregnant and the wedding was probably going to be a quick one in front of some government minister.

"It was a horrible death," she told Keith when she was safe in his arms later that night. "He hung himself, first shooting himself so that he would fall against the rope."

Keith whistled through his teeth. "Sounds like he wanted to be double sure he'd done the job."

"I think somewhere I guessed – especially when Marius was being so cautious about saying anything about Grandpa's later life – that he didn't have any later life."

"Well, now you know . . . maybe you can put the whole thing to rest." He cradled her. "Bad as it is, I feel it's given you back to me."

Kate decided to ignore the conflict between her interests and his. Right now she needed his support too badly.

"Mom must have been terrified after my brother's suicide . . . that there was something in our heredity. Maybe she thought if she didn't tell me, the crazy gene would somehow stay hidden and not assert itself." Kate shivered slightly. "Suicide does seem to run in families," she said.

"It's never been proven that it's hereditary. When it does run in families, it could be patterns people learn from their parents. Just because your mother is terrified doesn't mean you have to be. Besides," he added in a lighter tone, "you don't want to prove she was right to worry, do you?"

"If I knew why he did it, I'd feel better. As it is, I'm still in the dark. Maybe he had an incurable illness – though Marius said he wasn't aware of anything. But why do you think Marius wouldn't tell me?"

"It isn't something you tell people lightly. . . ."

"That's what he said. But I have the feeling something else was going on. He seemed suspicious that I wanted to damage Freud. And my mentioning that I knew Deutsch practically sent him up the wall. He accused her of being insufficiently analyzed. I think he was going to say she had 'penis envy.' I heard the beginning of the word, then he must have thought better of it and just said she had problems. Offhand, I'd say she was a lot more at ease with herself than he is."

"So what are you going to do now?"

"How did you know I was going to do anything?"

"I've known you long enough to know when you're building up a head of steam."

"I'm going to talk with Marius's brother, Emil. He phoned Marius while I was there. Anyway after I left, I looked Emil up in the phone book. He lives down in the Village. I'm going to see him tomorrow."

Marius called in the morning and said the photocopying was almost done – they'd rushed it for him – and he wanted to bring the diary back around lunchtime. When Kate said she would be out, he asked if it would be all right if he left it with the doorman. "I'll wrap it up and put it in a Manila envelope."

"There isn't a doorman," Kate said, "but you can leave it in the mailbox for 4A. If it doesn't fit, there's a table right in front of the boxes. No one will bother it." Kate told him the code for the outer door. She didn't mention that she would be seeing his brother.

Emil lived in an old brownstone on Horatio Street. There was no doorman and no elevator. Kate was sweating by the time she got to his top-floor apartment. He was standing by the open door wearing khakis and a woven blue shirt that set off his gray curls. His face, though lined, had a youthful, almost childlike freshness despite his being only slightly younger than his brother. "So you're my new niece," he said. "Welcome." He shook her hand, holding it for a moment between his – his hands, she noticed, were large and warm with short square nails – and ushered her into a large loft space with canvases stacked against the wall. The ones facing outward were covered by large irregular patches of strong color. In one corner there was a life-sized wooden statue of a man with an assortment of shapes coming out of his head.

"How extraordinary," she said, moving closer.

"They're his dreams," Emil explained.

On looking closer, she saw that it wasn't one piece, as it had seemed at first, but was constructed of thin layers of wood piled one on top of another and then cut and sanded to the shape of leg and torso. Each strip was brightly painted in brilliant colors. "I love it," she said.

"I do, too," he said, and laughed. "He's an experiment. I needed a rest from abstraction. These are Egyptian symbols for life," he said, pointing to some hieroglyphics on the statue's base. "And because this is called *To the First Americans,* I put in the American eagle."

She liked the frank pleasure he took in his work.

"I met your brother yesterday," she said, looking at the profile of an American Indian at the top of the dream structure.

"I know," he said, his eyes darkening, though he continued to smile at her. "But please –" he pulled up a black plastic cube and motioned her to sit, then he pulled up another and sat facing her. The dream man made a triangle between them. "You should know that my brother and I feel very differently about my father.

"To put it bluntly, Marius thinks our father was an irresponsible parent, a highly troubled man who could have been expected to come to a horrible end. I've had about all I can take of his psychoanalyzing. And the worst part of it is that he thinks he's being objective. 'Father was obviously this, father was obviously that.' Marius should get some more therapy himself, if you ask me. Not that I think it does anyone much good, especially if my brother's an example – but don't get me started. I could go on for hours."

"I didn't get the impression he was totally unsympathetic to your father," Kate said. "Ambivalent might be a fairer description. He did say he was angry at him for leaving your mother, but that seemed natural enough. I was angry at my father for leaving for a while too," she added ruefully. "But he did everything he could to keep in touch and show me he cared."

"Well, Papa kept in touch, too. We visited often. He wrote us letters and stories."

"Your brother said he kept the one about the tortoise-shell cat under his pillow. So maybe underneath . . ."

"That wasn't him, it was me," Emil interrupted indignantly. "I kept it and read it over and over. Marius used to shred Papa's letters and make spitballs out of them . . . either his memory is going or he's purposely trying to mislead you so you'll believe him when he tells you it was Papa's craziness that killed him."

"And you don't think so?"

"Papa wasn't cut out to be a lawyer. So? Is it a crime to have an artist's temperament?" He gestured widely. "The man had a beautiful talent. He wrote plays full of poetry. They had some flaws, but so does most youthful work. He was unhappy at being tied down with a wife and children, when he wanted to write . . . sure, what artist wouldn't be? But he wasn't irresponsible. He worked himself sick to get money for my mother after the divorce. He did hack journalism in the daytime for money and at night he kept himself awake with pots of coffee and wrote what he damn pleased. Does that sound irresponsible?" Repeating the word seemed to fuel his indignation.

"Not at all. But then why is Marius . . . ?"

"Sour grapes? Resentful that Papa and I were so in tune? Who knows." He gave a snort of exasperation. "The aggravating thing is, I accept his being so different from me. He is all straight lines, and angles . . . everything carefully arranged . . . and that's fine. Marius has a perfect right to be the kind of person he is, but not to insist . . . not to interpret every other type of behavior as sick. You think I'm exaggerating?" he asked her abruptly, looking up at her. His eyebrows, she noticed, met over his nose like rough gray wings.

"Well, perhaps he wasn't entirely candid with me, but he didn't call your father 'sick;' he said, 'stressed.'"

"That's a code word – code for crazy."

"Marius gave me Freud's obituary. He used the word 'stress' too, war 'stress.'"

"And I suppose he gave you the good-bye letter my father wrote too?"

"No, he didn't. . . ."

"Well, yes, he wrote a good-bye to Doctor Freud. Marius has never gotten over the honor Freud did him by inviting him into his studio and telling him about the letter. In it he thanks Freud for all the good Freud has done him and tells him he has no accusations against anyone, or any resentments. He told Doctor Freud that 'my suicide is the healthiest, most decent deed of my unsuccessful life.' He said his true motive was his inability to enter happily into a new marriage. . . . Oh, it makes me sick."

"New marriage? With Hilde, my grandmother?" She thought of Keith's urging her to marry him and felt an inappropriate giddy hilarity. "So fear of commitment killed him?"

"I don't believe it for a minute. Though now that I know Hilde was pregnant with your mother, it changes things somewhat. Maybe he didn't want to be trapped into caring for another child when he could barely support the ones he had. I'll need to think about that. But I do know that when he loved someone he loved all out. I saw him when he was deeply in love with someone in Vienna – we visited him there often – even a child could feel heat coming off him when he looked at her. Her name was Lou."

"I think he would have married her," Emil went on, "if she'd been free. And it wasn't just sex. They shared the same interests – though I didn't understand that as a child – poetry, philosophy, psychoanalysis. She was kind to us boys. It went on for about a year. They'd take us out to the zoo when she came and she would buy us cakes and wooden toys, little wagons, balls. I liked her a lot but Marius didn't. He was very loyal to our mother.

Mama was a completely different type from Lou, quiet, austere – a little like Marius's wife – did you know she's a psychoanalyst, too?"

"No," Kate said, "though I saw a photo of a woman on his desk."

"That's her, Ruth. They couldn't have children, which is a good thing from my point of view. She's a stiff person, obsessed with order, and Marius would have been a harsh father. Anyway, Papa often had to scold Marius for misbehaving or scowling at Lou. Finally, Papa and Lou quarreled. She went back to her home. I remember how desperate he was, always going out to the post box to see if there was mail from her and there never was. . . ."

"Are you suggesting that your brother frightened her away?"

"I'm not sure, but I think so," Emil paused, sucking in his breath. "I can understand that you'd be reluctant to take my view over my brother's, especially on such short acquaintance," he said, as he walked over to the partition that separated his bedroom from the rest of his loft, and returned with a dark leather notebook. "There is so little I have of my father's, mostly scraps. He left instructions for his papers to be burned and Marius spent much of the day doing that, but this diary with its engraved cover caught my eye and I took it. I made the argument to Marius that it was a bound book, not papers. Since it was the only thing we saved, it's a very precious memento. It's a diary of 1912-13 – the year he was with Lou."

"Have you read it?"

"I'm not a shrink, so I couldn't make much of all the talk about psychoanalysis and a lot of it seemed too personal for a son's curiosity, but right away I came on some passages about me and Marius as children – how we were with Lou – that was enough for me, I tell you. I'd like you to read it and tell me what you think . . . would you do that?"

"I'd like nothing better," she said. "It would be fascinating to see the affair from my grandfather's point of view. You sure you don't mind my seeing the personal parts?" He shook his head. "It just unnerved me – a bit too steamy . . . ," he gave her a mischievous half smile.

She smiled back. "I have a little more distance." She was wishing for a moment she hadn't given Viktor's breakdown diary to Marius. Hesitantly, she mentioned it to Emil. "I assumed he'd share it . . . ," she trailed off, twisting uncomfortably on the black box that served as her seat.

"Don't worry," Emil said with a smile. She noticed a small dimple at the corner of his mouth. His teeth were very white. "We don't like each other very much, but we preserve the civilities. I'm sure he'll give it to me if I ask."

"Good." She sighed, relieved. He got up and put an avuncular arm around her shoulder. "Call me when you're finished. I want to get to know you better. It's fairly unusual to discover a new relative so late in life, and to like her is probably even rarer. It's almost as though my father introduced us."

"I like you too," she said. She felt the smoothness of the diary against her palm. The cover was engraved with the same beautiful curving script as the earlier one. Emil walked her to the door. Looking back, she saw the statue with a branching tangle of dreams proliferating into the space above its head. A current of air struck the sculpture, making the shapes twirl. Below the eagle and the Indian, she noted a triangle, a compass inscribed with mysterious figures, and just before Emil closed the door, a beautifully shaped green and blue eye.

Chapter Six

W**hen she got back** to her own apartment, she threw herself down on the sofa and started to read. By now she had a sense of what her grandfather looked like, not only from the early photo but from seeing Emil, who was, she thought, one of the most handsome older men she had ever seen. He was very masculine but not at all macho and had the vulnerability that was becoming a requirement for feminists. As she started to read, she imagined her grandfather looking like a younger Emil with blond wavy hair instead of white and the same intense, dark, eyes.

October 30, 1912

I've started keeping a diary again though I've hardly the time for it. The most magnificent woman showed up at Freud's last Wednesday meeting, a statuesque, mature beauty – nearer to Freud's age than mine. She wants to study psychoanalysis with the Professor. He had already warned us that she was coming, noting that she was Germany's most famous woman of letters. She is best known for her excursions in philosophy but has also written innumerable stories, novels, poems, and essays. I imagine that Freud was thinking of the credit to psychoanalysis if she took it up since the health of our movement is always uppermost in his mind.

One of my colleagues, I think it was Federn, added sotto voce *that it was rumored that she had been the mistress of Nietzsche when she was little more than a girl, and much later of Rilke. Curious to meet this woman with an unerring nose for genius, I came early to the meeting, still in my white coat from treating patients at the clinic.*

She was there alone with Freud. When I entered, I felt her appraising me with her eyes, sweeping them boldly over my face and body. She carries her beauty with utmost casualness and a total absence of coyness. I'd actually read one of her literary novels, Ein Todesfall *– about the death of a gifted but unrecognized artist – and told her at once how much I enjoyed it. It occurred to me as I spoke that the despondent artist might well have been modeled on Rilke, who was* *notoriously delicate. She smiled at me warmly and then Freud took her arm, and, whispering something which obviously pleased her, seated her by his side. After a while the others came in and Freud introduced them. She seemed unconcerned at being in a room surrounded by men.*

Lou's hair is honey-colored, with streaks of gray that only serve to add a touch of gravitas to her beauty, and it is piled loosely on her head. She has a tiny waist and hips which have probably become more pronounced with age. Most astonishing about her is that her femininity and her intellect don't clash the way they do in some women – my ex-wife, Martha, being a prime example of someone who was at war with her body.

The description intrigued Kate. This woman, far from being a mindless movie goddess, sounded like a model feminist – both brainy and naturally beautiful. Kate began to visualize the group taking their seats around a table. She imagined it would be a long oblong table with Freud at its head, not, she thought, the more democratic round table. She pictured Lou at the other end where Freud could look straight into her face. Kate suddenly realized that she was imagining Lou incongruously in a '60's outfit; flaring skirt with narrow waist, neat jacket.

Not that it mattered terribly, she thought – you could put on a Shakespeare play in any era and with any costume. And this was clearly going to be a love story. Still, it satisfied her now to envision Lou in a proper Victorian dress, gracefully draped, dark blue, with embroidery on the dove-colored bodice. The men would be in stuffy suits, some with vests slightly bulging, stiff white celluloid collars imprisoning their necks, dangling watch chains. Except for her grandfather, not a particularly good-looking group. They were all, no doubt, having their different reactions to this splendid creature.

Kate knew what Freud's solid burgher's house looked like. She had seen photos of his famous couch covered with an oriental rug, the desk crowded with tiny figures dug from their hiding places in the earth. But though she would have liked to think of the meetings being watched over by these talismans from the past, she knew the meetings would have been held not in the inner sanctum but in the waiting room, and she found, by checking Jones's biography, that by 1911, they had been moved to the College of Physicians.

The location was not nearly as evocative as Freud's study. If she were a novelist she might be tempted to change it, but fact had its benefits. Kate continued reading.

Frau Lou was fascinated by the way Freud proposed to hook unconscious material between the shallows and the depths where it manifests itself in mental illness, and I was fascinated by the way her eyelids seem slightly swollen, as though she had had a night without sleep.

Adler was defended for his concept of organ inferiority and I could see it pained Freud to have this as the first thing she heard, but she leapt right into the debate and vigorously defended Freud's concept of the sexual origins of neurosis. That would ordinarily have been my role. If it had been a man who had taken it, I would have minded, but I had no sense of competition. I was reduced to chuckling when Freud later made a malicious remark about Jung, with whom he is having an increasingly galling exchange of correspondence. I admit that I'm not entirely unhappy about Jung's defection. Many of us are on edge , wondering who will be Freud's heir – perhaps no one. I don't think it presumptuous of me to think I would serve him well in that capacity.

After the meeting Freud was called away because of some trouble at home, and I walked Frau Lou back to her hotel, which was conveniently near our meeting place.

She had had several private talks with Adler, she told me, and was planning to attend his Thursday meetings – something Freud, who demands absolute loyalty, would not have tolerated from one of us. She was quite indignant about the way Adler personalized his disagreement with Freud, and, she added, laughing most delightfully, that Adler, though a clever man, has the face of a button. Her primary quarrel with Adler is that he exalts manliness, or the will to power, and makes the feminine into something negative, whereas she thinks a rich passivity is one of one of the foundations of ego function. I found this an interesting idea, especially coming from someone of her boldness. It made me fantasize about what she was like as a mistress.

Kate felt a cramp in her neck and got up to stretch it out, walking to and fro, swiveling her head gently from side to side. Once up, she felt hungry and went to the fridge, got out the raspberry jam and peanut butter and made herself a sandwich, which she ate rapidly standing at the kitchen counter, and then washed it down with a few mouthfuls of water and went back to the sofa.

November 5, 1912

Lou is attending my elementary course on psychoanalysis and I have managed to arrange for her to come and observe some cases with me at Frankl-Hochwart's clinic. Her curiosity is matched by her intuitive grasp of a patient's state of mind. Freud seems as entranced by her as I am. I could not help noticing in his lecture today that he fixes his gaze on Lou's face. When I asked her afterward if she noticed it, she said, yes, he had told her that he scans the audience to find her – that she is the one he directs his lecture to, and when she is not there – as happened last week – he suffers . . . I worry that he thought her absence at his previous lecture was due to her being with me.

November 10, 1912

She is mine . . . this astonishing woman. Her body is voluptuous, her skin flawlessly clear and white. She has no pudeur about any act of love but gave herself to me with complete ease and confidence. She caressed my body with the tenderness of a ministering angel. I have never had anyone open so deeply to me or felt so strongly merged with any woman. I asked her if she had felt it, but there she seemed to hesitate. I had a sense of her flowing back into herself – once more taking possession of herself. It was more than a little disconcerting to feel her slipping away from me but she assured me it was necessary for us both, the only way that a love as passionate as ours can be sustained. And in fact it is exhilarating to me to see her so proudly independent. It inflames me and makes me want all the more to conquer her. At the same time, I think I'm relieved that I cannot.

I persuaded her to come back to bed – she tossed out her cigar, yes, she smokes long thin elegant cigars – and dissolved once again in my arms, alternately fierce and soothing. This time she bit my shoulder so hard it left a purple stain. By the end of it I was wrung out but seemed to float in a greenish-blue atmosphere, an interior sky that buoyed me and enveloped me. Poetry is the only possible vehicle to express what she makes me feel.

Afterwards, I wanted to continue the marvelous intimacy – the floating – but she began, rather too abruptly I thought, to talk about Freud. She thinks he is a great man partly because he is willing to change his theories and let them develop. He isn't at all dogmatic, as she had been led to believe before she came. The topic did not seem chosen completely at random. She seemed to be suggesting that I should enjoy a similar freedom, that I was . . . how did she put it? Too precisely Freudian. It is true that I know his texts as well as I know my own thought. Was she implying I only mimic him, that my being able to quote chapter and verse anywhere in his work is a fault? She would not explain herself any more than that . . . turned aside my questions by complimenting me on remarks in my lecture about sadomasochism, saying they couldn't have been more congenial if she had made them herself.

Where does she get this enormous assurance of hers? She told me she had had it even as a girl. Even with the great Nietzsche. But she said I should not be deceived by her appearance of self-possession. She had it, yes, but there was another side. She confessed that she has always felt torn between independence and love, and that the thought of being mortified and even physically abused gives her a sexual thrill. She told me she had written about this in a short novella called Dissipation, which she will give me. As a child, the heroine observed a wet-nurse being lashed bloody by a valet and noticed the rapture in the woman's eyes. From that time on, she --and it seemed that Lou identified with this heroine of hers – felt menaced by sex. Seeing I was somewhat troubled by her revelations, Lou assured me that since then, she thought she had achieved a better balance between her impulses. I led her on to talk about Nietzsche and found that sex hardly entered into it at all. They were "soulmates" somehow driven apart by his jealous, mean-spirited sister.

November 11, 1912

I gave what I thought was an excellent lecture on artistic inhibitions but was distressed by Freud's really rather severe criticisms. He seemed annoyed that I was dealing with the subject of art at all, saying that with the persistent calumny of the movement – Jung's defection and the nasty remarks the Swiss analysts are now making about Freud's dirty-mindedness – we dare not move so boldly into new territories "leaving the rear exposed." If anyone else had used that metaphor it would surely have given me pause. Even Lou, who passionately defends Freud's concept of sexuality, was puzzled by his censure, calling me the most unconditionally devoted and outstanding of his disciples. In fact, the more diligently I try to take his thinking forward, the more I feel his irritation – for want of a better word – with me. Lou says I should talk honestly to him about it, but that is a woman's way. I cannot. Besides, I sense it would not do me any good. He would deny it and withdraw further.

To distract me, Lou took me with her to see Klimt's paintings. He is a great favorite of hers. I had seen them before, of course, but seeing them with her at my side, feeling the warmth of her body radiate through her clothes where our hips touched, was quite a different experience. There seemed to be some mysterious exchange of sexual energy going on between her and the paintings.

Lou stood for a long time in front of his painting of Danae. What an extraordinary work! The naked woman, lush and full-figured, lies curled like a fetus, her heavy thighs facing the viewer, her long red hair streaming. Her eyes are closed in a trance while Zeus, as a shower of golden coins, falls in a powerful gold stream between her legs. One hand claws her breast, while the other against her inner thigh is ambiguously out of sight. Lou whispered to me that it looked almost as if she were masturbating, that this "vision" of a golden lover was Danae's erotic fantasy. Feeling her breath against my ear and seeing the gold streaming between the voluptuous thighs gave me an erection and I had to put my hand in my pocket to keep it from protruding.

Lou was amused, and pretending to be a severe matron, rushed me past some sinuously naked water-snake-women to Klimt's painting of lovers kissing. Even though they are both fully clothed, it is even more sensually arousing than the other. Lou said it quite perfectly embodied her belief in a rich female passivity. I saw at once what she meant. The woman kneels on a fertile flower-strewn earth, her garment a beautifully intricate design of spheres – which Lou maintained was the eternal feminine – while the man's cape was decorated with darker phallic rectangles. Finding it difficult to concentrate with my erection throbbing against my pocketed hand, I wanted to go back to my apartment and make love, but she said rather mischievously that I had to wait until she had sated her visual appetite.

Pausing in front of a sinister painting of Judith and Holofernes, Lou reminded me of my lecture on the guilt behind artistic inhibitions and suggested that this was a fine example of what I was talking about. Klimt, clearly overcome by guilt for his sexual impulses, has become highly anxious and fearful of women. Lou looked at me slyly as she spoke, making me wonder if she thinks I am similarly fearful. I am not sure I like the way she scrutinizes me as though I were a patient in analysis. Though Freud's little band scrutinize each other incessantly, telling each other their dreams and discussing their self-analyses, I am not sure this is a good thing for lovers, who surely should leave some areas of mystery.

Just before we left, we looked at some posters from the first Secession show, when Klimt and others rebelled against their artistic fathers. It included a striking poster of a young Theseus fighting the Minotaur. Lou remarked that for Freud, the bull was the father. For once I did not want to hear his name.

I took her back to my apartment and made violent love to her.

Kate lifted her eyes as the door slammed and Keith burst in, threw his tattered briefcase on the sofa, and came over to hug her.

"You look beat," she said. She went into the kitchen and came back with a beer for him. "What's up, how was your meeting?"

He patted her bottom appreciatively, then tilted the can against his lips. "I'm not sure . . . ," he said after a minute. "Some of the student leaders are convinced we have to be more provocative."

"I don't get it," Kate said. Movement politics were so volatile these days; it was hard to follow. "I thought you'd been trying to avoid confrontations with the Right."

"Well, obviously it isn't working. They're ready to try something else. Wally – (Wally was one of the brightest of the student activists) – thinks there has to be conflict now. That we have to find ways to polarize the country, make the Right attack us. If they get really vicious, maybe the forces of reason will sit up and take notice, but it will take a lot of effort. Wally thinks we've got to calculate what they need to run this war – whether it's soldiers or taxpayers – and take it away from them."

"What sort of thing are they planning?" Kate hoped it wasn't something to endanger his job, or worse, get him locked up.

"They're thinking of various things . . . demonstrating at the Pentagon, destroying records. . . ."

"Sounds as though people will get hurt."

"Right now it's just in the talking stage, along with the mass burning of draft cards. To tell the truth, I'm afraid Wally and the others are losing touch with reality. They're ignoring the differences between what happened in the South and what will work now. There was a national consensus back then that we just don't have."

"Did you try to tell them?"

"I did . . . of course I did . . . someone called me a peace creep – under his breath, but I heard him clear enough. Well, we'll see how it plays out . . . SDS might self-destruct and I'm certainly not going to be able to stop it," he paused. "But right now I need a shower. I'm soaking wet."

While he was showering she went back to the diary. A few minutes later, with only a towel around his waist, he sat next to her, glancing at it over her shoulder. "How is it? Any juicy bits?"

"Some."

He took it from her and it fell open at the description of love-making, which immediately captured his interest. He read it, engrossed.

"Wow. This Lou was a pretty foxy lady," he said, after a few minutes. He reached out a long arm, pulling her down on the sofa.

She kissed him lightly but pulled away when he started to investigate her mouth with his tongue.

"That really turned you on, didn't it?" she asked him.

"It did."

Kate had been excited by it too – it was marvelously sensual – but somehow she resented his reaction, as if it were pornography instead of high romance.

"Remember, it wasn't just her beauty that attracted men," she said, rather primly. "They took her ideas seriously. Tausk was fascinated by her mind, too, And the fact that she loved her independence."

"So do you, my sweet." He stroked the soft skin on the side of her arm. "By the way," he asked, casually, "did you get your period? Is that why you don't want to make love? You must know how much I want you."

"I was having some cramps," she admitted, "and my breasts are swollen." She cupped her right breast in her hand, assessing its soreness. "I'm not too worried. I've been a few days late before."

"I wouldn't mind if you were pregnant. We'd have a beautiful child with your big eyes, my Dumbo ears." He put both hands up besides his jutting ears – his least perfect feature – and waggled them at her. "I know you think that having a baby can ruin a good relationship, but don't worry, our child will be an angel."

"Frau Lou didn't seem to feel the lack of children. I'm not sure I would either. I don't think having me has made my mother any happier."

"I'm not going to get sucked into that one – though I expect you know you're wrong. As for glamorous Frau Lou, she was probably too self-involved to feel the lack of anything."

"I like her," Kate persisted. "She was so strong, so comfortable being brainy; expressing her ideas didn't embarrass her. I don't think she would have minded wearing horn-rimmed glasses if she'd needed them. She was so sure of being attractive." Kate blushed, remembering how desperate she'd been to get contact lenses in high school.

"You have adorable glasses yourself," Keith said, reaching towards her and adjusting them slightly – "though they tend to slip down on your nose. With that provocative little slant at the edge, they make you look like Batwoman."

"Why do you have to turn everything into foreplay?" Kate asked, frowning.

"Sorry," he said, hurt. "I thought you needed a little relief from thinking. I certainly do. Your body wants to come close and cuddle; it's just your brain that's objecting. And if you are going to tell me that Lou got up after smoldering sex to talk philosophy, at least it was after sex, not before."

"You're impossible," she said, putting her face against his for a minute. "You don't really feel deprived, do you? We made love twice last night."

"And last night I was supremely happy. But you know the old adage, *l'appetito vien mangando?*"

She looked at him uneasily.

"Don't worry, love, dimwitted male that I am, I accept the fact that you're not receptive to my passion right now."

"I might be later," she said, thinking that he could be really sweet when he wanted to.

"I've got to go out again. I will be out until one o'clock at least, maybe two o'clock. I have a meeting."

"Another one?" An image came to her mind of the pretty women students who she'd seen clustering around him at the last big rally. She quickly suppressed it. He had never asked her for the sort of open relationship in fashion now.

"We didn't finish. I want to help them write a position paper. And we have to plan our stop-the-draft-demonstration. I told them I'd meet them up at my place after supper. I thought you'd be pleased to see me. What with trips to see what they're doing on other campuses and organizing here and my teaching, we haven't seen each other much lately."

"I know . . . and I am happy to see you," she said. "I'll go fix us something to eat."

Keith had kissed her warmly when he left, but when it came time for bed, Kate found she had trouble sleeping. She found herself going over parts of the diary in her mind. It had shocked her that Lou – this powerful, independent, woman – had admitted to wanting to be mistreated and abused. Helene would have liked that, she thought. It would have confirmed her idea that women had masochistic tendencies. And what about Lou's rhapsodic descriptions of fecund women and the female principle – coming from a woman who had never wanted a child? She puzzled over it until her thoughts took on a life of their own as images, and she fell asleep.

The next morning after Keith left, Kate took up the diary again. The first thing she saw was Helene's name.

November 14, 1912

Had a brief note from Helene Deutsch that she passed her second qualifying exam a few days ago. She passed with a "sufficient," which didn't seem to bother her at all. She just wants to get it over with and get her degree. Her final exam is in March. I like her and Felix enormously and feel badly that I have not made time to see them, but Lou takes every ounce of energy that is not given to work.

November 16, 1912

Freud seems to be almost obsessed with discrediting Adler. He argued against him again today, brilliantly, of course but still . . . for me it has been clear for months how vindictive and small-minded Adler is. If ever a theory indicated its maker's state of mind, the "Inferiority Complex" sums up Adler very well.

November 18, 1912

When Lou came to me tonight, I showed her some extremely beautiful South Slav ballads which I had translated. She seemed as taken by them as I had been, saying they made her happy. She particularly liked their lack of repression . . . their connection with the black earth of some primal heroic nature – Promethean – fully conscious of sin and its consequences, accepting them in an ecstasy of sacrifice. She thinks that in this respect, modern man – Freudian man, always working to expand the boundaries of consciousness – is sterile. She said that only women remain in touch with nature's rich subsoil by creating life and nourishing it with their breasts. To Lou, men, not women, are the inessential ones. She even thinks that women artists created the idea of maleness and God! She reconciles this idea with Freud's description of women as castrated men, emotionally and morally undeveloped, by emphasizing the parts of his theory that fit her views and reinterpreting the rest. I kept this insight to myself.

She works with me daily now at Frankl-Hochwart's neurological clinic. Together we are trying to analyze a paranoid woman. Unfortunately, our clinic chief, Dr. Hochwart, is absolutely set against psychoanalysis. Felix Deutsch, who happened to be at the Ronacher café when I was there yesterday, told me he ran into him one evening and Hochwart worked himself into a fury, cursing Freud and his company. He particularly castigates Freud for his high fees. He had just rescued two youths from Freud who had fought with their parents in consequence of a treatment by him. Hochwart reconciled them and sent them to the Graefenberg sanatorium to get straightened out, he said. Felix said it was terrible to listen to. I said I knew. I have to hear similar remarks all the time. I told him I was sorry to have seen so little of them since their marriage last April, and we determined to get together soon. Apparently Helene made a proposal to

Dr. Hochwart for an institution to care for young girls. Of course he said that if psychoanalytic treatment was to take place there, it would be no use. Felix asked me how I was doing in this atmosphere – with such hostility from the neurologists. Helene is wondering about how it would be to set up practice here in Vienna. I told him it is hellish. My case load is stagnating and I have to struggle to get paying patients. But despite my difficulties with Hochwart, I am determined to advance my understanding of psychotic patients. The one Lou and I were trying to help was yanked out from under our noses and committed to the asylum before we could make any progress.

The phone rang. It was Emily. She was bored at the beach because she could neither swim nor walk with comfort. Her daughter had decamped and left her feeling neglected and alone. "I've called Dr. Deutsch a couple of times to ask if she'd walk with me," she said. "If you can call my lurching along on my crutches 'walking'. She seems to be quite busy working on a memoir. Anyway, she's going back to the city next week to spend some time with her son and I asked her if I could come with her."

"You sure that's okay?"

"I don't see why it wouldn't be. It's a big car. Helene's housekeeper will drive.

They chatted a few more minutes. Kate tried to suggest that Emily was really better off where she was, with her aide. Though Kate felt mean, it had been a relief not having to worry about the day-to- day details of her mother's care. After Kate hung up, she dialed Helene. "I just wanted to make sure mother wasn't inconveniencing you. She can be pretty insistent sometimes."

"Not at all," Helene laughed. "I really need to come back."

Kate was dying to talk to Helene about her discovery and get her impressions, but she wasn't ready yet. She wanted to work through it slowly and then figure out what she thought before getting Helene's response. Still, she thought she might do a sort of cross-check on Tausk's narrative by referring to something Helene had already mentioned and seeing if she could get her to elaborate.

"I was thinking about your reading *Interpretation of Dreams* after you lost the baby," Kate started cautiously, "trying to use psychoanalytic principles with your patients. You said the neurologists were hostile. I wondered," she went on disingenuously, "if that hostility diminished, if you were able to win some support for your analytic work?"

The question was a reasonable one, but Helene noticed that Kate sounded strained, as though the phone she was using had a bad connection. Perhaps Helene had intimidated her somehow by breaking off the discussion about Freud's suspicions of Tausk. Aside from that, Helene thought they'd developed quite a good relationship, a friendship even. Maybe it was just some trouble with the boyfriend.

"Support?" she asked now with a touch of irony. "No not really. And it was difficult for me – and I'm sure for Freud too – to persevere in the face of such scorn. But I was determined to keep experimenting. Despite my supervisors' attitudes, the clinic provided me with a great variety of experience. In one day, I could see hysterical or psychotic women in the morning and then a quite ordinary young girl, suffering only from disappointed love, in the afternoon."

She paused, rubbed her arthritic thumb, then moved the phone to her other hand.

"Just then, I think I was most concerned about these ordinary girls. I suppose they reminded me of my disastrous love affair with Lieberman and my lost baby. I wondered how many other young girls had suffered the way I had and had received similarly inadequate care – perhaps other women were going mad because they had given away too much of themselves."

Helene remembered now with a certain poignancy how desperately she had wanted to help them.

"I was naïve then about the amount of opposition there would be," she confided to Kate. "I had the idea of founding a clinic specifically for troubled girls and women. I thought I could introduce psychoanalysis into the hospitals and revolutionize the way psychiatry was practiced in Vienna. Unfortunately, Vienna wasn't ready for me then. The eminent neurologist Felix and I consulted about my plan said he considered me 'infected by psychoanalysis.'"

Kate felt breathless. Tausk had written about Helene's idea of founding a clinic and had just confirmed Kate's suspicion that the idea came from Helene's misery over Lieberman. She was beginning to realize just what a godsend this diary was going to be for her thesis and the book that she hoped would come afterward. She might not only illuminate the women's roles in the early movement, the way theory and life went together, but recover Tausk and give him his proper place. She might even, if she were daring enough, reveal a new side of Freud's character. She suddenly saw, as if in an x-ray, the lives of Tausk and Lou, as closely connected as the veins and arteries in a maturing body, pumping toward and away from the powerful Freudian heart.

"We'll talk more when I see you," Kate said, finally, feeling faintly disloyal.

A few minutes later, she was back with the diary and her German dictionary.

November (here the date was smudged and she couldn't read it.)

Walking home from the clinic with Lou, we were talking about resistance to treatment and I remarked that analytic treatment is often alienating because it doesn't create a complete picture of the individual and is in this sense reductionist. She agreed, and even went further, saying she did not think that the scientific method could be applied to our inner experience. She then dropped a bombshell on my unsuspecting head. She is going to begin private meetings at Freud's house to talk about psychoanalysis one day a week. The only time he has free is after ten in the evening. I wondered – mildly, I thought – at the propriety of this, and no less at his offer to walk her home in the middle of the night. She was angry with me and accused me of jealousy and of wanting to limit her freedom. This was our first real argument.

Christmas, 1912

All this month we have been on good terms again. She made me see how important it is for her to be in close contact with Freud. How could I deny her what has been so inspiring to me? Still, it has not been easy. She will admit absolutely no protests or jealousies. But when I am generous, she is also. When the boys visited, Lou showed great sweetness, bringing them treats, a toy wagon and puzzles that she had picked out with great care. Emil is very fond of her. He stood near and leaned against her when she read him a story. Marius, though, has been more likely to create problems. He is distant and even rude, and avoids looking Lou in the face. I had to speak harshly to him about that and about purposely not seeming to notice her when he comes into a room. With her unusual sensitivity, Lou immediately noticed Marius's attitude and used all her charm to woo him. She asked him, treating him very much as a person able to make sensible choices, what he would most like to do. He brightened and expressed a desire to go to the children's amusement park, the Wurstel Prater. I had the unpleasant task of reminding him that, because it was winter, it was all shut down, his beloved merry-go-round covered by tarps. I suggested the Ferris wheel instead and Lou eagerly seconded me, but Marius would not be mollified. He dragged his feet, almost making us miss the tram, and not even the sight of the great wheel slowly revolving against the pale sky, its glass cars swinging, revived his interest. Emil, on the other hand, was excited almost to madness, dragging on our hands to hurry and then shrieking with joy when the wheel started to rise with us inside a transparent shell. The situation disintegrated further when Emil tugged at Marius, trying to get him look at the people walking below "like little toy soldiers," and Marius swatted him away. I lost my temper and cuffed him and then he started to howl. I could see how disappointed Lou was. But she did succeed in getting him to stop crying by promising that we would all go to Sacher's – a much too elegant place for children – and have cake and hot chocolate. Not having children herself, she doesn't realize that you mustn't reward them for bad behavior. Or perhaps she was so set on seducing them she did not stop to think of the consequences. Marius behaved just long enough to eat his sachertorte and then started to whine. I had been reluctant to tell Lou that chocolate overexcites him and makes him irritable. In short, the afternoon which started with such high hopes of coming together as a family, at least for me ended badly.

Later that night when the children had gone to sleep, we somehow got into a conversation about infidelity. Lou said she does not like the use of the word abandonment. That people do not necessarily desert one lover for another but, as she quaintly put it, are "driven home to themselves." I saw this as another – in this case distressing – example of her redefining things to please herself. She said that setting someone free need not be a gesture of abandonment but should be thought of as returning them to the world. I told her, half joking, that I, for one, did not want to be returned and began to kiss her neck, but she persisted in continuing our discussion.

Good for you Lou, Kate thought, make him listen to you. Women were often blamed for using sex to get what they wanted, but men clearly also used it to stave off hearing painful things. Kate imagined Tausk holding Lou close, passionately kissing her neck – just the way Keith had kissed hers last night – his body trembling with fear.

January 10, 1913

Freud gave a brilliant lecture on fairy tales. Afterwards we went to the Alserhof, and I got into an argument with Dr. Steif from Munich over Jung. Lou told me afterward that I am at my best in replying to someone's argument because even in abstract thought I bring things back to the living person: she would not have changed a single word of what I said. It could not have been clearer or more judicious. But she also observed that it is becoming difficult to speak about facts in any deliberation about Jung because of a desire in the group to preserve unity. She added that I should be careful not to make enemies – my comments had apparently made Rank suspicious of my intentions. Everyone is jostling for position.

In the evening, Lou received a telegram that her mother, Muschka – as she calls her – had died. It was not entirely unexpected but is still very painful, perhaps the more so because there seems to be much hatred mixed with her love. She talked to me for the first time about her girlhood, touching me deeply. Whatever her mother meant to her, her main passion was for her father, whom she imagined visiting her at night in her room as a thoroughly indulgent invisible god, the folds of his enormous cloak filled with toys. She told me – lying against my shoulder – that her story-telling had its source in those early days when she made up tales to relate to him and ended by believing it "reality." Once a small cousin called her a liar. After that, she said with that guileless look of hers, "I became scrupulous about my facts before transmuting them." I did not quite understand, and she explained that she would stalk strangers, day after day observing the facts of their daily routine, the way they walked, their appearance, and so on, before she wove them into fiction. The fecundity of her imagination astonishes me. Then, too, she has an egoism that becomes a sacred duty to affirm herself.

Kate realized with a start that she had done similar investigations as a child – once climbing high up in a maple tree so she could spy on lovers beneath, later enlarging the few bits of overheard talk into a gripping story. She, too, had been accused of lying as a young child – she flatly refused to admit she had bitten a playmate – and in fact, now she often had to rein in her mind when it lunged this way and that, tempted by an association or memory to amplify or redirect the fragmentary facts she was gathering.

January 11, 1913

Still Mardi Gras, the nights are filled with revelers and masks. The nobility play at being peasants while in the poorer neighborhoods, chambermaids and butchers' apprentices cheerfully imitate royalty. Freud refuses to be involved in the frivolity, sitting late at his desk over piles of paper. He might even be said to work harder during this festive season on his task of unmasking, though he is rather secretive about his thoughts just now. And of course none of us wish to seem less diligent than the Master. I lectured as usual.

After my lecture, Lou argued with me all the way home about a remark I had made. I had said quite simply that men as well as women like to remember the path to sexual fulfillment but find the act itself embarrassing. Lou insisted that men in particular were embarrassed because they have been raised to feel guilty about wish-fulfillment. Women, she thinks, share this embarrassment to a much lesser extent. This is clearly not true in my experience, and is another example of how she makes facts conform to wishes. She argued that because women don't isolate sexuality the way men do, they have less need to find it coarse. She has often remarked that women surrender their personalities in sex, and she now says that since their whole selves are involved, they cannot be ashamed of the act if they are to survive at all. A woman's emphasis on fidelity and marriage is just a defense against shame. A more erotically giving woman might have poured everything into the festival of love and had none left for morality.

The twists and turns of her logic are as dazzling as a magician's tricks. When I protested the dangers of unlimited eroticism, she threw it back at me that I, too, have refused to be shackled by convention and have had an abundance of mistresses, never hesitating to leave them when passion withered. The difference is that I really want to find the One Beloved and believe I have found it in her. I told her again that together we could find mutual salvation. Salvation comes from within, she said, if it comes at all. You are afraid to know your true desires, I told her. Part of her hesitation is fear of becoming submerged in me, but I believe I can reassure her of her essential freedom. If I try to bind her, I know she will slip like water through my hands.

Kate wondered if Tausk had it right. Was Lou's sexual freedom tied to a fear of being submerged? Lou just got up and ran when she felt herself getting too close. Kate certainly felt that way at times with Keith. What especially drove her crazy was when she felt herself wanting to give in to him. That was sure to make her dig in her heels. But Kate couldn't see herself escaping into perpetual new erotic adventures, as Lou advocated. Keith was probably right that Lou couldn't really love anyone – though Kate hadn't admitted it to him. She and Keith were both so stubborn . . . each wanted to dictate to the other. Maybe that was the trouble. . . . But Kate wondered if they were going to kill their love in the process of trying to make it work.

January 14, 1913

We were sitting at the Alte Elster after Freud's lecture, warming ourselves after the bitter cold outside. I remarked that I thought a failure in the ego realm and hence in the social sphere was an absolutely necessary condition for an outbreak of neurosis. Refuge would be taken in sexuality. The disharmony then results in illness. Lou said later that it was only through my formulations that she personally became aware of the equal significance of ego and sex. Yet now Freud agrees. Did she imply that I had helped him to see this, or was she only praising the flexibility of his thinking? At the close of the discussion, Freud referred favorably to a clarifying observation I had made earlier but failed to remember who had made it. When I pointed it out, he apologized, smiling. Am I wrong to suspect that he dislikes acknowledging my contributions?

February 1, 1913

Lou spent all of Sunday afternoon until evening at Freud's house. She talked about it freely over supper. At least I did not have the impression she was holding anything back. She admitted that the conversation was much more personal than it had been before and that he had told her about his life. She repeated, pronouncing it charming, a little story he had told her about a narcissistic cat. I was fascinated by this look at a more lighthearted, even playful Freud. The cat in question had climbed in through his office window on the ground floor. He did not care much for animals and had mixed feelings about the cat, especially when it began to walk around and inspect antique objects which Freud had temporarily placed on the floor. He was afraid that if he chased it, the cat might move recklessly and knock over one of these precious treasures. But when the cat showed its archeological satisfaction by purring and avoiding the objects with lithe grace, his heart melted and he ordered milk for it. From then on, the cat assumed a daily right to inspect the antiquities and receive her bowl of milk. However, in spite of Freud's growing affection, the cat paid him not the slightest attention, merely stared at him with cold green eyes as if he were only another object. If he wanted more from the cat, he had to remove his foot from his comfortable chaise and rub it with his shoe. One day, when the relationship had gone on like this for a long time, he found the cat gasping on his sofa. Though he gave it every care, the cat succumbed to pneumonia, leaving only a symbolic picture of the peace and playfulness of true egoism.

I laughingly suggested she saw herself in the cat – as she has always asserted narcissism as the base for creative endeavor. She flared up strangely. Afterward she confessed that Nietzsche, when their relationship was crumbling, compared her to a cat, calling her a monstrosity, "a beast of prey posing as a domestic animal." How bitterly he must have been disappointed to have said such things! I told her what she knew already: Freud's picture of the cat was clearly affectionate.

Yes, I think so, she said. After telling his story, Freud wanted to know the reasons for her involvement in psychoanalysis. She told him that analysis had enriched her life by showing its roots in the totality – the undifferentiated unconscious. Again Freud showed her his playful side, laughingly saying it seemed that she looked on psychoanalysis as a Christmas present, and she could only agree.

She was obviously immensely gratified by his confidences and interest and promised to bring photographs of herself and her family to their next meeting. How could I even think of telling her to deny herself that pleasure? Intense feelings of jealousy and shame. Striving hard to overcome them, I console myself with the thought that though he speaks with her intimately, I am the one she sleeps with.

Didn't her grandfather know that unconsummated love can be even more dangerous than a sexual affair? Kate guessed he had to suppress his anger for fear of driving Lou away, but it really was astonishing how hard Freud exerted himself to charm her.

February 3, 1913

Lou and I have gotten into the habit of listening in on the conversation of the others after Freud's lectures. After Freud's presentation of two childhood analyses last week there was much indignation – a feeling that he had left unresolved the opposition between nature and culture. Lou observed to me on the way home through the wintry streets that the princely education along psychoanalytic lines – being much more permissive of the child's impulses – hasn't so far accomplished much as the child still has the problem of what to do with his sexuality. In a society that demands renunciation, there is bound to be conflict. With Freud she is much more diplomatic. If she criticizes, she always mutes it by offering something else that he wants.

She went again to visit him the other night. Of course I had to wait up for her, anxious to hear what they had talked about. While I waited I could not stop imagining Freud sitting alone with her, the fire lit in the stove, cozily shielded from the weather, looking into her magnificent eyes. When she returned she professed surprise to see me still up. I blamed my wakefulness on heartburn, but I thought she looked skeptical. With all the casualness I could muster, I asked how her evening had gone. What had they talked about?

"Oh," she said, "we talked about his lecture on childhood sexuality. I told him it made me remember an incident from my childhood when I woke up and found my father's bed empty and became terrified that he was dead. My mother's moans convinced me that she was dying too and I let out a horrible shriek." She gave a little laugh. "Of course that brought both parents rushing in a panic to my bedside."

"Freud must have loved that," I said, "a perfect primal scene."

"He was interested, no doubt," she said, stretching her arms out towards the fire. Her face took on a rosy glow from the reflected light, and she herself was glowing with satisfaction. Apparently, he had

quizzed her about her older brothers. She told him – as she had told me – that they were chivalrous and protective and had made her open and trusting toward men, so that she looked on all the world as if it were populated by brothers alone. Despite this, she confessed to being lonely as a child and finding her chief joy in fantasy. As she told me this I wondered if she is being entirely truthful about her harmonious family – after her mother's death it was clear that Lou was deeply angry at her – or about being so open and trusting. But then I chastised myself for doubting her. She is a luminous being – and she loves me, that is the important thing. I truly believe that we have a deep and special bond that can't be hurt by her very different bond with Freud, and who knows better than I how difficult it is to resist him? Even when I feel unjustly rebuked by him, I love and admire him. Lou said she is going back to him Sunday afternoon to talk further about her childhood. Their encounters sound more and more like an analysis. I mastered myself enough to embrace her and was rewarded by the most loving caresses.

February 9, 1913

The boys were visiting again. There was a heavy snow last night, and in the afternoon we went out to the park and played in the snow. They made a marvelous snowman complete with carrot nose and a little crown Emil cleverly constructed out of twigs. I was glad to see them working together fairly harmoniously. I think Marius was pleased that Lou was off seeing Freud and that he had time to be with me alone. I asked him about school and he was noncommittal, saying with a shrug that it was much as usual, but brightened when he got to the subject of sports. He is going through a phase of liking ball games of all sorts, and I promised him that in the spring when the ground is clear, he could show me his kick. Emil was captivated by some long icicles hanging from the eaves, coming out of his trance only long enough to irritate Marius by boasting that he had chosen a lollipop with a better color – his was purple.

I grew restless as the afternoon wore on and Lou still did not return. Marius suggested that maybe she was not coming back. I told him that was definitely not the case. Finally, I took the boys with me to the flower shop to buy flowers for her. Marius sulked but Emil helped me pick out hothouse roses, a delicious peach color with huge velvety petals. When she finally came around six, my heart sank to see that Freud too had given her roses, a huge bunch in a deep deep crimson. I dispatched the boys for another vase with water, but not before I saw Marius regarding me quizzically as though to gauge my reaction. How quickly children pick up our emotions, even though we are doing our best to hide them.

After the boys had gone to bed we sat on the sofa. "You are positively radiant," I said. "Your talk must have been stimulating."

"Are you being sarcastic?" she asked.

"Of course not," I replied, not meeting her eyes.

"Good," she said, caressing my cheek with her hand. I felt for a moment as though I were a child being rewarded for good behavior. To recapture my manhood I tried to take her to bed, but she was not ready; she had to unwind first. She rearranged the flowers, took some tea that I had prepared for her and between sips culled bits from her afternoon and offered them to me.

She told Freud her childhood idea that a woman's internal organs are like the inside of a mountain filled with precious stones.

"There are so many descriptive terms for one's prick," I said, holding down my jealousy that she had revealed such an intimate fantasy. "There certainly ought to be something similar for womb, and that sounds like a splendid one. Do you know how you arrived at it?"

"I'd seen the Jungfrau on a trip to Switzerland once when I went down into a mine with my father," she said, and I could tell from the rapidity with which she answered that Freud had already asked her this. "My favorite fairytale was about a princess," she went on, "from whose mouth jewels gushed at every word." Here she smiled up at me as though to say: See, everything I offered him, I am sharing with you. And it was true that I felt better, though I had no way of knowing what she was suppressing. I asked her if she had played with her mother's jewelry as a child, and she told me that her first memory of jewels was of her mother's box full of many-colored fancy buttons.

Here her look darkened, and she went on to tell me that we attain our individuality only by repelling something and being repelled by it. I guessed that she was justifying her hatred of her mother. Does Freud know how much Lou dislikes rational modes of thought? She believes that the virtue of analysis is not that it gives man more control but that, through the unconscious, it restores us to our primal order of existence.

Emil called Kate and said he would like to see her again. They agreed to meet by the Sphinx in front of the Metropolitan. As usual, the museum steps were crowded with people, young and old, eating sandwiches, smoking, chatting in various languages. It took Kate a moment to pick him out standing on the far side of a group of teenagers. He was wearing the same blue work shirt as last time but with a sculpted silver necklace that glinted in the sun.

"Am I late?" she asked, shading her eyes with one hand and looking up at him.

"Not at all," he answered gallantly. "I've been enjoying the scene."

After her recent argument with Keith, it was pleasant to feel Emil's appreciative glance, which seemed to accept her with no demands. She smiled back at him and they went inside. Emil fumbled briefly in his wallet, then apologized for forgetting his member's card and making them stand in line for tickets. The line was fairly long – full of summer tourists intent on culture.

They inched forward behind a young woman with a mane of auburn hair and a peace logo on a thong around her neck.

"I've been reading the diary."

"You're the only person beside my brother who's looked at it. I'm curious to hear what you think."

"Well, I'm not finished yet, but I see what you mean about Marius. He certainly was a pain in the neck and he tried as hard as he could to make things difficult for your father and Lou, though I don't think that's what broke them up."

"Oh? What did, then?"

"I think it was Freud. He wanted Lou to himself and probably resented Tausk's being her lover. Freud did everything he could to bring her closer. If what Lou told your father is true, Freud created an intimate atmosphere in which he could elicit stories of her childhood. Told her playfully about his cat. Gave her bouquets of crimson roses."

"Ah, yes, the roses. I remember being sent to get a vase. And I knew Papa wasn't exactly pleased. But I didn't quite understand."

"How could you? You were just a child, but I'd say he pulled out all the stops for her. And there's no doubt she was fascinated by him. Did you ever meet Freud?"

"No, though I got the impression from my father that he was a great man, that it was a privilege to work with him. And I heard my father talking about him with Lou."

"Do you remember anything more?"

"Just that sometimes they argued and I'd hear Freud's name, but they always made up afterward. Or at least that's what I told myself. Lou was nice to me and I liked her. Once she stuck up for me when I told a whopping lie to avoid being punished. She said she was sure I believed in my inventions, and she refused to call that lying. She insisted I was going to be an artist. Anyway, I wanted them to get along, so I tried to ignore their quarrels.

"Once, though, I couldn't help noticing. My father was pacing around the apartment, distinctly upset, waiting for Lou to come back, and I saw Marius looking at him with a satisfied smirk. When I asked him why he was smiling, he whispered, 'She's with Professor Freud. She doesn't care how long she keeps Papa waiting' – he gave that sanctimonious little smirk of his, as if Papa deserved to be mistreated – and I threw myself on him. Being older and stronger, he held me off, and just at that moment Lou came back smiling . . . with those roses you mentioned . . . funny, I forgot them until now. I just remembered fighting with my brother . . . ."

Emil paused to retrieve the tickets and drop a few dollars into the Plexiglas contribution box.

"So do you think Freud was sleeping with Lou?" Emil asked abruptly, as they stopped in front of a sarcophagus with a bas-relief of an exquisitely robed priestess rising from the waves.

Kate had a brief image of Lou and Freud grappling together on his studio couch while his wife Martha was asleep upstairs.

"I'm sure she would have been willing," Kate said. "She loved brilliant men. There were Nietzsche and Rilke. Having Freud would have given her a trinity of geniuses. But I think he was probably too puritanical. He said that he gave up sex in his early forties, and when he met Lou he was about fifty-six."

Emil laughed. "Maybe it was just married sex he gave up." He studied the marble figure of a discus thrower, curving over in perfect control, gleaming stone muscles taut in arm and belly.

"I don't think so. Once when they were still on good terms, he told Jung that he was tormented by erotic dreams about prostitutes. Jung asked him why he didn't just go to one to relieve himself. Freud was shocked. 'I can't do that,' he said, 'I'm a married man.'"

Emil laughed again. "Funny business, Freud always thinking about sex and not able to do it. If that's true, my father was more of a man than he was. Though he worried about sex, too. I remember when Marius was an adolescent, my father made him write down his dreams and then he analyzed them. Marius almost died of embarrassment. It seems they were all about masturbation and showed some unhealthy elements. I never liked Marius, but I felt sorry for him. After that he shut down completely . . . poor stiff. I guess I'm lucky my father never asked to hear my dreams." He had moved on to an androgynously ringletted Apollo standing, languidly, stroking his lute.

"Why?" Kate asked, not quite following.

"Freud was pretty harsh on homosexuality, wouldn't you say?" he asked, walking around the figure to look at it from behind. "My father loved me but he would have been mortified to have a pervert for a son – even if I've done rather well as an artist. There aren't many of us who can live on what we make. Still, I'm glad my father didn't live to see me come out. I think he would have had to toe the party line, and it would have made us both miserable."

"Oh," Kate stammered, "I see." She had just noticed that in addition to the necklace he was wearing a beautiful ring – a half circle of silver that embraced his ring finger without trapping it. "But maybe you're wrong. Your father was ahead of his time in so many ways. The way he thought about war, for instance. Some of Freud's ideas were pretty primitive—about women too—and I know he thought homosexuals had arrested sexual development. But he also thought we were all bi-sexual. I think if he'd been around today he might have been more progressive. Actually, it was the later analysts who insisted homosexuality was an illness that needed to be cured by lengthy psychoanalysis."

"I didn't know that," Emil said. "My brother still treats me as if I'm sick and need to be cured. And it isn't just him. His analyst friends, at least the ones I've had the misfortune to meet, think so, too. I'd make a bet that it's still listed as an illness in their text books. Anyway, I made the mistake of going to one of his soirées – he has these little evening affairs sometimes with people playing the piano, sort of reminiscent of old Vienna, I suppose – and there were a couple of analysts talking about how the gay men they saw in their practice had more serious pathology than heterosexuals. I don't know if they realized I was gay, but they had the same maddening certainty that Marius has. It hurt my feelings."

"How can people be so stupid?" Kate said. She had read only one or two articles on homosexuality from the fifties and somehow assumed things had changed. "I'm sorry you had to go through that."

"Not your fault."

They finished looking at the gallery in silence.

Afterward, Emil walked her to the crosstown bus. He still seemed preoccupied. "I hope nothing I said has put you off," he said finally. "I'd hate that."

"You shouldn't even think it, even for a minute." Kate took his hand, "I'm glad you trusted me enough to tell me a little about yourself. I should be the one to be apologizing for bringing up distressing subjects."

"Actually, knowing more about my father's troubles makes me feel closer to him. I've had my share of heartache."

When Emil saw the bus coming, he opened his arms wide and gave her a bear hug, pressing his cheek first to one side of her face then the other, in the European way. She was touched. There was something intensely likeable about him, her newly found uncle. And vulnerable, too. She could see how bruised he must have felt by the remarks of Marius and his analyst friends. There were more ways than one in which theory could be used as a club. As the bus pulled away, Kate put her face close to the glass and waved at Emil.

Riding in the crowded bus on a warm day had made her thirsty, and when she got back to the apartment she drank two glasses of water straight down without stopping for breath. Then she filled a small bowl with cashews. Though she knew they were fattening, she needed the salt. There were still hours of good afternoon work time left before Keith was due back, and she was eager to return to the journal. The nuts in one hand, she headed to the sofa, curled her legs under her, took the journal from the coffee table and started to read.

February 12, 1913

Lou returned very late from supper at Freud's – one o'clock in the morning – and at first refused to tell me anything, saying she was tired and needed to sleep. Toward morning, though, we were both awakened by the sound of a stray tomcat mewling out back, and when she got up for something to drink I followed her. Finally she told me that they had spent most of the evening talking about me. Though she was somewhat vague, it is clear that Freud feels justified in his harshness toward me, thinks of me as having a neurotic disposition. She said she had defended me.

Ah, thought Kate. That's what she says, but is it true? Perhaps she considers it something of a game to raise the tension between her admirers. Kate was curious to see what Tausk thought.

The diary continued:

Lou came away feeling afraid that any independence around Freud makes him uncomfortable. My fighting spirit apparently worries and wounds him – particularly when it forces him into premature discussion. In telling me this, she couldn't disguise her great admiration for him, describing his egoism as the "noble egoism" of the investigator. I had long suspected that he felt threatened by me, though I constantly reiterate my belief in him and my loyalty. It hurts me more than anything that he feels most threatened when I try to advance his ideas. Lou observed that he prefers men like Rank who are intelligent and able but function as sons and nothing more. He asked Lou, "Why can't there be six such charming men in our group instead of only one?" She told me that when Rank lectured on regicide the other day – when I was sick and couldn't attend – Freud scrawled a note to her saying, "R disposes of the negative aspect of his filial love by means of this interest in the psychology of regicide; that is why he is so devoted."

February 13, 1913

At the Wednesday meeting, I gave my paper on masturbation and its relation to adult sexuality. When I wrote it, I thought it good and I still believe my conclusion: That difficulty in renouncing masturbation, even when incestuous fantasies have been made conscious, expresses unconscious hostility towards the father. But Lou told me afterward that I did not seem myself in this paper. She even hinted that perhaps my patient's feeling of being forced back into infantile modes of sexuality by a harsh puritanical father resonated in my unconscious because of my troubles with Freud. She had the distinct feeling that I seemed paralyzed. The thought chilled me. Am I in a mental straitjacket?

February 14, 1913

Lou was invited to a dress rehearsal of Wedekind's "Pandora's Box" by the leading actress. She asked me to accompany her, and though I had the beginnings of a bad headache, I agreed. At the last minute I thought of asking Felix and Helene if they would like to join us. I know they love theater, and I have often gone with Felix when Helene was away. Helene was too busy studying for her final exam in March, but Felix came gladly. We had good seats in one of the boxes. Lou looked ravishing in black velvet with an antique necklace. The writer Schnitzler was there too and kissed her hand, exclaiming that the stones of her necklace resembled tears – or drops of blood. He was clearly fascinated by her. I gathered that he has long been one of Lou's admirers. Wedekind was probably once her lover. Maybe Schnitzler, too. Surprisingly, I did not mind – felt rather proud of possessing the treasure coveted by such brilliant men. In the intermission I had the opportunity to tell Schnitzler how psychologically acute I found his novels and stories. I told him that one would almost have to invent Freudianism to properly describe them. Then suddenly I saw why Freud avoids this man like the plague while simultaneously praising him so highly – he finds him too close for comfort, an unwelcome double. It makes me wonder again about his attitude toward me.

The play, though technically brilliant, depressed me by presenting a morass of grotesque, joyless sex. The heroine, Lulu, is a sexually insatiable mistress without moral scruple. Her appetites lead to a string of horrors ending with her death at the hands of Jack the Ripper. None of Schnitzler's nuance. Rather a portrait of pure unconscious impulse bubbling furiously to the surface, like some witch's brew. Lou did not share my feelings and rather liked, I suspect, Lulu's sadistic power over her lovers – though she denied this – and defended Wedekind's attack on society's bourgeois ideals and hypocrisy. The only thing we agreed on was that the actress who played Lulu managed to exude sensuality from every pore.

February 20, 1913

Lou loves the movies, and often when we have just an hour to spare we sneak off to one like naughty children. Yesterday we took the boys to the Urania theatre to see a movie – "The Student of Prague" with a screenplay by Hans Ewers. The story of a Faustian student who gives his image to a demon in exchange for wealth was admittedly a little over the boys' heads, but they seemed mesmerized by the moving images. Lou said over tea afterward that she thinks movies, with their rapid change of images, more closely approximate our minds' imaginative faculty than theater, where the illusions of movement are often so clumsy. She is amazing in what she can assimilate, how she takes in everything and seeks to place and understand it.

Marius, though enthusiastic about the film, wasn't at all interested in hearing his sensations analyzed. Not daring to say he was bored, he played with his teacup, tilting it too and fro, sprinkling in sugar and ended by spilling some tea on Lou's lap. She took it good-humoredly, but it pains me that he cannot be brought to like, never mind love her. Nevertheless, the day ended well. When the boys trundled off to bed, we closed ourselves in my room and enjoyed the most delicious love-making, kissing each other all over with tantalizing slowness – not coming to the sex until we were both mad with passion. Having to suppress our moans because of the children in the next room only made it more exciting. Lou's climax was so strong, she wasn't able to hold back a cry. Marius said he had heard a scream in the night and asked if it was Lou who had screamed. I explained it, blushing, as a nightmare, which he seemed to accept because he has them often himself. Freud says we must be open with children about sexuality, but in this instance it would have raised more questions and anxieties with them than it answered.

God, they were passionate, Kate thought, and the children seemed to serve as an aphrodisiac rather than a brake – she noted with interest that her grandfather questioned Freud's idea of complete openness with children about sex. Kate thought he was right – though not being stupid, the boys probably figured it out. She could imagine Emil being intrigued by the scream while Marius was scared to death.

February 23, 1913

Lou returned from her session with Freud with the look of a cat who has swallowed a canary. She said he had spoken about a sadness and decreased euphoria as he ages. I sensed she was holding back something but couldn't get her to tell me what . . . until finally I managed to pry out of her that he had told her a "fantasy" not yet put on paper. She wouldn't elucidate and I felt it was beneath my dignity to press her further.

March 2, 1913

Lou got a letter from him after breakfast complaining of being deprived of her presence at his Saturday lecture. Clearly, he suspects it was because of me. He said that without his fixation point, he spoke falteringly, and that she spoiled him by her understanding, which goes beyond what is said. So why does he not value this same quality in me? The answer is perhaps only too obvious: because I am a man and he sees me as a rival.

March 14, 1913

I gave my last lecture – on the father problem. Freud seemed restless, one could almost say agitated. He rejected my paper practically in toto, saying it failed to apply psychoanalysis to the neuroses – though I had made clear from the beginning that I was excluding them. Lou explained to me later that Freud's "fantasy" topic – the one she had refused to describe to me – was the importance of parricide for civilization, and that when Freud saw me taking up a similar question he became fearful that she had relayed his embryonic ideas to me. I've observed that he likes being able to develop ideas slowly without interference, but can he blame me for seeing the same things as important? Does he immediately think I am filching his ideas? Lou told me that during the lecture he had passed a note to her asking "Does he know all about it already?" But of course she had told me nothing. Isn't father-murder a natural subject for anyone in our field? Lou says she wrote back, "Of course not, he knows nothing, nothing at all." I'm not sure if I should believe her. Not sure that at bottom she does not side with him. It would be farcical if it did not have such potential for tragedy.

After my talk, Lou did not wait for me but went ahead and walked with Freud. The next night he invited her for supper, and when she returned, she told me they had talked at length about me. In the end she thought she had soothed his fears. We promptly got into a discussion of negative attitudes toward life. Sounding positively Nietzschean, she inveighed against a culture obtained by a deficit of life: a culture of the weak. How does she see me in this? Master or slave? I have the feeling that she is critical of me for my depressive moods. She sees herself as always affirming, though I sense this may be a cover for her own depressions. The same with her belief in God, which exalts her, the creative artist, along with Him, since she believes that human imagination created the idea of God.

Just then Keith came home and Kate just had time to give him a hug when the phone rang. It was Marius – he was in the neighborhood and wondered if he might come over. He had something to say to her.

"He didn't sound any too happy," she said to Keith. "I wonder what's up." She hastily made the bed and folded it up into its daytime form – it did double-duty as a sofa – and hastily arranged a few pillows covered with the remains of an Oriental rug she'd gotten at a flea market. Then she washed the dirty dishes, gave them a perfunctory rinse and put them into the rack to dry. A few minutes later the phone rang and it was Emil, warning her that his brother had found out that he'd lent Kate the diary and had been talking to her about it, and he was very angry.

"I wanted to warn you. Maybe you should be out when he calls."

"Too late," she said, "he's on his way." She heard a groan from the other end of the line. "I'm afraid that's him now coming up the stairs. I'd better go; the last thing he needs is to find me having a conversation with you."

Marius was panting slightly when he finished the five flights of stairs. Kate shook hands solemnly, introduced him to Keith, and ushered him to her best chair – the only one with fairly intact upholstery.

"Are you all right?" she asked politely when he had caught his breath and his face was less alarmingly red. "Would you like a glass of water?"

He nodded and she went into the kitchen and poured him some from a bottle in the fridge, adding a twist of lemon. He didn't seem angry. Perhaps Emil had exaggerated. In any case, she was genuinely curious to hear what was on his mind.

"I'm afraid my brother made a serious mistake," he said when he had thanked her and taken a few sips.

"Oh?"

"You must know what I am referring to. My father's journal. Emil had no right to let you see it without asking me for permission."

"I'm sorry," she said. If she told him it was just an impulsive gesture on Emil's part, that would only make things worse. "He probably thought that because I was family. . . ." There was no reaction.

"I need to have it back."

"Of course, I'd be glad to give to you, but I'd like to make a copy first."

"No, I'm afraid I can't allow that."

"But why?" she asked innocently. "I let you copy mine."

"You seem like a fine young woman. I don't think you intend any harm, but there are things in it that unscrupulous people might use."

"There is nothing in it that's discreditable to your father. In fact, he comes off rather well, I thought. Though it did make me wonder what could have happened after the war to make him want to kill himself. He never mentions suicidal thoughts or being deeply depressed. Even when Lou seems about to abandon him."

"Abandon him? You see, right there is a misunderstanding. I feel sure he exaggerated his importance to her. Frau Lou rather quickly discovered his weaknesses and distanced herself . . . her true loyalty was to Freud and psychoanalysis. It hurts me to say it, but I'm afraid my father was a sick man, possibly schizophrenic – a harsh fact my brother understandably denies."

"But what makes you say that?" Kate asked. "From the diaries and everything else I've read, he doesn't seem especially sick to me." She was perched precariously on an edge of the sofa back, not wanting to sit. Marius was a tall, severe man, even seated, and she didn't want him looking down on her. "I mean, no sicker than the rest of us . . . if he sometimes exaggerated his importance, well, that happens often enough when you're in love, but his analytic work, at least the paper of his that I've read, shows a probing, lucid mind."

"I don't deny he was brilliant."

"And brave, too. Dr. Deutsch told me he intervened to prevent the shooting of deserters in 1915 – that can't have been easy at a time of intense patriotism during a world war."

"Freud generously mentions that in his obituary. Too generously, perhaps. What he doesn't say is that my father rebelled against all authority, not only his own father's."

"Just like that, without any reason? What was his father like?"

"My grandfather was a cold, taciturn man. I have to admit that he mistreated his wife, had numerous affairs, failed to support the family."

"A callous philanderer! Well, then. . . ."

"He may have had some justification there, but the fact is he extended his rebellion to a struggle against fathers in general. And it quite naturally included Freud."

"I don't quite see how you can say that. Tausk's diary shows how valiantly he defended Freud – and his work is studded with references to him. If anything, he seems excessively loyal. Overscrupulous."

"He couldn't bear to admit his own competitiveness."

Kate began to feel dizzy. It seemed in Marius's way of reasoning as if everything could be either itself or its opposite.

She tried again. "He admired Freud tremendously. He was the only one of the disciples who taught a seminar on the basics of psychoanalysis. He knew Freud's work by heart."

"I have spent some time thinking about my father's relation to Freud. Believe me, I would like to find him blameless, but I believe he sometimes cited Freud's thoughts as his own and it is certain that much as he admired Freud, he also accused Freud of taking his ideas."

"Really? But isn't it possible that Freud did sometimes borrow from him?"

Marius grimaced. "Freud was always generous and most correct in citing predecessors."

Kate had a moment's sense that there was a trial going on – that Marius felt it was important to establish his father's faults. But why? What was at stake?

"Perhaps their ideas just ran along similar tracks, as Lou seemed to feel. Maybe he was capable of developing ideas that Freud had only sketched out. Perhaps when he'd done that, Freud would absorb his contribution and make it part of his own thought."

"As I said, Freud was always most correct. I should try and

explain to you the sort of harm you are likely to cause if you speculate this way in public. There are many people who would like to draw Freud's personality to their own liking. Many who would like to find he had feet of clay. I would urge you not to be unwittingly party to this calumny."

Kate began to feel that there were definitely things he was hiding.

"You know I have a purely personal motive for finding out about my grandfather," she said softly. "I'm certainly not part of any group wanting to discredit Freud. On the contrary. But what I hoped you could help me with – purely for my own information – is what happened to my grandfather after the war? I know post-war Vienna was in a terrible state. Did he have money worries? Trouble getting food? Or was there something more specific? A man doesn't kill himself for no reason. Please, if you know anything more, I wish you'd tell me."

Keith had been sitting on a footstool, quietly listening. "Would a promise not to reveal anything help? I'm sure Kate wouldn't mind." Kate shook her head energetically.

"Times were hard, true. It was difficult to keep his place heated. Food was scarce, but I can assure you he wasn't starving or destitute. He even had a few patients." Marius hesitated for a moment, as though on the verge of saying something else, then went on. "I'm afraid there is nothing more I have to add. I think I told you that he didn't want to marry, wasn't up to it. Didn't want to be burdened by a child . . . forgive me, your mother."

The mention of her grandmother seemed to dry up Kate's thoughts. She hung her head. Keith got up and squeezed her shoulder. "I have a feeling there was more to it than that. Wasn't Dr. Deutsch in Vienna when your grandfather came back?" Keith asked, thinking aloud, "Perhaps she'd have another take on it."

"Of course, you can ask her what you like, you are perfectly free to do so, but I don't think it's wise to show her the diary."

"Are you implying that Dr. Deutsch is one of the people interested in causing harm to Freud's memory?"

"Not consciously, perhaps, but I think I mentioned to you before that she had her own ambivalences and jealousies. She never forgave Freud for dropping her from analysis so he could take on 'the Wolf-Man.'"

Oh, that was a surprise. Kate had not known Helene had been

in analysis with Freud. Kate wondered why she hadn't mentioned it.

Marius got up and, after looking around the room, walked to the other side of the bed where the diary was lying on the bedside table. "I'm sorry, but I'm afraid I really have to reclaim this. . . ." He tucked the diary under his arm and headed towards the front door, his jacket flapping awkwardly.

Keith stood up and moved quickly to block his way.

"Kate's his granddaughter, she has just as much right to the diary as you do. . . . The decent thing to do would be to let her keep a copy. It's one of the few pieces of her grandfather she has."

Marius tried to walk around him, but Keith politely but firmly held him back. He stared for a moment, blinking helplessly through his thick glasses at Keith.

"I've tried to explain that people are trying to denigrate Freud and psychoanalysis. It is far more than a personal issue, I assure you. Much more is at stake than either you or me personally."

"Since this discussion is hardly over, you can't just walk away with the diary," Keith said. There was a brief scuffle in which Marius almost fell. Keith immediately put a hand under his elbow to steady him and then gently relieved him of the diary. Marius straightened his tie and, reminding Kate a little of Don Quixote after an unsuccessful encounter, walked in a halting but dignified manner to the door. Once there, he turned, "*Aufwiedersehen*," he said. "Till we meet again, Fraulein," and he gave an abbreviated bow.

"Thank you, sweetheart, you really saved the day," Kate said to Keith after she heard the elevator door clang shut.

"What an uptight stiff. I was tempted to take him by the shoulders and shake him hard, just to loosen him up."

"I'm glad you didn't. He is my uncle, after all. I don't want him even more paranoid about me than he is already."

"Violence is never a solution."

"I'm glad to hear that," Kate said. "Though it's beginning to look as if the students' tolerance for nonviolence isn't as great as yours."

"There's every shade of opinion from blasting the pigs' heads off to lying still under a beating the way the peaceable draft protestors did in LA this summer. I'm somewhere in the middle . . . some self-defense may be acceptable. But I have to admit it's frustrating when mannerliness doesn't pay off."

"You've worked so hard. With everything else you have to do, I think you're heroic."

He laughed. "Maybe I can accept that better after some self-administered medicine." He took a joint out of his pocket, lit it and took a drag. "You sure you don't want to try? I used to think weed was demonic, but it's really very nice."

"No thanks. I'll stick to music."

She went over to the record player and put on the Doors', "Dance with Me Baby." Singing along with it, she danced back over to him, and kept on dancing until he took her into his arms.

The next day, still shaken by Marius's surprise visit, Kate returned to the diary.

March 15-16, 1913

Helene and Felix Deutsch went out for a drink with us last night. We toasted Helene's graduation from the University of Vienna. In the course of conversation, Helene mentioned that though her father hadn't shown up for the ceremony, her old lover Lieberman had. This interested Lou, and she got Helene to talk a little about the grand passion of her early youth – I knew about it already from our mutual friend Reinhold, who had often told me how it was dragging this bright capable young woman down. Felix, by contrast, is a rock of stability and glows with pride in her. I got the impression that the two women didn't care for one another. The night was cool and clear and we walked part of the way with pleasure – a half-moon above the lamps.

When we got back to my place and were going over the evening, Lou opined that Helene would tire of Felix, whom she saw as feminine, and long for a more highly sexed man. This led into a renewed discussion of fidelity/infidelity. We had spoken of it before – I thought rather lightheartedly – but now she said straight out that a woman had no choice than to be unfaithful or to be only half herself.

I confessed I couldn't understand her logic. I would have thought a woman enhanced by fidelity rather than diminished. Lou wasn't interested in logic; she offered me a metaphor. Woman in love is like a tree waiting for the lightning to sunder it. Also like the tree, she desires to blossom abundantly. Since she can only be one at the expense of another, she needs to make the compromise of being only half herself – unless she can start life afresh, plant the whole tree again, sinking a new seedling deep within the soil. She went on to observe – as though she weren't talking to a man who adores her – that the quality in a person that delights us and the quality which later alienates us come together. A gesture may tell the tale, or a walk, or the line of his neck. At the time when we still believe ourselves faithful, we may perceive such traits that limit our liking, but we may consider them harmless, just as a cold doesn't cause a healthy man to think straight away of pneumonia. Later, it is more sinister . . . a person at the height of passion, fearful of being undone by it, may search for these tiny treacherous loopholes, which then permit him to escape and find freedom.

"You won't be undone by love," I said. "Not undone, not riven in half." Her eyes narrowed like a cat on the verge of skittering away. I took her hand and brought it to my face, kissing it gently. "Don't I leave you enough freedom?" I asked. "I was not talking about us," she said, "just thinking about a problem." Can she really feel constrained by me? With her husband Andreas back in Loufried, Freud here, and former lovers attending her at the theater? I suppose she can. She is a being whose ways are unique to herself. I was awake half the night wondering what traits of mine were going to make her stop loving me . . . what defects were gradually becoming more obvious.

She returned home from her last visit to Freud's with roses and told me she thinks that partly due to me Freud has come to stress the ego more than he had before, and that this has brought him closer to those who have defected. That way she left me with a compliment.

May 8, 1913

She is going home for a couple of months but reassured me that she will write often and that we will see each other in August – she is coming back here for several weeks before the Munich Congress. We both sense Freud means to bring his struggles with Jung and the Zurich school to a head there.

July 5, 1913

In her last letter, Lou mentioned a surprise visit from Rainer Rilke, leaving me in anxiety about whether they are lovers again. She says only that he is physically ill and she is afraid for him, adding that he has produced some new work – elegies – of great power. If she had freely included some of his poetry, would I have felt better? If she'd shared her experience? I am trying to lose myself in work.

August 3, 1913

She is back and I accompanied her to her hotel room, the old room, No. 28, which I had made sure had many new flowerpots in the window to welcome her.

She was hot and tired, the whole town is suffering under August heat, but beautiful as ever, and after dinner we made love very sweetly. I almost wept with gratitude and relief. I confessed my fears about Rilke, and she said no, that was long over, but she was still fascinated by his combination of personal frailty and lyric strength. She continued to caress my face gently as she told me about this so it was somehow all right. She was close.

In the morning, though, she was another person, completely focused on work – our joint investigation of narcissism. She spoke of her belief that it is more than some immature stage to be superseded but is rather where ego and libido interact to creative purpose. She thinks neither Freud nor I adequately emphasize this point. We began to argue. She accused me of using psychoanalytic thought to block my powers of synthesis, reducing everything to logic.

"You have a philosophical head by nature," she said, "but you cut it off instead of using it." Here I think she saw me pale and added more gently, "at least on holidays."

I didn't agree. "I've always tried to see the philosophical implications of analysis, you know that, we've talked about it many times – though of course I may not be aware of my inhibitions."

"You are not. Whenever you find yourself thinking synthetically, you get an attack of bad conscience and torment yourself."

"I know you think I need analysis – maybe that's true. All of us have our share of neurosis. But you've heard my criticisms of Freud. You know I can be critical."

"Critical and too accepting at the same time. You know I speak as a friend, but this is painful for you . . . should I stop?"

I shook my head. Perhaps that was a mistake, but I wanted so much to know how she sees me.

"You are always tackling the same problems as Freud . . . always making similar attempts at solving them. You don't need to do this. You could step aside and give yourself some room, but you don't. Why?"

"You're implying that I make myself 'the son' and then hate him for it. But I'm afraid it is he who is threatened by the similarity of our thought. It is he who worries that his disciples have death wishes about him. Look at the debacle with Jung, his chosen heir. Didn't the Professor faint when Jung told him a dream about skulls – so sure that Jung imagined him dead?"

"Jung has since broken with him. You could say it was prophetic."

"But I haven't broken with him. And you know how hard I defend his sexual theories against Jung's dismissal of them . . . . Doesn't it matter to him that it's in his service?"

"I know you love him," she said, putting her hand on my arm to calm me, "that's not in question, and I don't want to get into a fruitless argument. But deep down, there is also resistance . . . your conflicted feelings confuse you and sap your natural energy. And it doesn't need to happen. I have a vision of you freed from conflict, whole and glowing with energy. You are already a brilliant analyst. You've come upon profound discoveries in your analyses . . . but can't you see that they are displacements of your own longing to be known – to be analyzed yourself? And though you see so deeply into your patients, you pass right by the things in front of you if they involve yourself. Remember when I told you about your hidden maternal side – how relieved and free you felt?"

I was tempted at this point to flee. Is this how my patients feel under my probing? "Yet afterward I felt worse. Much worse."

"You were resisting the insight, afraid you were showing a tendency to inversion . . . but motherliness isn't homosexuality, you shouldn't have been so afraid. How beautiful it would be if you let it flower into the tenderness and ardor of understanding."

"Don't leave me," I said kneeling and putting my head in her lap. "I am struggling. . . ." She ran her fingers through my hair but didn't speak.

"I have so much on my mind just now – the boys, their mother, my final medical exams –" I lifted my head but was afraid to look into her eyes and read my fate – "that I haven't been able to do as much as I could in the way of self-analysis. I don't even have time to read the papers relevant to my problems . . . but I will. . . . I promise you."

"I am not your judge," she whispered. "All human creatures struggle. I too. . . ." She seemed deeply moved. With her by me I will raise the lantern and hold it unflinchingly to all the dark corners of

my ghost haunted mind.

Kate paused, confused. What exactly was going on here? Lou seemed to be implying that Tausk was partially responsible for his troubles with Freud, that he did somehow follow or parallel his thought too closely. Kate had a different idea: that Freud had cast Tausk as Oedipus, the potential fatherkiller. Once he'd done that, it was easy to misinterpret anything Tausk did. She imagined Freud watching Tausk the way the stag watches a younger buck who is coming too close to his females. Eventually she'd have to ask Helene what she thought of all this . . . but not yet. She wanted to have her own ideas clear first, or at least as clear as she could make them. Didn't want to risk being swayed or driven off course, the way she often felt she had been by her thesis advisor, Professor Downes, who made her write and rewrite until she was blue in the face and in danger of losing her original idea.

Sept 6-8, 1913

I went to the Munich Congress with Lou a day before it began. The train was hot and stuffy but the countryside outside through the window was beautiful. As we passed the farms and villages, the trees rich with fruit, I kept imagining that we were going to some pastoral retreat to be together. I could even see the cottage sheltered by elms just beginning to turn color. I was jolted out of my dream when we arrived at the Bayerischer Hof station and Freud was there to meet her. He embraced her warmly, then almost as an afterthought, shook hands with me. Lou went off to see Rilke at her friend Gebsattel's house, leaving me not a little jealous. Gebsattel seemed a grandiose, sneering sort of person, spouting Nietzschean sentiments while looking at Lou with open lust. How can she tolerate his company? I'm afraid because she can't pass up such a tempting candidate for her counseling. I contented myself with going to the hotel bar with some of the others and looking over the advance notice of the papers for the congress.

Seeing the name Bjerre on the program, Fenichel, who had drunk too much, told a tale about him and Frau Lou that made my blood curdle. According to his story, which is probably untrue if not vastly exaggerated, Lou seduced Bjerre after befriending his invalid wife and then laughed at his scruples.

When Lou came back from Rilke I told her I had heard a scandalous tale about her that I had done my best to dismiss. She made a face, and said that, angered by her rejection, Bjerre was undoubtedly spreading stories. She knew he felt injured but hadn't thought he would stoop that low. "He's an arriviste," she said, her voice heavy with scorn, "a banal and brutal man posing as a noble helper." She forbade me to mention his name again. She looked so beautiful in her fiery indignation that I could not press her further.

That evening we spent with Freud and our group together in the lobby bar, sitting in the semidark with candlelight throwing wavering shadows on the walls, talking mostly about our feud with the Zurichers, who are not only accepting Jung's innovations but refusing to credit Freud with his original discoveries. Jung apparently had the cheek to say he no longer thought it necessary to mention his name in print because everyone knew he was the founder of psychoanalysis. Rumor has it that when Freud first heard this, he fainted. Surer than ever, I suppose, of Jung's death-wish against him. I find it rather remarkable that he should do this, and for the second time. Is he, then, more vulnerable than he seems?

I admit I am not a little envious of Jung; the man has nerve and a kind of belief in himself that I have only too rarely. Last year when he toured America, he told them what he damn pleased . . . ticked off the changes his school had made in psychoanalysis. He began by calling the Oedipus Complex merely a metaphor and ended by rejecting the need to delve into a patient's past – all the time denying a schism. Then he had the brass to write Freud, boasting of his new converts among people uneasy at Freud's emphasis on sex.

As we talked among ourselves, I found myself hoping that Freud, so disappointed in Jung as son, will still eventually turn to me. Didn't he want Jung to apply to the study of psychoses what the Professor has begun for neurosis? And the psychoses are just what I am so determined to understand. I tried again to reassure him by my look that I was wholly and devotedly on his side.

The next day at the Fourth Psychoanalytic Congress, all the Zurich members with Jung at the head sat at their own table, opposite Freud's. There could have been no clearer symbol of our relations. Lou sat next to Freud like some Norse goddess protecting her hero. I sat close by. Jung presided over the sessions in an unpleasant and overbearing manner, arbitrarily restricting the time allotted to each speaker. His paper made clear that he was no longer a disciple. It is not so much that

Jung diverges from Freud but that he does it in a way that suggests he has taken it on himself to rescue Freud by these divergences. At the meeting two years ago Jung exhibited a sort of exuberant vitality, even gaiety; now it is all turned to pure aggression, ambition, and intellectual brutality. He managed to suggest that it was Freud who had caused the break by his narrow obstinacy.

I took the floor and spoke strongly against the way Jung and his group have behaved. It is quite plain to me that Freud wants to have nothing more to do with them. After I sat down, I expected at least a glance from Freud acknowledging my effort but felt only a radiating coldness.

Kate went to the kitchen for a glass of water. It upset her that Tausk kept trying to get Freud's approval, fighting for him when it was so clearly impossible. What made Jung strong enough to tough it out, she wondered – some sort of survival of the fittest? The only thing she could think of was that it was Tausk's wish for Freud's approval that did him in, finally . . . he just had to keep trying.

Jung continued making one-sided and offensive comments on the papers being presented. It was so extreme that when it came time to vote for his reelection as president of the society, twenty-two of us – there were only fifty in all – submitted blank cards. Jung was incensed at not receiving a unanimous vote and lashed out at Jones, saying that he thought Jones had no moral principles. He seems to have assumed that as a fellow Christian, Jones would support him.

Despite my perception of Freud's coldness, I felt pleased that I had done my part in chastising the erstwhile son and heir, who has assured himself total banishment from the psychoanalytic family. I was shocked to hear from Lou later that Freud admitted to her that he was holding me off but that in this new and threatening situation, I was the right man . . . clever and dangerous, someone who can bark and bite. Am I reduced to a dog, then, who will be put down when his usefulness is ended? He goes too far . . . and for the first time I felt a wish to break away as Jung and Adler have done.

Lou angered me by attempting to defend Freud, saying that he was under incredible strain. She tried to suggest that Freud had to distance himself from my attack even though he wanted it because he had to keep himself above the fray – and for the moment at least continue working publicly with Jung. All that does not matter to me, I said. What matters is that he is treating me badly. And I don't deserve it. Lou tried every means to soothe me and finally diverted me by lying down with me. I could not in the end make love to her.

Tomorrow I return to Vienna.

Sept 9, 1913

Lou saw me off at the Munich station. She is staying on for a while with her friends. I opened the compartment window and looked back at her standing on the station platform. She stood very still, reminding me oddly of my mother, who had once seen me off on a journey and had stood a long time with her hand raised, waving. Lou waved only once, then stood, getting smaller and smaller as the train clanked and roared, gathering speed, oblivious to my distress. There was a strong breeze and she was wearing a little hat with a white veil that blurred her features as I strained to make them out. For a moment I was tempted to jump off and run back to her, but it would have done no good.

Chapter Seven

Three days later, Emily returned to New York City and Kate went over to help her unpack. Emily was obviously happy to be back in her apartment among familiar things.

"So much for vacation," she said, as Kate helped her hang up her sun dresses. Kate wanted her to lie down and rest, but she limped slowly around the apartment holding her Siamese cat on her shoulder like a baby, putting her clothes in drawers and checking the mail, which a neighbor had brought in. When Emily approached her desk, Kate's heart started thumping against her ribs so loudly she was sure Emily would hear. She considered a diversionary activity: she could offer to make her mother some coffee and lure her away to the kitchen. But before she could say anything, her mother leaned over, jettisoning the cat, and pulled open the wooden desk cover and tucked her mail neatly into one of the cubbyholes. To hide her momentary panic, Kate bent down and picked up the cat and cradled him in her arms, scratching him behind his dusky ears.

Her mother was looking at her affectionately. She obviously liked seeing her cuddling Ali Baba. The cat had been Kate's gift – a guilt-offering when Kate moved out. She'd gotten a pedigreed Siamese, she joked to Keith, because of her mother's status anxieties. Her son had deserted her. Her daughter had picked the wrong profession. Now she would have the ideal child. Emily fed him prime beef and only the white meat of chicken. He was spoiled rotten.

"So how was the drive down?" Kate asked. They settled themselves on the sofa with fresh brewed French roast.

"Not too bad," Emily said. "Actually, Dr. Deutsch and I had something of an adventure. A car right in front of us ran off the turnpike – the driver must have gone to sleep for an instant – hit a tree and turned over, and a couple clambered out of their car, looking dazed. Helene told Mrs. Dubrovsky to pull over on the shoulder so we could see if they were all right. Mrs. Dubrovsky was very much against getting involved, but Helene insisted. We thought at first it was a man and his wife, but it turned out she was the man's daughter come from Poland to visit her father. She was holding her chest and crying, almost hysterical. I tried to ask her what was the matter, but she spoke only a few words of English. Helene was wonderful. She started speaking Polish to the girl, felt her all over for broken bones, and calmed her down in two minutes flat. Then we drove them to the nearest gas station and Helene called an ambulance.

"The more I see of your Dr. Deutsch, the more I like her. She's not at all the way I imagined an analyst to be. I told her she was going to make me revise my opinion of the profession. She isn't just normal and sane, she is a real mensch."

"What did she say to that?" Kate asked, viciously scratching a bite on her wrist.

"Oh, she just laughed, told me not to idealize her." Emily hesitated, seeing a black look on her daughter's face.

"Don't you think that was a little rude? I mean, did you have to suggest that analysts are a bunch of lunatics? Why didn't you just say you really enjoyed her, she seems like such a nice person, and leave it at that?" She dropped the cat abruptly, and he yowled in protest.

"I don't think she minded," Emily said meekly. "If she had, we wouldn't have had such a good conversation afterwards. She told me a little about her family. Did you know that her son had three analyses? She told me that once when her son was small, she asked him what he wanted to be when he grew up and he said a patient. I thought that was awful. I told her I thought poking around in people's psyches could actually hurt them, and you know, she didn't disagree."

"Well," Kate said, trying to hide her own horror, "what is she supposed to say? She obviously didn't want to argue with you, she likes you." God, did they use the poor kid as a guinea pig? She'd have to ask Helene about it. Perhaps her mother had misunderstood. Looking at her mother's expectant face, she felt suddenly angry. "I suppose her mentioning her son gave you a chance to talk about me and complain."

"I didn't say that." Emily nibbled her lip, wishing she hadn't mentioned Helene's son. She had such an impulse to share things with her daughter, but half the time the tidbits she offered only served to annoy her.

"You don't need to be defensive. I know you can't help saying whatever pops into your head," Kate said. "It's the way you are. But don't imagine it doesn't get back to me. I can tell by the probing little questions your friends ask that you've been soliciting their advice." She mimicked her mother's voice, feeling more and more irritated. "I don't know what to do with Kate, she's so stubborn, so touchy."

Her mother sighed and Kate struggled to control herself. She took five slow breaths, repeating her secret mantra. When that didn't work, she tried visualizing a Van Gogh field full of sweet-smelling hay, but she couldn't block her mother's voice.

"Don't mock me, Kate, I don't like it," Emily was saying. "It's true that you're touchy – like a firecracker waiting to go off – that's not very pleasant." She stopped a minute and gave her daughter a scrutinizing look. "But I can't see the point in quarreling, can you? If there is something really bothering you, tell me and we'll talk about it. Well, is there?"

"No," Kate said, blushing. She had the feeling – had had it as a child, too – that her mother could read her mind. She'd always seemed to be lurking outside her room, looking at her with big eyes waiting to hear – what? For the first time, Kate felt she understood that her mother wanted to be close but didn't know how. She thought it was from knowing Kate's secret thoughts. She didn't realize she was scaring her daughter, making her scurry underground like some furry mammal.

Kate felt an abrupt pity for Emily waiting eagerly at the entrance to a burrow from which the occupant was long gone. She had a sudden urge to reveal herself, throw herself into her mother's arms and cry against her neck. Tell her mother that she knew who her grandfather was and how he died, and maybe have a good cry together . . . close and warm with arms around each other.

But no, that was a crazy idea. Emily would be furious that she searched her things – intrusion went only one way in her mind and she herself was an extremely secretive person. Kate guessed that after that her mother would refuse to discuss it. Emily wouldn't help her find out what she needed to know about the last years of her grandfather's life. Emily would certainly refuse to meet her half-brother, Emil, lovely as he was. Nor would Emily have wanted to meet Marius – after all, Emily had had both their names in her desk for God knows how many years and had never called or spoken to them. To her, it was all a matter for embarrassment – even humiliation. She felt tainted by having someone sick in her family, someone possibly mad, a suicide. And the fact that Kate seemed so upset would just confirm her mother in the view that her father's suicide was something that should be closed away and forgotten, certainly not investigated further by his granddaughter.

For a second Kate wondered whether it was possible she was wrong, whether she could be so sure what her mother would do. Then she felt a strong cramp and excused herself to go to the bathroom. The bathroom light was florescent and it made her skin take on a bluish tint in the mirror as she bent to examine her underwear. There was a tiny stain of dark blood that she hoped was the start of her period. What a relief! – though Keith would probably be disappointed.

When she came back from the bathroom, her mother came up and put her arm around her. "You know, I really appreciate your getting the house ready for me," she said.

"Thanks. I'm glad," Kate muttered, trying to regain her sense of dignified independence.

"And I'm sorry if I offended you. I certainly didn't mean to."

"I know . . . something sets off a bad dynamic, and then – then it just keeps on by itself." She knew these were just words, they didn't really explain anything, but they made her feel more in control. The cat was mewing, rubbing against her legs, and she picked him up. He opened his mouth and took her finger, playfully biting. The two women stood for a moment not quite touching, both engrossed by the cat's rumbling purr.

When Kate got back to her apartment she called Copy-Brite, a photocopier she knew near the University, and asked whether if she brought the journal in the afternoon, they could have it back to her by the end of the week. Even if Marius was behaving badly, she was going to get a copy so she could give him back the original when she finished reading.

After she talked to the copier, she settled herself on the sofa with some pillows, reached for the diary, which she'd left on the little end table, and started to read.

Kate had hoped that Tausk would change his mind and jump off the train at the last minute. But his own appraisal had been more realistic. It wouldn't have done any good. From then on entries were spotty. Tausk noted his letters to Lou but not her answers. Perhaps, Kate thought, she didn't answer.

October 3, 1913

I've heard that she has taken a new lover, that obnoxious Gebsattel.

Here there was a long gap, until April of the next year.

April 25, 1914

Jung has finally resigned as head of the International Psychoanalytic Association. I hear that Freud says he is tired of leniency and kindness and is prepared for any reprisals that Jung can dream up. I wondered at Freud's holding his fire all this while, then realized that he was waiting, watching to make sure he could handle the breach without harm to the Movement.

"Tired of leniency" made Kate remember his disciple Sachs' comment about Freud's vindictiveness, but Tausk didn't seem to be alarmed; in fact he seemed calmer than he had been while living with Lou.

June 14, 1914

I passed the Rigorosum. My medical studies are complete and I can now devote myself entirely to psychoanalysis. My practice is going well – Freud seems to have relented toward me, at least to the extent of sending me patients. I wonder myself whether this is due to Lou's absence – whether she wasn't in some way a wedge between us, not, as I thought then, a force for bringing us closer. This idea struck me forcibly after seeing Lou's new play, "Tor und Ur," in a small experimental theatre. Felix went with me. We were both charmed by the pastoral setting, the richly colored surreal costumes and the oddly glowing cave which the two children use as their retreat. I was touched at what seemed to be her construction of our romance – Tor, a softhearted wild boy, falls under the spell of Ursula, a passing visitor in his little town. But when the children begin to play master and slave and seal their enthrallment bond with blood, I became disturbed – even more so when Tor kills his detested headmaster in effigy. I saw at once that the headmaster represented Freud and that Lou remains convinced – as she implied to me at

Munich – that I am locked in rivalry with Freud and unconsciously want him dead. I broke into a sweat when I realized this. How lethal a weapon psychoanalysis can be, especially in the hands of a friend – I almost said when a friend goes over to the enemy. But that would be wrong because Freud is not, never has been, the enemy.

Kate stopped for a moment to jot down the name of Lou's play. It occurred to her that there might be other stories or plays of hers that might throw light on the last phase of Tausk's life or at least give her interpretation of them. She'd have to look.

June 14 (continued)

I asked Felix to join me for a drink afterward. I would have liked to talk to him frankly, he is such a kindly fellow in addition to being learned – but of course I couldn't. So I tried to put the whole thing out of my mind and asked about him and Helene. He told me Helene is in Munich finishing up her project on word-association. She uses a stop watch and asks patients for pleasant and unpleasant associations; apparently depressives have more pleasant memories than the others. Not at all what she expected. God help Schopenhauer! Man remains utterly optimistic even when he is depressed.

When Felix told me in confidence that Helene is pregnant, I shook his hand, congratulating him – though it sounds to me as if she is ambivalent about the prospect of being a mother. Felix laughingly reported that she feels like a fattening pig, consumed by a totally animal existence – a lethargic instrument of nature. He has encouraged her to keep up with her work, though I think he hardly needed to. I feel sometimes that she takes her work much more seriously than she takes her marriage.

Interesting that Tausk thought that. Kate wondered if it was true. She made a note to explore Helene's feelings about motherhood and having a child with Felix.

June 10, 1914

Helene is planning to take my seminar on psychoanalysis next fall. As for me, I told Felix that my situation, particularly in regard to patients, was improving. He was glad to hear it both for me and because Helene wants to know what her prospects might be here.

So Helene wanted to be Tausk's student! That meant, Kate thought, she must have considered him an authority. Kate was finding it more and more unaccountable that she hadn't seen him referred to – or only in passing – in any of the accounts of the beginning of the movement. Then, just as Kate thought she might be going to get some explanations, Tausk's reports of analytic doings in the inner circle were pushed aside by the shock of an assassin's bullet – a real, not fantasized, parricide.

June 28, 1914

Archduke Ferdinand has been assassinated in Sarajevo! All of a sudden, the bands all over Vienna stopped playing. The silence was followed by a murmuring as of thousands of bees awakened from their hives. No one knows what the consequences will be. His coffin was conveyed through Vienna without ceremony in the dead of night. His enemies were no doubt rejoicing to see him snuffed out. Too brilliant, too arrogant, too indifferent to protocol. I'd felt an odd chill when I heard he was going to Sarajevo on Serbia's National Holiday – as if he were tempting fate. When I was a boy growing up in Sarajevo, my father, as chief of the press office, was always trying to explain Vienna to the Croatians. I was forced to listen to his endless harangues about the beauties of the monarchy, listen to him read his articles out loud to my long-suffering mother. Even as a child, I favored Slav independence. To be more accurate, I loved the words used to describe it, "autonomy" "self-rule" – how beautiful they were – how I liked to see my father's face grow red when he saw those words in some socialist newspaper. But I was never for violence. Never. What is so pitiful is that Ferdinand would have made the empire into a federation, giving all of the Slavic people autonomy. And this is the man the extremists killed. But few in Vienna understand this. Not even Freud. I saw him at the coffeehouse late in the afternoon. I think he was relieved. I overheard him say that if Archduke Ferdinand had become Emperor there would have been war with Russia.

July 28, 1914

Austria has declared war on Serbia!

August 15, 1914

It is horrifying to see the degree to which people have turned into saber-rattling patriots. The Freuds were taking their vacation in Karlsbad and rushed back to Vienna. Freud announced that for the first time in thirty years he feels himself to be an Austrian. He seems positively invigorated by the idea of war – who would have thought it? And I hear he refuses to help patients avoid the draft by writing them certificates of mental illness. Both his sons have enlisted for "the noble cause." I saw them looking very sharp in their tunics with gold stars. It is quite astonishing the way Ernst resembles Freud, same cut to his beard. I felt for a moment as if it were Freud going off. Martin will be a gunner.

How strange, Kate thought, that Freud would be such a nationalist and for the war, while Tausk was the one with insight into the madness of the whole thing. Kate would have to tell Keith.

October 14, 1914

Short note from Felix that Helene had a miscarriage and is distraught. He doesn't even mention the war. As though it isn't taking place on our borders.

Ah, so she didn't have that baby. Her son must have been a later pregnancy. And if she was distraught – though Kate thought that might be open to interpretation – she must really have wanted it. As she read on, things seemed to be worsening for Tausk as well, but in his case it was because of the war.

October 20, 1914

It is astonishing how fast things can change. This war has been a disaster for me. Patients are vanishing on all sides and practicing psychoanalysis is becoming all but impossible.

December 5, 1914

Dr. Sachs has been rejected by the army because of nearsightedness, Otto Rank is fighting against conscription . . . when will they come after me? I received a note from Lou in response to my letter. She is worried that Freud is depressed, says he asked her if she still believed that big brothers were good. I gather she tried to be optimistic for his sake. That must have been hard, given the dismal state of affairs.

Just as suddenly as she had disappeared from the diary, Lou reappeared as Freud's guardian spirit. Tausk doesn't say how it must have made him feel that Lou was writing to him about Freud's depression just when Tausk was going through such difficult times himself. Kate assumed that it made him feel rotten. In any case, the diary was interrupted again, just as it had been previously, leaving her tantalized by what went on in the interval. Only four years from his suicide, everything became more significant, offering clues to why he felt he had to kill himself. The diary resumed after six months.

July 20, 1915

I am assembling a collection of my poems. So my sons will have something to read if I'm killed? Or just for myself . . . to show what I could have done. The boys are safe in boarding school but Martha finds it increasingly difficult to bear the responsibility for the boys' education. My mother – bless her – invited her to stay with her in Zagreb where food is cheaper.

August 10, 1915

I've been called up as medical officer. I'm to be stationed as army psychiatrist in Lublin. It may not be so bad. It seems I will have some time for my private patients and if I have the stamina to write at night, some time for that too.

September 20, 1915

I received a letter from my sister Nadia. Father suffered a stroke that has left him in very bad condition and she is desperate – poor girl, she has always been the most delicate of my sisters mentally. I have no money for a leave. I wrote to Martha that I'm not equal to the misery at home because I am mobilizing my last forces to keep myself going. We shall see with what a skeleton I shall start a new life after the war for the nth time. Despite the hardship and grueling work, I feel more at peace with myself than I have in a long time. Could it be because I am away from Vienna? I work from 8:00 in the morning to complete exhaustion.

December 4, 1915

I'm working on a paper on the war psychoses, sketching it out in my mind when I am waiting for a patient, or in line at the mess hall. In the seven months I've been here, I've seen approximately 1,500 cases, mostly sent to me from the front. I approached my job with loathing at first because it meant that I became part of the judicial process, which I had rejected when I gave up law. But the work gave me access to a group of patients that presented me an unusual challenge. The first is simply language. The soldiers come from all the language groups of the monarchy, and often I needed the service of an interpreter. Then too, they lack the sophistication of patients at a big-city clinic. It's hard to exaggerate the primitiveness of certain popular classes. A peasant from Lower Austria represents a high standard of cultural development by comparison, for instance, to a Ruthenian peasant, whose interests and outlook on life we can describe in words but cannot enter into with emotional understanding. For that reason, some cases of schizophrenia seemed inaccessible for me. The incommunicativeness of these people, the poverty of their ability to convey what is going on in their mind even when normal, has to be experienced before the difficulties involved in making a diagnosis can be appreciated. All the ways in which schizophrenics living in European cultural conditions communicate abnormal body sensations, e.g., when they say they are electrified, hypnotized, influenced, and so forth, are not available. These patients do not do the brooding so characteristic of schizophrenia; they are simply bewildered and unable to put anything into words. It is a relief when one comes across a definite, clinically characteristic symptom, such as when a patient suddenly gives his neighbor a terrible box on the ear for no reason and then takes no further notice of him, or wets his bed or smears it with feces, because, if general paralysis has been excluded, it is then possible to diagnose schizophrenia.

I gradually realized that some cases refuse to fit the psychiatric system and are occasioned by the war itself and contain a mix of melancholia – acute feelings of wickedness and unworthiness – with paranoia. My clinical training gives me no clue to these strange syndromes. It occurred to me that it would be easy to become famous by laying claim to the discovery of a new psychosis – paranoia cum melancholia – though one would run the risk of being told that it had been known for a long time. I am avoiding this risk by saying that every psychiatrist has seen symptoms of both melancholia and paranoia but never such large-scale development of both. I am going to present a number of such cases in detail at the Conference of Medical Officers here in January. As always, I have been extremely careful to give credit to Freud's unpublished conjectures and verbal remarks.

Meanwhile my paper on the psychology of war deserters has been accepted by the Internationale Zeitschrift! *It is, I think, an original contribution. No one, to my knowledge, has written about the subject previously. If I were to express myself freely about military institutions or political conditions, I would have more to say. But I hope that what I do say will reach the ear of future legislators. I shall try to persuade them that there are universal human values that could be of greater value to the country than killing off a few deserters.*

In every case I studied, the desertion was part of a pattern set from childhood of running away from family strictures. Every dependent relationship arouses these men's unconscious rebellion . . . therefore, I argue, they are acting from a compulsion, their reasons for desertion are infantile. Of course, there are subgroups within this general one, but a disturbed relationship with the father – often strict or cruel – and displacement onto father-figures and eventually onto army superiors, is a constant factor. While one group is always on the run since childhood, another submits totally to the paternal authority and is then so terrified of punishment that he deserts to escape it. A third category, perhaps easiest to defend, are more or less feeble-minded peasants with no relationship to the idea of the state or service to the nation. Their army duties are meaningless to them and they can't understand why they shouldn't return to harvest their crops.

If only the just sat in judgment, there would not be enough judges to go around.

Ever since the war began, Tausk had seemed to be sinking, but now inexplicably he seemed to be leveling out. Kate wondered if there was a chance that he had some sort of mood disorder, something physical . . . or should she accept his idea that he was at peace because he was away from Vienna and, presumably, from Freud. Obviously, he was fascinated by the problems of dependency on parents or parent surrogates. But though he complained about the burdens of his army life, he was clearly full of energy, doing strong and what seemed to Kate strikingly original work. Why, then, weren't his papers translated or quoted?

January 10, 1916

My sister Nadia telegraphed me that my father died in his sleep. I wish peace to this much-tested man. For my part, I feel liberated. He was like a fog hovering always in the background of my life. The night after I heard of his death, I dreamed I was resting on Freud's couch, my army boots kicked off, feeling perfectly at ease. I woke with a feeling of confident vigor.

What a coincidence that Tausk's father would die just when he had put some distance between himself and Freud – completing, on the biological plane, his feeling of liberation. But the diary didn't end on a positive note. The last entry was the rough draft of a letter he had written to Lou in Munich after the war. It was dated 1919. Kate read it eagerly.

My dearest Lou,

I am resigned to the fact that you won't let me visit you in Munich. But I wish you could permit yourself to answer my letters. My urgent last still goes without a line from you . But in my mind I still talk to you . . . I build continually on matters we once thought about together. I know my asking for word will only annoy you, but things have come to such a pass. . . .

The next paragraph was inked over with heavy black lines and he resumed in a restrained way, talking about his continued work on paranoia as what he called "a local psychosis." It sounded as if he had been writing to Lou regularly, though Kate couldn't know how many of his letters she had answered. The letter ended with the cryptic and sorrowful remark that "no one will sit down at table with a wretch like me, not even you." What could have happened in the interval to make him feel like a pariah?

Kate put the diary down, overwhelmed by a multitude of unanswered questions. She would have given anything to have him sitting there across from her in his military uniform – the stiff collar with stars tight around his neck, saber at his side – just to be able to talk to him for two hours.

It struck her that her knowledge of him had come full circle.

The first time she'd heard of him was when Helene – neither of them knowing Tausk was Kate's grandfather – had brought up his war service, his heroism in protecting deserters from the imperial Austrian army. Now the diary ended with the war bringing him a feeling of liberation, and a fantasy of coming to rest on Freud's couch.

Chapter Eight

H**elene had agreed** to let Kate continue interviewing her in New York. They were to meet in the tea room at the Hotel Stanhope, where she was staying. She liked it, she told Kate, because it reminded her of a Viennese café, with its lamps and dark wood and an unspecified old-world charm. Before Kate got on the crosstown bus, she'd dropped the journal off at Marius's building. She had no wish to see him, so she just gave it to the elevator man along with a tip and asked if he'd be kind enough to take it upstairs.

Kate still arrived a few minutes early, to find a slender bespectacled man just getting up from Helene's table. He was frowning, and when Helene introduced him as her son, he offered his hand with a brusque movement before excusing himself.

Kate was used to taking the temperature of her relations with her mother and decided that he and Helene had been engaged in some sort of disagreement. How disappointing. This physicist son of hers seemed a formal, rigid sort of man – a little, she couldn't help thinking, like Marius. Helene had mentioned that she was staying in a hotel because her son's apartment wasn't large and she felt you should never impose on your children. Now Kate was thinking that if someone like Helene couldn't get along with her children, who could? Probably not Kate.

"I'm sorry I came a little early," she said, keeping her face bland. "I hope I didn't interrupt something."

"No, nothing to speak of," Helene shook her head. She'd been to the hairdresser recently and her silver hair set off her face with serenely shining ripples. "But I have been wondering about you since you left . . . I missed you. Talking to you helped me organize my thoughts. In fact, I'm beginning to find a shape for my memoir."

"I'm glad it's going well – I missed you too," Kate said, feeling a sudden rush of warmth.

"But you have been busy."

"Yes," Kate said simply. She hadn't finished digesting what she had learned and still didn't feel ready to talk about it.

Helene stayed still for a moment, studying her. Kate's face was tense but not at all sour – as if something were quietly bubbling under the surface, percolating. Ah well, maybe Kate would tell her about it later. "So what would you like to talk about today?"

"I think we'd gotten up to the 1914 war. What was that like for you? You were married . . . but your son wasn't born?" Kate was curious to see if she would mention the miscarriage Tausk had written about in the diary.

"Not yet. Neither Felix nor I paid much attention to the war at first. He had a chronic liver problem, so we knew he wouldn't be drafted. There were a few changes –" she hesitated and Kate noticed a faint blush suffusing her face. "But," Helene continued evenly, "our lives went on much as usual. In many respects, things were better for me than they had been before. I was offered a post at Warner-Jauregg's clinic in Vienna. Women couldn't hold high positions at the University, but with the men away fighting, I had opportunities I would never have had otherwise."

Kate admired Helene's *sangfroid* . . . only a blush had indicated a gap – a personal grief – in the narrative of success. Kate had a vision of the war as a giant machine that shunted men like her grandfather aside and elevated this petite, self-confident woman to a position of unheard-of responsibility.

Just then the waiter came over. "May I take your order?" he asked Helene.

"I'd just like a little more hot water to refresh my tea, thank you."

"And you, Miss?" He had an old-fashioned air that she wasn't used to. Apparently it went with the café's décor. Kate quickly scanned the teas and decided on a tisane with fresh mint. "And I think I'll have a tea cake . . . the one on the tray with the sugar coating."

"So on the home front, war had a liberating effect," Kate said when the waiter left. "I know that was true in the Second World War as well – what an irony."

"Well, yes, the military needed doctors. Before I knew it, I was made assistant to the hospital chief, Warner-Jauregg. At the time, he was probably the most important psychiatrist in the Austro-Hungarian Empire. I was put in charge of the women's division. There I became increasingly interested in the psychoses." She sighed, feeling the word "interest" hardly described the sense of strangeness and discovery she'd felt when faced with psychotic patients. "I will never forget a mute patient I had in the ward. You can't imagine what it's like seeing a human being lying motionless without expression day after day. Convinced something must be going on behind her frozen mask, I courted her for weeks until one day she greeted me with a smile. I came toward her full of excitement, but at the same moment she plunged forward, punching me in the face. Warner-Jauregg was unable to explain this, but I was sure the smile and the punch were connected. Freud believed that in seriously ill patients, love and hate were intermingled in a sort of witch's brew . The punch was the reverse side of her smile."

"How did your chief take to that idea?"

"Not well. I should explain that Warner-Jauregg was a bright man, a humane man and good clinician, but he was utterly scornful of Freud's ideas. He often joked with patients, asking them if Dr. Deutsch had told them yet that they wanted a baby from their fathers. Freud, for his part, was resentful that he never got a university appointment, so there was always tension between the two camps."

"I know that the talking cure got a big boost from the successful treatment of shell-shocked patients during the war. Did you get a chance to treat any of the wounded soldiers with analytic methods?"

Helene shook her head. "Someone else was in charge of the men's division. He was quite sadistic and treated soldiers with conversion symptoms as malingerers, shaming and abusing them. I once saw him kick a man with a hysterical paralysis. His only concern was returning them to the front. Luckily, I was responsible for diagnoses in both divisions. I decided who would stay with us and be treated and who would be sent home or to an asylum. I was able to save a number of men from being brutalized."

And she had been appreciated. Her clinic chief, Warner-Jauregg, had praised her self-sacrifice and diligence. Well, it was true; she had worked hard and at night when she finally fell into her bed, she was too tired to think of her lost baby. Helene sighed and concluded cheerfully. "By the time I started my analysis with

Freud, you might say I was well-seasoned."

Kate perked up her ears. "You had an analysis with Freud?" she asked, somewhat disingenuously. She'd been curious about Helene's analysis ever since Marius had mentioned it the other day. "You were one of the lucky ones then! How did that come about?"

"Well, in those days there was no rule that analysts had to have a training analysis before they could practice and become full members. Instead, you joined the Psychoanalytic Society before being analyzed. Toward the end of the war, I started going to some of the meetings of the Society. I admit I didn't find the group remarkable – in fact, some were pretty odd birds. I remember one of them – a particularly unkempt man with dirty nails who gave a paper on the sexual symbolism of flowers in dreams, and I found myself thinking, good heavens, can't a flower sometimes be just a flower? So, as I said, I wasn't particularly impressed. But I understood right away that Freud needed followers to corroborate his findings, and of course he shone, he stood out like a giant among pygmies. So I was honored when he asked me in 1916 to comment on a very difficult paper by Lou Salome. I knew how much he valued her."

"Uh huh," Kate murmured. So Helene was aware of their ongoing closeness. It would be interesting to hear whether she would say more about the tension between Freud and Tausk.

Kate vaguely remembered Tausk and Lou working together on a paper about some aspect of narcissism. "What was the topic of the paper?" she asked.

"It was about the connection between anality and narcissism. Frau Lou had the theory that a child's rage at giving up soiling is what first makes him conscious of having a separate self. Her reasoning was quite complex, but basically, she thought that the child's hatred of the toilet-training mother was a precursor to later Oedipal hatred and rivalry."

Helene's fine lips curved slightly upward – the ghost of a smile. "I had the irreverent thought at the time that Lou was trying to justify her own matricidal impulses. We had talked together about how much we hated our mothers."

Kate found it disconcerting that both these powerful women had so much anger against their mothers. It crossed her mind that it might not be deserved. Perhaps a mother – hers too – was just the best available target for free-floating discontent – an ever-present dart board.

"How did Freud take Lou's idea?" she asked after a moment."

"Well, as a matter of fact Tausk had connected anality and narcissism in a presentation he gave before the war. I heard that Freud criticized him sharply. But he seemed delighted with Lou's paper – and it was evident that she wanted to please him." Helene pursed her lips. "He was generally delighted with Frau Lou. Even when she suggested theoretical modifications."

"But this is interesting! So would you say that Freud accepted things from her that he wouldn't from Tausk?" Kate leaned forward, intent on hearing the answer.

"At least in this case," Helene said cautiously.

"What did he say specifically? Do you remember?"

"I do remember because I thought then that he was criticizing Tausk for daring to lead, to assert a new idea. He said he was being 'too boldly assertive.'"

"But he didn't censure Lou."

"On the contrary. He praised her for her subtlety and originality and what he called 'the greatness of her bent for synthesis.' He didn't even seem to mind when she criticized the way he conflated what she thought were two distinct types of narcissism – one selfish and the other, life-enhancing. Lou was – in my opinion – more on the selfish side. And she was quite clever in the way she presented herself. She almost never spoke up in the Society meetings. If she did, it was to clarify or mediate, and she always let Freud see her papers before she thought of publishing them. Whereas Tausk . . ." she shook her head, lips pursed.

"It sounds like a male-female thing," Kate said. "Freud could tolerate more from Lou because she was female . . . and she knew how to approach him. He seems to have had trouble with most of the strong men in his circle, but with none of the women. Even Karen Horney didn't openly oppose his theories until Freud was dead." It was a little like the war: while men were fighting among themselves, women rose to positions of power in the analytic movement. Helene was the prime example.

"Do you have Tausk's paper?" Kate asked, trying to keep the excitement out of her voice.

"No I'm afraid I don't. It was a presentation to the Society. But I know that Freud wrote Lou that as far as he was concerned 'Tausk's constructions were wholly unintelligible.'"

"That sounds pretty snide to me," Kate said. "Not worthy of a great man. Did you happen to notice how Freud received other things from Tausk?" Again Kate leaned forward.

"His paper, 'On the Influencing Machine,' was well received when he presented it in 1918 – I was one of the discussants, and as I told you, I wrote a paper in response. But perhaps the positive reception was because Tausk's work was concrete and centered on a single case."

"And so less threatening?"

"Perhaps."

Though Helene seemed somewhat reticent, Kate had no doubt that she was an acute observer of the undercurrents in Freud's circle. And like Lou, Helene had observed that Freud was particularly harsh with Tausk. "Was that your only contact with Tausk during the war?" Kate asked softly. She wasn't sure where this was going but had the unnerving sense that her grandfather was just beyond her, in the shadows, waiting for her to fill in the blank pages of his last years.

"I'd heard him give other papers, one on the psychology of deserters," Helene said, glad to be getting away from the subject of Freud's injustice, "and early in the war, he sent his youngest sister Nadia to me for a consultation. Of course, we had become good friends by that time. Before the war he often brought his women friends to visit Felix and me. There was one we particularly fond of, Lea . . . she became quite a famous actress, I believe."

"Oh?" Kate breathed, the skin on her neck tingling the way it did when she was startled. How incestuously tangled these relations were becoming. And it seemed triangles were sprouting everywhere. Tausk-Lou-Freud was the most obvious one, and now it seemed there was another: Tausk–Helene-Freud.

"He must have trusted you a great deal to have sent you his sister."

"Yes. I think he did," Helene said. "She'd become engaged to a man she didn't love. When I told her that she herself was full of doubts and suggested she break with him, she became outraged and fled. Perhaps I interpreted too quickly. I'd be more patient now. In those days we expected insight to be almost instantaneous," she laughed.

"That's fascinating," Kate said a little too warmly, and Helene gave her an appraising look. "I mean, how interconnected everyone was in those days. People analyzing their friends even family members. It's hard to imagine being in a group where everyone knew each other's psyches so intimately. But I want to hear more about your analysis. You were telling me about beginning."

"Well, I had my first session in 1918 – I'd joined the Society formally in the spring – a year to the day after my son was born."

There was something about the casual way Helene dropped the fact of her son's birth that way at the end of a sentence that gave Kate the feeling Helene's wish to be analyzed had something to do with having a baby. "How was it being a mother and working full-time?" she asked with equal casualness. "It always seemed like a death-defying aerial act to me. I'm not sure I could do it."

"You would if you had to. It was difficult, but Felix was wonderful with Martin, he was very involved and calm . . . and we had a good nanny. I loved being a mother, though I have to admit I was not as calm as I would have liked to be." She gave a dismissive laugh. "If Martin got sick it threw me into a panic."

"Really, I find that hard to believe. You were so terrific with Mother when she fell, and Mother told me how you took care of the girl who had the car accident."

"They weren't related to me," Helene said and sat quietly for a moment. "But believe me, it surprised me, too. I thought there was nothing I couldn't manage, and then this baby comes along and gets a fever or a cough and I'm demolished. It seems amusing now, but then I felt as though I'd been swept up in a cyclone. I couldn't keep my balance. Once I took Martin to the country for a vacation when he was about a year old. He got a terrible fever and I was frantic, I thought he was going to die. If the nanny hadn't been there, God knows how I would have stood it."

"Having a nanny is sort of a luxury now," Kate said. "You were fortunate." She noticed Helene frowning. "Or, didn't it go well? What was she like?"

"She was a peasant woman, not at all like me, illiterate and practically a dwarf." Kate heard a muffled tone of resentment. "But she put all her passion into nursing my son."

"Was that hard for you?" Kate thought that if she ever had babysitters, she'd want them to be young and educated, as much like herself as possible.

"It gave me a pang sometimes to see how much he loved her. And she was possessive, too, she did everything for him. Too much probably – he came to think of her as his mother."

"I imagine you talked to Freud about her," Kate offered.

"He wasn't very interested in that aspect of my life," Helene said matter-of-factly. "Babies and problems with my nursemaid tended to bore him. He was interested in Felix, in my marriage and my total involvement with his Movement."

"But what if there was a conflict? If your work impinged on your mothering?"

"He felt my mothering, my femininity was good enough," Helene straightened her shoulders. "He didn't want to analyze it. He told me that I'd gotten as far as I had because of my identification with my father. He didn't want to touch that because he felt it was so good for my career. Sometimes I thought that he only cared about conflicts of professional loyalty."

"I don't understand."

"Well, at first I thought that my working at Warner-Jauregg's clinic – providing a link to psychiatry – might be helpful to Freud, but very soon I understood that he saw it as divided loyalty. I felt I had to give it up – I couldn't serve two masters."

Kate remembered that one of her friends told her that her therapist wanted her give up yoga for similar reasons, sensing a rival guru. "For a supposedly rational science there was a lot of passionate feeling going around. It sometimes seems more like a religious sect than a rational science."

"I wouldn't go that far," Helene said calmly, "though I do think now that some analysts were saved by it, as they might have been in earlier times by a vocation, that they might not have been able to survive in a less protected realm."

"But then wouldn't being 'saved' depend a lot on being in Freud's good graces? Wasn't Freud passing judgments all the time, sending the sheep to one side, the goats to another?"

"Possibly," Helene said looking down at her plate. "But you know I'm very tired now. I need to stop for awhile, relax . . . and you must have other things to do."

Kate hid her disappointment. "I don't really. I left the afternoon free. I thought I'd walk over to the park. It's such a beautiful day. I'd be delighted to have you join me."

"I'd like to, but I'm just too tired, now," Helene said. "Let's do it tomorrow. Is that all right, are you free?" She called the waiter over and got the bill – she wouldn't consider letting Kate share, and after she had paid, she went up to her room to rest, agreeing they'd meet again the next day.

Helene lay down as soon as she got upstairs, but she couldn't seem to relax. The talk about Freud's single-mindedness – Kate had implied it was a sort of despotism – had disturbed her. So had remembering Freud's attitude towards her problems with Martin.

She got up restlessly and looked out the window, watching tiny brightly colored figures playing in the park. Just before Kate came, her son had said with a slightly ironic intonation, that he was leaving Helene "to her work." As though, she thought, he was reminding her that she, like Freud, had made work the top priority. And now, with Felix gone, she wanted more of him – well, you reaped what you had sown. Martin was always polite, but more distant than the brightly moving figures below her engrossed in their play.

She turned back from the window to the desk scattered with notes written in dark ink in the fine hand she had prided herself on in school. Though she had told Kate her memoir was moving forward, the material actually seemed increasingly intractable. Almost more, she thought, from the pressure of things she wasn't saying than from what she had so neatly chronicled.

She picked up a faded photo of herself, slim and beautiful in a white wedding dress surrounded by a flowering porcelain frame. It suggested a new beginning, the illuminated first letter in some precious manuscript. But the story that followed wasn't about love, was it? After her marriage it was her career that blossomed, starting with that decision to leave Felix for a year to work at the famous neurological clinic in Munich she'd boasted about to Kate. "Blossom" was hardly the metaphor for that, she thought. Her career had rolled straight ahead, gaining power as it went, like a steam engine going downhill. She could count the stations and tick them off. The clinics, the patients, her gradual –then, as she had told Kate, sudden – rise, when the men were away at war.

She sat down, took up a fresh piece of paper and began to write.

It was no good. Her thoughts dragged her unwillingly backward to the miscarriages she hadn't told Kate about, and before that to the other lost child, and the misery of her last year with Lieberman. Like malignant gnomes in a Munch painting, the fetuses curled at the edge of her successful life mocked her.

She stopped fighting, leaned back in the chair, closed her eyes, and gave herself up to her memories.

She was sitting on the bed holding Lieberman's hand and looking into his face. He had been telling her how much he loved her, she was his darling Halusia, his divine girl. Breath of his breath. His soul. He'd decided never to travel without her again. His sensual lips smiled at her under his golden mustache. Taking courage from the passion in his voice, she'd told him she was pregnant.

At first he refused to believe her. It would come, it always had when she was late before. But when she insisted, told him that she'd started feeling sick in the mornings, his face went white with horror. True, he quickly rallied and took her in his arms to soothe her, but it was clear he didn't want the baby. She knew as well as he did that it was impossible. With a sick wife at home, a daughter of his own. But still she'd assumed he would yearn for this love-child as much as she did. Would cry with her, agonize. After all, for so many years they had spun out the fantasy of taking his young son and making a new life for themselves. She was too young to realize that this was just romantic talk, a titillating dream of life in a small rose-covered cottage – the saved child little more than a prop for their love-making – innocent, smiling flesh.

Yes, she'd been disappointed in love – so long ago now but brighter than anything in her shrinking future. Despite the fact that her lover had let her down – had been a somewhat selfish and narcissistic man – she still missed the intensity of what she'd felt for him. It was incredible, really, the way her mind wanted to skip over the years with Felix – all those peaceful productive years when her career had flourished, making her the most prominent expert on female psychology in the world. If by some miracle she could relive some bit of her past life, what she'd want back wasn't her kind Felix but that early, febrile passion for Lieberman, the eager wetness between her thighs that came from just thinking about him. She missed her madly beating heart almost more than she missed her taut smooth skin.

It made sense that her major discovery had been the often fatal attractions of self-abnegation in certain women. Not that she had ever admitted she was her own prime example. How willing she had been, back then in her glossy adolescence, to suspend herself. Suspend was a good word, she thought, her intelligence and insight and drive all held in suspension, waiting not for a prince's kiss but for a break-up to liberate them.

It was ironic, really, that when she left in 1914 for the Munich clinic, only Felix, left alone in a partially furnished apartment, was steadfastly behind her. He never complained, never reproached her. In fact, from the beginning he'd urged her to do what she had to.

"If you believe you must get away, then go. But go with strength, not in tears and sorrow."

And when she heard the reproachful voices of her mother and her sisters in her head speaking the Polish of her Victorian childhood, she ordered them to be quiet. Who were they to dictate how she ran her life, insinuating that she wasn't a proper woman, or murmuring that her husband would stop loving her? But when she banished them from her waking life, they came back in dreams. She increased her endearments to Felix, her "faraway darling."

Did she still love him, then, or was she already regretting her lost passion? She scanned the letters Felix had saved, rather surprised at how genuinely loving they seemed. He became her "darling boy" – though she wasn't older than he, she was certainly more experienced – just as she had been Lieberman's "beloved girl."

No, she thought, she couldn't or shouldn't try to fit these fragmentary thoughts into her memoir. It didn't matter to the world's view of her achievements that she had called her husband "dear boy" – or even whether her restlessness and craving for excitement had sent her to Munich that first year of her marriage. The important thing for the world to know was that Felix supported her decisions, difficult as they were for him. He never put pressure on her to hurry back home, certainly not to get pregnant, though he loved children.

Pregnancy was just one of the topics that she had trouble fitting into her narrative in any meaningful way. Especially her two miscarriages after she married. Was it shame that made her so reluctant to write about it, she wondered?

Though she had spent hundreds of hours freeing women from their oppressive mothers, and even though she could appreciate the irony and smile, her own mother's criticisms still echoed in her head. You're not the woman I was. Look how easily I had my children. You may be defining femininity for generations of women, but when it comes to life you are not the real thing. She could still see quite clearly her mother's lips pursed in disdain, arms crossed on her full bosom. Oh no, you are no match for me. If she'd for a moment hoped that being pregnant would make peace between them, she was disappointed. The young Helene couldn't stand the idea of being like her mother in any way, and watching her belly swell couldn't help but remind her of their similarity.

If Helene had seen such a tangle of contradictory wishes in a patient now, she'd have talked it out, tried to find out how much the woman really wanted a baby. Not the idea, but the living, dirty-diapered, empty-bellied, squalling reality.

Still, without knowing what she really wanted, the young Helene persisted. She wanted to have this experience that not only her old-fashioned mother and sisters but the revolutionary Dr. Freud thought was woman's highest goal. Freud, of course, went further: not only was it woman's goal, but it was her only compensation for not having the valuable male organ. What pernicious nonsense, Helene said now under her breath – though Freud was long dead and there was no one there to hear her.

In Munich in the long months away from Felix, Helene had been working on a word association project. The Munich doctors were all hostile to Freud and looking under every rock for evidence to disprove him. They set up the parameters of her experiment in such a way that she could only skim the surface. She was frustrated at not being able to really get at the deeper thoughts of her subjects. She thought it would have provided lovely material for psychoanalysis. When she was offered a good job at Warner-Jauregg's clinic back in Vienna, she took it. She didn't expect her pregnancy – for despite mixed feelings she had conceived – to interfere with her work.

What if she'd given the association test to herself? Mightn't she have gotten a shock?

Milk – poison – she'd never liked it, made her break out in hives.

Mother – pillowy breasts – huge and suffocating.

Baby – parasite, an alien being eating you from the inside.

Birth – death.

Helene still hated to think about her miscarriages. It was almost as though they had taken place in another woman's life, or more exactly, as if two women alternated inside her body. The worker – competent and in control – and the vulnerable, emotionally labile breeder . . . dependent and needing her husband.

She tried now, just for herself, to remember her feelings when she first found she was pregnant. The exhilaration of having successfully conceived was soon replaced by a heavy weariness. When she visited her sister Malvina, she wrote Felix that she felt estranged from herself, a lethargic instrument of nature, "a fattened pig, a well into which all cares and slaveries are swept."

The habit of analyzing everything made her search for something or someone to blame for her miscarriage. The fact that her sister had just given birth to a mentally defective child seemed to explain her rush of fear that something would be wrong with her own baby. In all her thoughts about pregnancy she had insisted there was a strong psychological component to being able to bear a child successfully. That a woman had to identify successfully with her mother or a surrogate. She had kept to her view even when it had been ridiculed and denounced. Now she wondered about her sacred dogma. Could it be that losing a baby was easier to accept if there was a reason, something mental that could be controlled or eliminated? She thought of all the women who tried every way to dislodge their fetus: immersing themselves in boiling baths, jumping from a height, taking poisons even, and still their pregnancy endured. She would have said because somewhere they deeply wanted it, but now she wondered.

The pains had started in the middle of the night. She'd been sleeping curled against Felix's comfortable back when she felt the first twinge. She'd ignored it and tried to go back to sleep, but the twinge developed into a cramp. She'd gone for a hot water bottle. Changed her position, gone to the bathroom. At first she'd thought it was indigestion. She'd eaten a heavy dinner of roast meat and something she'd developed a craving for, stuffed cabbage, cooked the way they'd done it in her childhood. But when the cramping continued, she woke Felix. He rubbed her back and belly gently, trying to get her to relax, then brought her warm milk, but nothing helped. The doctor was called and rather callously informed her that she was probably having a miscarriage. There was nothing he could do, but there was no reason why she couldn't stay at home. If she did miscarry, she should simply bring the fetus with her to the hospital in the morning.

After that the pains became stronger and she panicked and started to moan and toss from side to side in the bed, writhing to escape the pain. Felix brought cool cloths for her head and tried to tell her to relax, that tensing against it probably made it worse, but she couldn't – she was more frightened than she had ever been. Then about four in the morning blood gushed out, soaking her nightgown. Felix picked her up and took her to the hospital, where she was given something to stop the hemorrhage and sedated while her doctor did a curettage . . . the doctor told her the next day that there didn't seem to be anything grossly abnormal in the tissue he had recovered.

Still, she agonized over whether her abortion a few years before had injured her body in some way. When she became pregnant again a year or so later, her fears multiplied. When she noticed spots of blood, she became hysterical. She worked on a couch in their cramped living room, trying to hold on, to think positive thoughts, but images of a deformed fetus with a misshapen head or tiny finlike arms kept coming to her mind. It couldn't happen again, she thought, but it did.

She miscarried not once but twice more before she finally bore her son, Martin.

In thinking about it, Helene blamed her mother, who, she was convinced, had wished she'd never been born. If she hadn't gotten pregnant with Martin at the same time that her good friend Hannelore became pregnant, Helene was sure she would never have had a baby. Hannelore had a generously warm mother who fussed over both "her girls." Helene was convinced that only finding this mother surrogate enabled her to complete her pregnancy. After Martin's birth, she and her friend got pregnant together once again. But Hannalore's husband was transferred and he left town unexpectedly. Helene miscarried the next day.

She was never able to carry another child to term. Analysis with Freud hadn't seemed to help. The truth was, it might actually have been inconvenient to the Movement if she'd had other children. She was one of the few disciples with clinical experience – Tausk was another – and Freud would want her to direct the training institute in Vienna in the not-too-distant future. She was a loving but over-anxious mother. One child was distraction enough.

The next afternoon, Helene and Kate made their way down Fifth Avenue to the zoo.

Helene, who hadn't slept well that night, rested for a few minutes on a stone bench at the entrance while Kate went to the ladies' room. Then they strolled around slowly, breathing in the mild air – Kate resisted an urge to buy a balloon, she had loved this place as a child – and drifted to a stop in front of the chimps. There was a small crowd of children and parents admiring some new babies. Helene was intrigued by the tender expressions on the chimps' faces as they brooded over their offspring, their very human gestures as they groomed, picked out fleas, suckled their young.

"We could learn something from them," Helene said. "They don't waste precious time being anxious." Kate laughed, but she found herself oddly moved by the tender way the chimps cradled their babies and the tiny wizened faces with huge eyes. Her arms began to curve themselves around an imaginary baby. She could almost feel it pressing softly against her.

If Keith had been there, he would have taken advantage of her sentiment. He was pleased that the spotting had stopped, and her period hadn't arrived after all – it was now almost two weeks late – and just that morning he'd caressed Kate's stomach in bed, leaning over to kiss it.

"If there's a baby there, I want it," he'd said, leaning his ear against her belly as if he were listening.

She had pushed him off. "If it's there – and we don't know for sure – it's just a pinprick of cells. Please Keith, don't be all sentimental, you'll just make it harder for me if I have to have an abortion."

He'd been dismayed, then angry. She'd calmed him down. Promised to keep an open mind. Now she gave herself a vigorous shake and moved away from the chimps. But she still felt in a softened mood. And Helene too seemed somehow more open.

After a few minutes they found themselves in the area of the predators. They stopped in front of the lion's cage and watched the animal pace back and forth.

"Poor creature," Helene said, "how he must hate being confined." A small child escaped from its mother and ran forward toward the protective railing, waving a popcorn box. His mother rushed up and pulled him back. "I just wanted to share," the child wailed. Just then a keeper came out with a wheelbarrow full of meat and deposited it in the cage. The lion crouched down eagerly and started to tear it apart.

"He has his proper food, you have yours," the mother said to the child. "Besides, he's dangerous."

"You better mind your mother or that lion will have you for dinner," added a white -haired man standing next to her. He squeezed the boy's bicep appraisingly. "Mmm, what a tasty morsel." He laughed and put his arm around the boy.

"He won't eat me, Grandpa," the child said. "The lion likes me because he knows I'm his friend."

Helene smiled at the boy and his grandfather.

"Point of view is everything, isn't it?" Helene asked. "That little boy saw the lion as a friend." She sighed. "I'm reminded of something Frau Lou said about Tausk."

"Oh, what?" Kate looked at her eagerly, hoping they were about to resume their conversation.

"Freud thought of him as a predator, but she saw him more as a berserker, a warrior with a soft heart. A suffering fellow creature, *Brudertier,* a brother animal."

The lion in front of them, tired of pacing, flopped down on his side, exposing his dark fur underbelly, which reminded Kate of a moth-eaten rug. "How do you know that?" she asked.

"Lou told Freud after the war . . . and he told me."

Kate's mind flashed back to all the late-night talks Freud had had with Lou about the Tausk problem. "But weren't you Freud's patient? What made him tell you that?"

"I'll explain, but tell me something first. Do you have some special interest in Viktor Tausk?"

Kate, caught off-guard by the abruptness of her question, looked down avoiding Helene's eyes, while she tried to think of what to say.

"I wondered because every time I mention his name, your eyes brighten. Frankly, you look a little like a cat about to pounce."

"He seems like a fascinating man," Kate started. "So full of contradictions. Volatile, passionate." She could hear herself stammering. "And he seems to have been a more important part of your life than I realized," she finished lamely.

"You are interested in my connection with Tausk?" Helene asked. "Why? Is there something you are looking for?" Kate sensed that she was suddenly wary.

"I'm interested in your relations to all the members of Freud's early circle," Kate said, innocently. "There was such jealousy, so much jockeying for power among the men. I need to know how the women – how you – fit into that. You told me in our first interviews that Lou had an affair with Tausk – she seems to have felt close to him, at least for a time. You just said she thought of him as a suffering fellow creature. I can't help wondered if she – or if you – sensed that he was doomed. Not a lion but a goat," she added jokingly, in an attempt to lighten the mood. It didn't work: she saw Helene visibly stiffen.

"I imagine Frau Lou was aware of Tausk's problems, though I doubt she saw him as doomed – but of course I'm not a mind-reader. In any case, I think you are attributing too much power to Freud with this metaphor of the doomed and the saved. Freud wasn't God," she finished in an irritated tone. "Tausk was a grown man, you know. What he did with his life was his responsibility."

"I'm sorry . . . I'm making you angry."

"Kate, I like you, I want to trust you, but I'm beginning to sense you have a hidden agenda. It makes me uncomfortable." Just then, a red ball tossed by a rambunctious child hit against Helene's legs and she stumbled. Without thinking, Kate reached out to steady her, took her arm and guided her to a sunny bench.

Elderly women were seated on the benches across from them feeding pigeons while nursemaids bounced their perambulators. Helene sat in her trim suit like a small gray bird poised for flight. Kate made an instant decision. If she was going to keep Helene's cooperation, she was going to have to confide in her.

"I've been waiting for the right time to tell you," Kate said, as a loud screech came from the direction of the aviary.

Helene nodded gravely.

"Where to begin? You know when I came into town to get mother's insurance papers?" Kate asked.

Helene settled back down and rested her eyes on Kate's face.

"Well, I found a mass of old papers and letters as well." She decided not to mention that she had opened a locked drawer. "It took a few minutes before I realized what I was looking at –" she paused, "but then I understood that I'd found what I'd been searching for for so long. I found out who my grandfather was."

"You did?" Helene asked. "But what does that have to do . . ."

"It was Tausk." Kate burst out. "My grandfather was Viktor Tausk."

Helene let out her breath in a sharp exhalation. "How extraordinary. I knew there was something . . . but . . . who would have imagined this underground connection between my world and yours." She smiled hesitantly at Kate. "Amazing. I'll have to start thinking of him as your grandfather. He would have been glad to know you, I think."

She put out her hand and Helene took it and held it for a moment.

"I'm sorry I didn't tell you right away," Kate started apologetically. "I needed to mull it over."

"Perhaps you wanted to hear what I had to say," Helene said, a glint in her green eyes, "to see if it jibed with what you knew."

Kate started to protest, but Helene held up her hand. "It's natural, natural that you would want to find out what more you could about him without prejudicing your source. And of course, it must have been a terrible shock," she paused and seemed to reconsider. "But perhaps you just found his name, some letters – or was there more?" Helene studied her face intently. "What exactly do you know?"

"Well, I've found out a lot. More than I can assimilate. You must be wondering if I found out about his suicide, and I did and you're right, his death was shocking. Inexplicable. Horrible. I could see why my mother didn't want to tell me about it. It could really make you worry about bad genes and when you add my brother's death, I can imagine how scared she was." Kate realized this was the first time she had had a charitable thought toward her mother for a long while.

"It was a tragedy. He was an immensely gifted man. But I always think that knowledge gives power. I hope that will be true for you. Did you," Helene asked in a different, less certain voice, "find any clues to his state of mind?"

"There was literally nothing after the war . . . that's why I hoped you could help me. I did find an early diary of his sanatorium stay in 1908. I forget the name of the clinic, someplace on the Dalmatian coast."

Helene looked surprised. "I hadn't known about that. How long was he there? What seemed to be wrong?"

"A few months. I think he was exhausted mentally and physically. He wanted to find something he could put his heart into, and I think he was depressed that he had to put so much of his energy into making a living."

"He never told me he'd had a breakdown," Helene said uneasily. "But of course, many people have an incident of depression and fully recover. Go on to do important work. He seemed so buoyant when I knew him, full of life, outgoing, warm. No more neurotic than the rest of us."

"I'm glad to hear you say that." Kate said, smiling as a group of pre-schoolers in matching red hats marched by hand in hand, singing. One small boy stopped to examine a pebble and a counselor rushed back and scooped him up. "It was the impression I got, too. Even though one of his sons seems intent on proving him crazy."

"So you met Marius?" Helene asked, excitedly.

"And Emil too. They couldn't be more unlike each other. Emil seems to really love his father. He was very open. He showed me my grandfather's suicide letter to Freud."

"I'd heard there was one but I never saw it. What did he say?"

"I don't remember it all – I can show you next time we meet, but I was struck by how calm, even generous it was, considering what he was about to do. He thanked Freud for all the good he'd done him, said he had no accusations, or resentment, and that he took leave of this life knowing that he had 'witnessed the triumph of one of the greatest ideas of mankind.'"

Helene's face twisted into a strange grimace, as though she had tasted bitter medicine. "No resentment," she repeated, "no accusations. Ideas are all very well, but they're never worth a life."

"I don't understand." Kate had never heard such sorrow in Helene's voice. "Do you think it was exaggerated? I admit I thought it was strangely positive when he'd clearly been having his troubles with Freud."

Helene sat up very straight. "Being around a genius is never easy. Or were you referring to something specific?"

"There was another diary," Kate went on more slowly watching Helene's face as it settled into its usual frank expression. "A diary of my grandfather's year with Lou."

"Aha, and was that interesting?"

"It was. I felt I really got to know him – and I liked him. But that wasn't all. I think . . . I think, though maybe I'm wrong, that Freud's discomfort with my grandfather started during that year when Lou and my grandfather were having an affair. Lou reported that Freud had long talks with her about Tausk and what a problem he was. Freud was clearly fascinated by her." Kate decided not to add "and probably jealous." The image of Freud was so zealously guarded, Kate had no way of knowing if it was the journal's suggestion of human weakness that made Marius so eager to hold it close to his chest.

"Marius was furious that I'd read the diary at all. He actually came to my house and tried to take it by force. I feel as if I've gotten into something way over my head."

"I see," Helene said calmly, not letting Kate see how eager she was to read this journal. There was so much that she still didn't understand about what happened to Tausk. She'd heard fragmentary, often conflicting accounts of this affair and Freud's growing animosity, but she had never been quite sure what was true and what was fantasy. A journal kept at the time would be invaluable . . . but she mustn't press.

"Can you tell me anything about Marius," Kate was asking, "that would help me understand what he's so worried about?"

Helene studied her young friend. "Nothing you couldn't find out in the library. Marius has always been an active psychoanalyst. He is the editor of one of the most important analytic journals, *American Imago*. He helped set up an archive of important material from the early days, including interviews and such. You might say he has set himself up as a guardian of Freud's memory." She felt there was no point in adding that he had the reputation of being a fanatic. Kate would find that out soon enough, and Helene wanted to preserve at least the semblance of neutrality.

"But not of his father's memory?" Kate said, caustically.

Helene winced slightly. The young could afford indignation. They didn't realize that people made all sorts of compromises when they felt their goals threatened. She herself . . . she didn't complete the thought. "When Tausk committed suicide," she went on quietly, "some of the early analysts worried – probably rightly – that his death might reflect badly on psychoanalysis. It wasn't the only suicide of a disciple – Silberer killed himself too, and Federn, and there were some nasty rumors going around. I don't think you need to hear them."

"No, please, any detail might help me at least to get a sense of how people saw it. Even if it's a rumor."

"The rumor was that before he died, Tausk castrated himself. Someone who'd noticed the tension between them said that if Tausk hadn't done it, Freud would have done it for him."

"Oh, my God!" Kate exclaimed, "how gross."

"Of course, it was preposterous. But that sort of thing – well, it might be reason enough for Marius not to want to revisit the subject, aside from the fact that it's still painful to him."

"I get the feeling that there is something more," Kate said. "Something that happened after the war. Do you have any idea what it could have been?"

Helene sat for a moment, worrying the ring Freud had given her as a sign of his special favor. "Vienna was not an easy place to be after the war for any of us," she said, with a slight sternness that Kate interpreted as defensive. "Food was scarce. I myself brought goat milk to the Freuds – I was lucky enough to have procured a goat to provide milk for my baby, for Martin – other patients and friends supplied various necessities. Crucial supplies like coal were hard to come by, the currency was ruined by inflation, and as you can imagine, it was difficult for Tausk to find patients willing to invest in a personal analysis.

"In those days, analysts couldn't make extra income by taking on patients for short-term therapy. He would have liked to get a university appointment as a docent, but his connections to Freud wouldn't have been a help there and he may also have thought Freud wouldn't like it."

"The question of divided loyalties again? And I suppose he had to depend on Freud for referrals?"

"We all did," Helene said and paused, looking at some sparrows that had flown into a cage and were picking at scraps. "We were all dependent on him in some way. Tausk maybe more than most had trouble with that – in some respects, he was a little like an adolescent boy." She sighed. "He'd swing away and then he'd want to be close." Kate had taken her pad out of her purse and started to doodle, it helped her to concentrate. As Helene described Tausk's need for Freud, Kate sketched a tiny winged figure and right behind him, much too dangerously close, a huge round sun. "Genius", she wrote in the sun's center. If she'd had her pencils she'd have colored it blazing orange, shot with red flames.

"That wish for closeness, Tausk's dependency wish, was probably one of the reasons he asked Freud to take him into analysis."

"He did?" Kate looked up from her pad, startled. So that was the meaning of the dream of lying on Freud's couch – with the touching detail of boots kicked off.

"Yes. Right after he came back from the war. Of course, there were other factors as well. He was feeling depleted. He needed to put his life together all over again. It probably felt as if he were back to the beginning of his career. Living in student quarters, trying to build up his practice to what it was before. The curious thing was that he had a chance to take another route. A beautiful Serbian widow had fallen in love with him and offered to set him up in practice in Belgrade. At first, apparently, that seemed like a good idea. But though she was charming, she was ignorant, without culture. The moment Tausk returned to Vienna with all its cosmopolitan riches, he realized it just wouldn't work. Still, breaking with his widow was painful to him. He wanted help."

"So he asked Freud to analyze him," Kate repeated as she sketched two hands reaching out of her sun disk to sustain the winged figure. This wasn't what she'd expected. She wasn't sure what she had expected, some sort of more open quarrel perhaps. But she hadn't really expected that Freud would try to help him. Maybe she'd misjudged.

"It made sense in a way," Helene was saying. "Tausk was the most brilliant member of Freud's circle. He had produced significant work. He felt entitled. There was no one else really in a position to take him on. But Freud refused. He felt that Tausk was dangerously aggressive."

So her first expectation had been right. "I still can't understand that," Kate said, bitterly. "Whatever aggression he used was to defend Freud against his critics."

"Freud felt it could easily be redirected against him," Helene replied. "He told Lou that Tausk was 'a dog on a leash' who would 'bark' at him or worse, 'eat him up.'" Kate quickly drew a small dog with a heavy muzzle and collar looking up at a man with a big stick. The dog had big sorrowful eyes that almost filled its face. Hungry eyes.

"Besides," Helene went on, "he felt uncomfortable around him and believed that Tausk was taking his ideas and developing them before they were fully formed. He knew that Tausk thought similar things of him, and perhaps correctly predicted that if he took him into analysis, Tausk would just become more paranoid, more certain that his ideas were being stolen. One thing you have to know about Freud's way of working was that he played with ideas for years, digesting, mulling. He couldn't accept other people's ideas unless he had absorbed them, chewed them over and made them part of himself. In a way, then, Tausk couldn't make an original contribution, and it was quite possible that Freud took hints or ideas from him and worked over them until they became part of his system. In that sense, it would have been almost impossible for Tausk to get credit for an original contribution."

Kate suddenly understood what Lou had said about the tragedy of Tausk's being unable to take a step to the side of Freud, to make some separation between them, the way he insisted always taking the same direction, running parallel. "It sounds like a continuation of what was happening in 1913 when Tausk was with Lou, but still, Tausk had devoted so many years, been so loyal, couldn't Freud have tried . . . ."

"Remember, he was an older man by now, he wasn't well, he had recently lost a daughter. He also had an influx of new followers."

"So he didn't need him anymore? How did Tausk take his refusal?" Kate began to see what might be making Marius anxious.

"He didn't have much of a reaction, certainly no observable depression, though he did complain to one of his sisters. But I don't want you to think that Freud left Tausk stranded. He suggested several other of the well-known male analysts. Tausk refused them all." Helene moved her head abruptly from side to side, as if shaking off some nagging insect. "I'm afraid I'm getting a bad headache," she said massaging her temple. "It happens sometimes when I'm overtired. I think I should lie down a little before dinner. My son is coming later."

Kate, looking up, noticed that the sun was moving down to the tops of the trees. They must have been outside for at least two hours. Helene seemed suddenly like an old lady. Her eyes got that slightly glazed look Kate had seen on her dog, Lupe, when she'd gotten cataracts. Kate noticed patches where Helene's make-up had worn thin and there were dark circles under her eyes. She felt a sudden panic that Helene was going to have a stroke. And how much of what she needed to know was locked in that frail vulnerable body! Chastising herself for such a selfish thought, Kate jumped up and offered Helene her arm.

All the way back to the hotel, Kate thought about how, when Helene was talking, she had no trouble picturing her as young and vibrant. Her voice was strong; sometimes it even had a seductive throaty appeal. If you had heard it on the phone, you would have thought you were talking to a young woman. Kate had several times sketched the woman Helene's voice evoked: Helene glamorous in a huge flowered hat, Helene head resting on her hand, slender and winsome, listening to a patient.

Gradually, as Helene talked, her youthful self and that far-away time and foreign city Kate had seen only in books – had come to feel as real, as contemporary, as Kate herself. That's what people meant, she supposed, by the phrase "making history come alive." So it was shocking, in a way, to find Helene suddenly old.

Kate carefully deposited Helene, blinking with the pain of her headache, into the hotel elevator. As she watched the red floor indicator numbers move slowly upward, she found herself wondering what young woman, in an era she couldn't yet imagine, might be interrogating *her* half a century from now. The thought was idle enough, but thinking of herself as old gave her a chill, almost as if a sharp wind were blowing in the midst of summer.

What would she ask? Wasn't the most difficult question one age might ask of another: "If you had it to do again, would you make a different choice?"

They had agreed to meet again the next morning if Helene felt better. Apparently, her headache was still with her – she called and apologized. Kate had the feeling she wasn't eager to meet again. Something was bothering her. Kate's first thought was that it had to do with Tausk. Maybe she felt disloyal telling Kate that castration rumor and the fact that Freud had refused Tausk's plea for analysis. Especially if that was what Marius didn't want bruited about. If he were as vigilant as Helene suggested, he might be worried that people would blame Freud for Tausk's suicide.

Kate knew Helene had been shocked that Freud refused him so bluntly, wouldn't even try, but then Kate guessed Helene was biased – but what about Marius? She supposed that if he had blamed Freud in any way for his father's death, that might have damaged his career. Certainly he might not have been put in charge of important sensitive documents from the early days.

Even now, when psychoanalysis was so firmly established, it wasn't considered good form to blame Freud, not even for his egregious errors like interpreting hs patient Emma's bleeding as a hysterical symptom when it was caused by a botched and pointless operation. It would take feminists to point these things out – the conversation was just beginning. But, Kate thought, she mustn't let her suspicions run away with her. She wasn't on a witch hunt. An analyst had a right to reject a prospective patient.

Chapter Nine

T**hree days later,** Helene was sitting at the little table in Kate's apartment while Kate prepared brunch. She scrambled some eggs with herbs and was frying up some sausages. The nutty, hearty smell was one she had loved as a child, but now it made her queasy. She found she couldn't tolerate it. She opened the kitchen window, which helped a little, but not enough. The next minute she lurched past Helene into her bedroom and threw up in the bathroom at the far end. Afterwards she splashed cold water on her face, dried it with a towel and went back to where Helene was sitting.

"I'm sorry," she told Helene, "but I don't feel well all of a sudden." Above all, she didn't think she could deal with the sausages.

Helene looked concerned. "Do you think it's something you ate?"

"I had what I thought was a mild flu yesterday, but after I threw up I felt better, so I thought today would be fine – but I'm afraid I feel too queasy to cook." It occurred to her that she really was pregnant, but she pushed the thought away. She'd had a relapse of flu, that was all.

"Maybe you should go back to bed. Sometimes that's the best idea."

"No, no, I think I'll be all right. And I don't think I'm contagious."

"I'm not worried in the slightest. Now, you just sit down," Helene said briskly. "I'll bring you some tea with lemon."

"This was going to be such a nice brunch," Kate wailed. "Strawberries and scrambled eggs with sausages." Meekly, she sat down and Helene got up and patted her shoulder.

"That's a good girl. Now, if you'll tell me where the teabags are."

"In the cabinet right over the stove. Bottom shelf. But really . . . you don't have to do this." For some reason she felt ridiculously weepy.

The kitchen was really nothing more than a little alcove in back of the table, with sink and fridge and stove, the basics of a city apartment. Kate could see Helene opening cabinets, looking for cups. "They're in the next one over," Kate called, "and please have some eggs. They're on the stove, they're probably still warm."

"Will you try some?" Helene asked, "eggs are bland."

Kate shook her head, then, thinking she felt a little better, she pushed back her chair and stood up. But as soon as she took a step toward the stove, her stomach contracted. "This is ridiculous," she said with a puzzled frown, "I've always loved sausages, but the smell is making me feel nauseous. Maybe they've gone bad."

"They look fine to me," Helene said spearing one with her fork, "I'm willing to try one. I'll be the guinea pig."

Kate's stomach heaved again at the thought of sitting anywhere near a sausage.

"No, please," she said, "would you mind just throwing them down the disposal? I seem to have gotten preternaturally sensitive to sizzling pork. Maybe it's some ancestral taboo springing to life."

Helene didn't laugh, she just raised her eyebrows, gave Kate an appraising look, and shooed her back to her seat. Then she went over to the sink, scraped the sausage into the disposal. When the sausage had gone down she found the whole-grain bread – which Kate revealed she stored in the freezer to keep it fresh – and put two pieces in the old toaster. After the toast popped up, she brought a slice to Kate with the tea, then she put some egg on a plate and brought it in for herself.

Kate bit a tiny piece of toast and chewed it tentatively. The dryness and lack of flavor were soothing. She ate a little more.

"Does that help?" Helene asked.

"It seems to. Thank you."

"But you still feel queasy?"

"A bit . . ."

"Is there anything more I can do?" Helene asked in such a concerned voice that Kate blinked back tears. They kept coming. Kate was mortified to find herself starting to cry. "Excuse me," she sobbed, putting her head in her hands. "I can't seem to stop." She could feel her nose starting to run. She had a sudden image of a shrunken Alice standing in a puddle of tears.

Helene got up and put her arm around her. Patted her the way you would a crying child. "Do you want me to help you back to bed?"

"No . . . no," Kate hiccupped. "I'm all right."

"Can you tell me what's the matter?" Helene's voice was soothing, maternal, tender. The way, Kate was aware, through a blur of misery, she must be with her patients. "Tell me, it might make you feel better, no need to be stoical about it. Perhaps I could help."

"Maybe you could . . . ," Kate said, wiping her eyes with a napkin. "I'm afraid I've really messed things up. I think I'm pregnant."

She had a sudden image of her mother, intrusive as ever, trying to find out if she was protecting herself. "I'm not a child," she'd snapped, "give me a break. And anyway, I don't think I should be talking to you about my sex life." It was one of the few times that she'd been able to push back, set up a barrier and tell her mother to stay on the other side.

"And is that so terrible?" Helene was asking with a smile. Clearly, she'd already guessed Kate's problem.

Kate tore a loose thread off the sleeve of her blouse and rolled it into a ball and flicked it onto the floor. "I don't know. I think I want to get an abortion."

"What does your young man say?"

"I'm not sure I want to tell him. He wants me to have it. He thinks we can get by. . . ." Kate lowered her voice to almost a whisper. "I thought you might know a good doctor."

"I do. I know several . . . but it's quite a process. Two doctors have to interview you. You'll have to pretend that you would harm yourself if they didn't agree to an abortion."

"That I'd kill myself, you mean. . . ." Kate started to tremble.

"Yes. The interview can be very difficult, and then, they'd probably put you in Bellevue for the procedure – on the psychiatric ward."

"Oh," Kate stammered, "the psychiatric ward?" It would be ironic if all her investigations of her grandfather's self-destruction, not to speak of her own efforts to be a balanced, normal person, ended up with her in a loony bin being poked by young interns. Would they have to diagnose her? What would it be? Hysteria with suicidal tendencies? Kate pictured the doctor examining her, surrounded by interns perhaps still young enough to be embarrassed at the farce, while other, truly insane patients, drifted like ghosts along the corridors.

"I'm not trying to frighten you," Helene said, "but I thought you should know what to expect. But for now, that's how it is. How late are you?"

"Almost two weeks."

"It's very early." Helene said. "You might even miscarry naturally, and the procedure can be done any time in the first trimester. That gives you some time to think. You could wait a month, six weeks – until you're sure."

"But you'll help me?" Kate persisted anxiously.

"I will. But do you mind if we talk a little more about it?"

"Not at all. You're being very kind. I'm grateful."

Helene went into the kitchen alcove, brought back the kettle and poured Kate another cup of tea. "May I ask what makes you think you don't want to have the baby? Is it that it seems like the wrong time, or is it something deeper – are you afraid that this isn't the man for you?"

Kate hung her head. "I don't know, actually. Keith is wonderful in so many ways . . . and I do love him, but we have some pretty major differences. I have a feeling he thinks I'll forget about my work if I have a child. His mother did, so why wouldn't I? It just makes it all the harder for me to think straight.

"And I have enough fears on my own," Kate went on, "without his threatening to change his mind unless I do everything perfectly. I'm not sure myself that I can have a baby and still have a life. I'm not even sure I'd be a good mother, whether I have it in me. My mother was always worried about one thing or another. She never seemed relaxed. That was partly because of what happened with my brother, but even before that, I never remember her being mellow."

She could be brave, Kate thought, the way she was after she broke her leg, funny even, charming, but mellow?

"Once when I was in college, I brought home some hash from a party," she went on with a little laugh. "I had the idea that if I got her to smoke a joint every day, it would change her life."

"And did it?"

"No, she wouldn't even try. I forgot she didn't know how to smoke – I should just have baked it in some brownies. And she ended up interrogating me for hours: 'How often do you do this? With whom? What other drugs have you tried?' On and on . . . I think what bothered her was less the drugs than the fact I hadn't confided in her."

"I don't want to sound like your mother, but are you afraid the drugs you took might damage the baby?"

"I haven't done anything serious for quite awhile," Kate said, alarmed. "Do you think a joint or two could have hurt?" Without thinking she crossed her arms over her belly.

"I wouldn't smoke just now," Helene said, "but I'm sure no harm's done."

Just the sound of Helene's voice was soothing. You're all right, it seemed to say over and over, just fine. "But even if Keith was perfect," Kate ventured, "what I'm most afraid of is" – she rapped her chest with her knuckles – "me. Well, you told me how hard it was to keep calm with your baby, with Martin? I'm a pretty nervous person already. What if I really can't cope? If it was so hard for you . . . how will it be for me?"

"For one thing, you don't seem so very anxious, or if you are, you've already learned how to manage it."

"Is this managing it?" Kate asked with a wry smile.

"You have some real-life problems to work out with your young man, that's not neurotic – and most people would have trouble with an unplanned pregnancy." Helene paused and looked up at the ceiling, where the paint was peeling back in flaps, then she stretched herself and smiled. "You seem to think I am a special case, but I'm not."

"Yes you are," Kate insisted, "you've done so much. . . ."

"A woman can be a queen and still, as a private person, make mistakes. In fact, being a queen may make it that much harder for her as a private person. That's one of the ironies of being a psychoanalyst, because you are set up to tell other people how to live their lives." Kate heard a note of bitterness that she hadn't heard before.

"Profession isn't everything. If I got a second chance at life, I'd do it quite differently," Helene went on. "I'd have worked less, for one thing. I'd probably have stopped work entirely for the first years of Martin's life. Perhaps then I wouldn't have felt so overwhelmed . . . and if I was still anxious, I would have made more of an effort to deal with it. I could have insisted that Freud help me . . . not because it interested him – it didn't – but because it was at the center of my life. I'm not sure it would have worked, but I would have tried. You know, when I die, I'm not going to be grieving over one last book left unwritten, but I will be grieving that I didn't have more children, and that I didn't spend more time with the one I had. . . . All I'm saying is, give yourself some time to think."

"Thank you for telling me that," Kate said. "I appreciate it, it helps." She wanted to say she felt very close to her but was suddenly shy, not quite sure where they were now. Helene hovered in Kate's mind somewhere between her friend and her subject – her motherly advisor and the still formidable Doctor Deutsch.

When Helene got back to her room, she kicked off her blunt, sensible shoes, lay down on the bed and shut her eyes. How honest had she really been with Kate? Wasn't the truth more complicated? True, she had tried to have more children. It wasn't her fault that she had miscarried, but would more children have made her less anxious than just one? Or a better mother? She had imagined herself using the best educational measures, giving the best informed care. And yet what mistakes she had made as a mother. Mistakes that, as a therapist, she should have been most aware.

That was one true thing she had told Kate. Whatever you are in your profession, queen or psychoanalyst, it doesn't affect your mothering – ironically, being a therapist might have made it worse by reviving her childhood and urging her to dwell in it. The episode of her storytelling, for instance. Surely that had come from thinking about her relations with her siblings. But she'd been totally unaware of the connection. It had all seemed like good, harmless fun.

Against her closed eyelids, Helene saw the four giants she had invented to amuse Martin while he ate – he was a poor eater, and they, the giants, could eat an ox at one sitting or a cauldron of soup. What had induced her to tell him they were her grown-up sons who lived in Russia? It had seemed so innocent at the time, and she thought he'd be pleased because she always squeezed him tight and told him she loved him better, much better than those clumsy louts dressed in skins . . . that he was her precious, her bright and wonderful, sensitive darling.

The stories reminded her of how happy she'd been to be her own father's darling, chosen from out of her lumpen siblings – and she couldn't understand when Martin had refused to eat and begun to be afraid of going to sleep, saying in a tiny voice that the giants didn't like him and were coming to get him. Any child analyst now could have told her what a bad idea the story was. Told her that the child would consider these giant "sons" rivals he couldn't possibly vanquish. What little child could eat an ox, why even try? And Martin was still angry with her for her storytelling.

Whisking Martin off to Berlin with her in 1923 when he was so young, leaving Felix behind, had been a mistake too. She'd thought it would only be for a short time, to study the teaching methods of the Berlin analysts before becoming head of the Vienna Training Institute. But it had dragged out for over a year, partly because of her reluctance to return to her marriage.

She'd persuaded herself Martin was happy, though the German governesses were strict – tyrannical about manners and cleanliness, always trying to get him to eat – and he missed his father terribly. And though she made sure his physical needs were taken care of, she was so often distracted. She had a painful memory of Martin sitting on her lap while she put the finishing touches to a paper she was going to give on mistrust, of all things.

"Mama," he'd said, "Mama," reaching up to touch her chin, tilting it down with his small hand to make her focus on him. She hadn't been able to; she'd put him down. She sighed.

Felix was the one who could be totally warm and loving with Martin. He had a special knack with children. He was a little like the boy who flew away to Neverland. It had even made her jealous at times to see how unconflicted Felix was in his "mothering," how easy and natural, almost a child himself. For him it seemed as natural as breathing. Whenever Felix went to a party, he filled his pockets with sweets for the children. Sometimes when she quarreled with him, she would blame him for that, for being like a second baby, for never taking the lead in decisions that affected them both.

Helene opened her eyes and observed the gilded cornice that ran around the room, a remnant from a gaudier age. She wondered if she were being too hard on herself. If a patient had told her these things, she might have admitted they were mistakes, but she would have pointed out that most people make mistakes with their children. Some made worse mistakes, and the children seemed to emerge unscathed. In her old age, she thought genetics had a lot more to do with it than the severity of any trauma.

She could feel her habitual cheerfulness reasserting itself. And though she had taken Martin away, she had tried hard to keep up his connection with his father. They wrote Felix letters together. Martin invented a game where there'd be a knock on the door. The maid would answer, "Good day. Does a lady with a big boy live here?" – "What are their names?" – "Frau Doctor Deutsch and Martin." – "Yes they live here." Then he and she would pop out, find Felix and tussle over who would be first to embrace him. She tried to stop the memory there, to keep it positive, but it kept on. Martin would push against her, trying to elbow her out of the way as they ran toward the door. She'd push back, laugh, enjoying the fun, acting out the game. But then, as she'd written Felix at the time, "Martin, quite tired and with a sad disappointed face declared, 'Yes, but he really isn't here, so why are we tussling?'"

But it wasn't just ambition that drove her to Berlin, Helene thought, getting more heated as she responded to an inner interlocutor. Freud had terminated her analysis abruptly because he wanted to take on a more interesting patient – the famous Wolf-Man who dreamed of his parents copulating like dogs. That still stung. There was nothing half so interesting that she could produce. No dreams of wolves in a tree, no primal scenes.

Twice she'd even caught Freud napping during her session. His cigar had dropped to the floor and she'd picked it up and handed it to him with a smile. She knew he liked her, there was no problem with that. It was just as a case for research that she bored him. He told her bluntly she didn't need anymore analysis, could do the rest herself. She'd accepted that, though she felt she hadn't really worked through her problems, not just with motherhood but with Felix.

Hadn't it been a secret wish to get out of her marriage that made her ask Abraham – a highly respected member of the Berlin Society – for a second analysis? Helene opened her eyes and looked out the window, where two pigeons were cooing loudly on the sill, the male fluffing out his feathers. And then to find out that Freud had written Abraham and told him he didn't want her marriage with Felix disturbed. She could see Freud's dark, preternaturally intelligent eyes boring into her, trying to hold her to him.

Divorce *verboten.* Helene felt anger flare in the middle of her chest, so strong she could taste bile. What kind of a chance did that give her to figure out what to do? Freud didn't seem to care that Felix was as good as impotent with her, that he climaxed so fast she was never satisfied and that she had almost ceased to desire him, but had still to cradle him like an infant against her breast. Just because Freud himself was no longer interested in sex, was it right to expect her to be a nun for the rest of her life?

She felt a sudden rush of tenderness toward Kate. Her radiant skin and eyes and just the way she inhabited her body made Helene surmise that she was satisfied with Keith sexually, just as Helene had once been with Lieberman. There were clearly problems about priorities, but she had a sense that Kate could figure out how to make it all work – if she wanted to. Kate wasn't just a lovely girl, she was a brave one. She wanted to understand what had happened to make her grandfather take his life. Whether it could help her choose well or badly how to lead her own life, wasn't the point really, wasn't – crudely put – Helene's business. And apart from what her grandfather's untimely death meant to Kate, Helene had her own reasons for revisiting it. She began to see that what was keeping her from giving a proper shape to her past was just this unexamined part of it.

Helene could sense her final memories of Tausk as a tightly knit ball, a tumorous growth that proliferated inside her, sending out roots and shoots while she pretended not to notice, looking the other way. It still frightened her now – she couldn't be sure how Kate or other outsiders would react. Certainly, the analytic world had been as intent on keeping quiet about it as Helene was. But after so many years, perhaps it was time to go in with the knife, get the whole mess out and have a look at it.

Kate was at the Columbia library skimming through the catalogue. It had occurred to her that letters might be a good source of information about Tausk's death. She was particularly interested in Freud's correspondence with Lou. She'd seen how close they were in 1913, and their friendship had obviously continued after the war. Jones had mentioned her as Freud's favorite postwar confidant. So, maybe, he had told her things he wouldn't have told anyone else, even Helene.

She had to stop from time to time and stand with her eyes closed to still her queasiness. Finally she found what she was looking for: a new German version of the Salome-Freud correspondence.

She took the book to a relatively uninhabited table and started skimming the letters from Freud to Lou, starting from the date of Tausk's suicide. The days after Tausk's death came and went with no mention. Kate worked her way slowly through the next weeks. A month passed in the correspondence and she was about to give up when Tausk's name leapt out at her. There it was, "*der arme* Tausk." Poor Tausk. But why had Freud waited a whole month to tell Lou – back in Germany with her husband – about the suicide? Dictionary in hand, Kate read the salutation and innocuous opening remarks, moving slowly down until she got to her grandfather's name:

Poor Tausk, whom you distinguished awhile with your friendship, put an end to his life on July 3. He came back from the horrors of war exhausted, set out under the most unfavorable circumstances to reconstruct the existence he had lost through his military duty, made an attempt to take a new woman into his life, was due to marry . . . but decided otherwise.

Kate was struck by the fact that the announcement of Tausk's death began with an allusion to his relationship with Lou. The tone was easy and informal. By now, Lou was obviously someone he felt he could confide in almost as if he were talking to himself. At the same time, it echoed parts of the obituary: so far, there was nothing surprising. Kate went on:

His farewell letter to me is affectionate, attests to his lucidity, blames no one but his own inadequacy and bungled life – thus throws no light on the final deed. In the letter to me he avers his steadfast fidelity to psychoanalysis, thanks me, etc. But how it looked behind that is not to be guessed. So he fought out his day of life with the father ghost.

I confess I do not really miss him; I had long taken him to be useless, indeed a threat to the future. I had a chance to cast a few glances into the substructure on which his proud sublimations rest; and would long since have dropped him had you not so boosted him in my esteem. Of course, I was ready anyhow to do what I could for him, only I have been quite powerless of late, given the degeneration of all relations in Vienna. I have never failed to recognize his significant gift, but it was prevented from being translated into correspondingly valuable achievements. . . .

Kate put the letter down and shook her head in disbelief. It seemed so heartless. Brutal. This was a man Freud had known for ten years, with whom he'd worked closely – and what danger could he possibly have posed to psychoanalysis? She got up, taking the book with her, and walked to the front of the room. She needed to stretch her legs. As she reviewed the letter in her mind, she was so absorbed that without at first noticing who he was, she almost bumped into Marius standing at the information desk.

"I see you are still investigating," he said, looking sideways at the book.

"Just reading." She turned the book over awkwardly, so the title faced away from him.

"You were so involved in 'your reading.'" He gave the words a slight ironic emphasis. "You didn't see me when I walked right by your table a little while ago. I wonder what is so fascinating." He was obviously trying to sound avuncular, but underneath she could hear the anger.

Kate could have said she wanted to check out something about Lou for her thesis on women; she could have insisted it had nothing to do with Tausk, but she was too angry and upset to censor herself.

"I found a shocking letter that Freud wrote to Lou," she said, "about Tausk's death. I imagine you've read it."

"As a matter of fact, I've read some of Freud's letters to Frau Salomé in an edition of selected letters that's being prepared for publication. But I didn't see anything shocking, as you put it. Why don't you show me what you have there?"

"Shush," said the librarian at the front desk, putting her finger to her lips for emphasis. "Please go outside if you're going to talk."

Kate considered telling Marius she didn't want to discuss it further, but she was curious about what he could possibly say in Freud's defense, so after checking out the book, she followed him to the library steps.

He motioned her to a ledge running alongside the steps and she sat down easily. He looked at the steps for a moment as though he was wondering if they were dirty – or perhaps whether his knees would allow him to get up again in a dignified manner, then stayed standing in front of her. Whatever his reasons, it made Kate uneasy to have him standing that way, looking down at her.

"I need to refresh my memory before we talk," he said, "so, if you'll show me the letter." Then, with an attempt at lightness when he noticed her hesitation, "Don't worry. I'll give it right back." He stretched out his hand and she reluctantly handed him the book. She'd stuck a piece of paper between the pages to mark the place of Freud's letter. Marius opened to it and read the letter quickly.

"Ah," he said, "just as I thought. This is a corrupted text."

"What do you mean?"

"There are several things here that don't appear in the original, the version that will appear in the *Selected Letters.*"

"What things?" Kate asked, remembering the series of corrosive phrases.

"I don't remember exactly, but I'm almost sure Freud didn't say he was relieved that Tausk was dead, felt he was a threat, any of those things."

"I don't believe this is a corrupted text," Kate spat back. "There's no reason to think that. It's much more likely that the worst parts have been censored in the *Selected Letters.* Censored because they make him sound so heartless, ruthless. In addition to refusing to analyze him, he's practically gloating – saying he only kept him around anyway for Lou's sake, . . . and after Tausk had tried for so long to gain Freud's approval. You read the diary where he said he hoped Freud would finally see him as a worthy heir."

"If he really wanted to be a beloved son, he should have been proud that his father imago is using his ideas . . . yet for years, he accused Freud of stealing them."

Kate thought there might be a grain of truth in that. She stayed silent for a moment.

"He begged Freud to help him with his problems, to analyze him."

"Tausk was already hostile, and what's more, he thought his attitude was realistic. Freud probably realized he would have gotten nowhere in an analysis – and please remember how much Freud had helped him with money that made his medical studies possible. No, I'm sorry, but from the beginning my father's demands were insatiable. At the very beginning of his association with Freud, I remember personally that Freud had sent him a considerable sum. He complained that it wasn't enough to pay for his planned vacation. Freud had to draw the line somewhere; he had no obligation to take him as a patient."

"Even if his refusal caused Tausk to kill himself?"

"I repeat, Freud cannot be blamed. Sometimes I think his disciples expected too much of him – just because he was a genius, that didn't give him magical powers to keep a self-destructive person alive, and I'm afraid that's what my father was – probably a schizophrenic. I know, I know how hard it is to accept. Imagine how it was for me. I loved my father very much when I was a child, but after he killed himself, I hated him. He deserted the people who loved him. I can't forgive him."

"And Freud didn't desert anyone?" she asked, echoing his word.

"He has always been a model for me – from the first time I met him after my father's death – of a genuinely great and deeply moral human being. And I think just before my father's death he came to terms with the fact that Freud was so much his superior. He wrote in his farewell letter that Freud's work was genuine and great and thanked Freud for all the good he had done him. For the first time, my father realized that his accusations against Freud were false, but he couldn't stand the insight . . . and he killed himself."

"That's what you think?"

"Yes, I do . . . and I beg you not to keep on dredging up this sad history. Let it go. Whatever it may have meant to your grandmother, she's dead. It can't be important to you now, and speculations, incorrect interpretations of Freud's behavior, can grievously impugn his reputation."

"I see," she said, though she felt quite thoroughly confused.

"I hope you do." He gave her a slightly ironic bow with clicked heels, turned away from her and without another word went down the steps.

When he'd gone, Kate felt herself unaccountably trembling. She sat there for a moment watching the procession of students with their glasses and unkempt hair and "Get Out Now" buttons pass in front of her. She had always felt a little surge of agreement when she saw those slogans, but after listening to Marius, being right seemed suddenly more complicated. She wondered what brilliant Lou had made of Freud's cruel dismissal of Tausk. Would she have defended him, told Freud he was mistaken?

Kate went slowly back to her seat and opened her book to Freud's letter. On the next page was Lou's answer. She wrote back very simply that she was sorry to hear of Tausk's death. She'd been fond of him and had never imagined him as a suicide. She admitted that he had a vulnerable side, but she thought that was part of his charm. She called him a berserker with a tender heart.

The phrase echoed in Kate's mind. Helene had used that phrase at the zoo. Kate hadn't known exactly what it meant. She'd assumed it had something to do with being crazy, berserk. Now she looked it up in the OED. It was a reference to Norse warriors going into battle frenzy. Kate remembered how Tausk had read heroic ballads to Lou – by his account, she'd been quite excited by the idea of supermen committing exorbitant crimes.

Lou could well have protested that Tausk's battles – though perhaps undertaken with too much intensity – were against Freud's enemies, that he'd always thought he was doing what Freud wanted. But instead, she agreed with everything Freud said, including his statement that Tausk was a danger to the future of the Movement. How could she? She must have known that wasn't true. Kate had thought of her as a wild bird, proud and free, and now she was behaving like the worst stereotypical female – deceptive, manipulative. Kate slammed the book shut.

Kate had compiled a list of the early analysts when she started her research. Several lived abroad and the rest were scattered across the country. Many of the old guard – stalwarts like Berta Bornstein, Kurt Eissler, Mark Brunswick, Jeanne Lampl-de-Groot, Heinz Hartman, and Rudolph Lowenthal – lived in New York or Boston. The secretary at the New York Psychoanalytic Institute had helped her track them down. The rest of the afternoon she spent calling anyone who was old enough to have known Tausk, and after telling them she was doing research for a book on her grandfather, asked them what they knew about Tausk's death.

She was able to reach only about fifteen. Several didn't answer. The ones she got hold of simply said they knew nothing except that he had committed suicide. She was nearing the end of her list when someone mentioned a Dr. Brinner who had been Tausk's friend. "If anyone would know, it would be he."

When Kate called, she got Dr. Brinner's daughter, who told her he had had a stroke and was in a nursing home in Brooklyn, She gave Kate the number.

"I've never been so sick that I didn't want to have visitors," Dr. Brinner said. He seemed glad that she'd called – "so few people do nowadays. I feel quite alone." He readily admitted to being a friend of Tausk's.

Kate took her seasickness pill as soon as she woke up, but the motion of the subway packed with commuters made her feel horribly queasy, and by the time she managed to find her way to the nursing home in Brooklyn Heights, her skin was clammy with perspiration. The home was in a section of old Victorians, several of which had been linked together to form an elegant complex with leafy gardens in the back.

Kate reminded herself that she had taken a final examination when she had 102 degree fever – certainly she could cope with a bit of nausea – and told the pleasant-faced woman at the front desk that she was here to see Dr. Brinner. He was expecting her. A young aide walked her to the room which was on the ground floor overlooking the garden.

Dr. Brinner was sitting slumped in his wheelchair, though as soon as he saw her he tried to straighten up. He must have been tall when he stood; his knees were raised now to make room for his long legs. Kate was shocked when she saw him. His skin was practically translucent, white and thin as parchment, and his high forehead, covered with yellow-white hair, made her uncomfortably aware of his skull.

She had the feeling he didn't remember their conversation the day before, so she started slowly, asking him how he was, about the food, the garden, the care, and only then reminding him of Tausk.

"We had good times together," he said in heavily accented English. "He was brilliant but never aloof, never pontificating, warm, a lovely person. But he had some problems. Mostly with women. . . ." Here, Dr. Brinner looked at her blankly. "My own wife died last year," he went on after a moment, "Matilda would never would have let me go to a place like this . . . *die gute weib,* she cared for me fifty years . . . but Tausk didn't have luck with women . . . he liked the brainy ones."

Kate had the feeling from his fragmentary speech that he was about to fade out entirely, like a radio succumbing to static.

"Do you have any idea why Tausk committed suicide?" She asked touching his arm gently to focus his attention. "Freud thought it was because he was depressed by the war."

"*Narishkeit,*" he said using a Yiddish expression, and then in a voice that was suddenly much stronger. "Nonsense. It wasn't just the war that depressed him. It was Freud. If Freud had showed him some human interest, he wouldn't have killed himself."

"What do you mean human interest?" Kate asked.

"Well, he gave him a certain measure of respect, but as a person, as a man, he rejected him. I loved them both and I repeatedly urged Freud to take Tausk into analysis."

"Oh," Kate said not wanting to interrupt for fear he would wander off on a tangent or sputter to a stop.

"I have to tell you that I'm a great admirer of Freud's and I've never told this to a living soul, but I'm an old man," he paused, "I'm going to die soon and I feel very strongly about this. . . . Someone needs . . ." He looked at her for help.

". . . to tell?" Kate prompted hopefully.

He nodded. "I had been urging Freud more insistently on Tausk's behalf, telling him how much he needed him, how there was no one senior enough to analyze him. We were at the Café Ronacher, having coffee. He told me frankly there was a very good reason why he couldn't take Tausk into analysis – because . . . if he did, Tausk would kill him! Then he put his cup down hard, and I realized that the subject was closed. I must never bring it up again."

"Do you think he meant he would die from the effort?"

"No. I think he meant it quite literally. He had a streak of paranoia, you know, that became more pronounced as he got older – or at least it seemed that way to me."

"It makes a certain sense, if you think every son is out to kill his father when he becomes too weak to defend himself," Kate said, excited by the unexpected corroboration of her own idea about the link in Freud's mind between Tausk and Oedipus.

"And after the suicide," Dr. Brinner went on, "it was almost uncanny the way Tausk seemed to drop into a hole or into a deep well – as if he had never been born. It became psychoanalysis's family secret. 'Our shame,' Federn called it, that we couldn't keep him. No one would talk about it. Or if they did, it was only in whispers. None of the older analysts would talk to you about it even now." He stopped and looked at her, triumphant at having delivered his memory safely. Now he could relax and forget. He slumped back in his chair, and his eyes took on the slightly glazed look they had when she first came in.

Kate thanked him profusely and left. Clearly he was right. No one had been willing to talk to her. Helene was the only exception. After hearing Dr. Brinner's story, Kate admired Helene even more for being so candid. She must have known as well as all the others that it was a taboo subject for the faithful.

In the middle of the night, Kate woke up with a start from a frightening dream. Unable to get back to sleep, she started going over her conversation with Dr. Brinner and his revelations about the cover-up. Suddenly she had one of those midnight revelations that often seem banal in the morning. She saw – literally as crimson ink on a white storyboard – a shape for the Tausk material. It would be – had to be – part memoir, part mystery. She stayed up the rest of the night writing a book proposal for Rachel, the young agent she met at her women's group who'd liked her earlier article and suggested they stay in touch. In the morning Kate mailed off her proposal without reading it over because she was afraid she'd lose her nerve.

The next meeting with Helene was at Kate's apartment – this time in the afternoon when Kate thought she'd be feeling less wobbly. And in fact she felt fine though she was bristling with questions. She had put the kettle on to boil and set out two teacups, milk and sugar and a small vase of yellow and purple pansies.

Kate noticed that Helene seemed slightly breathless.

"I hate to make you climb my stairs," Kate said as she pulled back a chair at the table for Helene to sit.

"Nonsense, it's good for me to move. I don't do it enough. At my age the body favors the horizontal all too much. But how are you?" she asked warmly, eyes flicking from Kate's face to her belly.

"I'm fine," she forced a smile. She was going to have a blood test in a few days, that way she'd know for sure. But she actually felt certain enough. She'd been nauseous again this morning and taken a motion sickness pill to ensure she didn't go over the edge. But right now, all that receded under the pressure of her curiosity.

"So," Helene murmured, "where are we?"

That's how she must have started her sessions Kate thought. Her voice had a soothing, inviting tone.

"I've been trying to make sense of it all," Kate said, "but I still don't know what to believe about my grandfather. Was he a loyal defender of Freud or an aggressive, envious, competitor? I ran into Marius again at the library and he insists that his father was a psychopath. I'm sure that's what my mother thought. Do you think that's why she wouldn't tell me about him?" Kate hadn't planned to talk about her mother, but she'd suddenly imagined her listening to Marius and fearfully accepting what he said.

"You'd have to ask her, to know exactly what she was afraid of," Helene said, looking, Kate thought, as if her mother were present at the table and she could simply turn and inquire. "But what her father did – killing himself that way – obviously produced shock waves that resonated through your family." She made a gesture suggesting the expanding circles.

"Trauma is a loosely used word these days," Helene raised her eyebrows, "but I think it's apt. I could imagine that Hilde wouldn't want to speak of the suicide for a long time, but some of her feelings – grief, fury – must have been passed on to your mother without explanation. There's an expression we used in my village in Chemesh – 'nursed on the milk of sorrow.' And when Hilde did speak she probably impressed on your mother the need for secrecy. Your mother already felt uneasy – unloved – she interpreted the suicide as shameful or dangerous, maybe even as her fault. Since it had done so much damage already, she wanted to erase it and protect you from anything connected with it."

"I think I can understand that," Kate said, shivering slightly as she thought of the milk of sorrow. "Poor mother. It was hardly her fault. She didn't ask to be born. But if she suffered so much confusion as a child, you'd think she'd have been more straightforward with me." Kate had a fleeting awareness that as often happened in her relations with her mother, she had quickly veered from sympathy to criticism. Not nice, she thought. I'm not a generous person. Just then the tea kettle let out a shrill demanding cry and she got up to fill the pot.

"She well might have been more open," Helene said placidly, when Kate had come back and set the pot down to steep, "but honesty isn't always so easy."

"It may not be easy but I think people should make the effort," Kate said. "Hidden things are like abscesses, they fester and in the end probably cause more pain than if they could come to the surface. Besides, I think it is a sort of duty to tell the truth."

"Not if it's hurtful, I hope," Helene said easily, reaching out to take a cookie.

Kate blushed suddenly self-conscious. "I don't know. I have never possessed a momentous secret. When I was young I used to reveal things my girlfriends told me, but my revelations were more embarrassing than harmful. Like telling the boys that my friend Louise wore a padded bra."

Kate was suddenly aware that this hadn't been an idle question: Helene was wondering about her, wondering how scrupulous she'd be if she knew – what? To hide her momentary confusion, Kate peeked inside the teapot to see if it was ready, then slowly poured two cups.

"Oh, well," Helene smiled benevolently and helped herself to another cookie, "that's hardly catastrophic."

"No, just that my motives aren't as pure as I'd like them to be."

"Whose are?" Helene asked. "I'm sure there's a healthy dose of voyeurism in the choice of analysis as a profession," she continued cheerfully. "I know I have some. Being locked in close quarters with someone telling you things the dearest people in his family don't know – it's powerful. But there has to be the urge to help.

"Freud may not have had enough of that," Helene went on. "He was so compelled by his discoveries – the Oedipus Complex, childhood sexuality, free association – more interested in research than therapy. Once when I was agonizing over a patient who had made no progress, he said rather bluntly that 'only a few patients are worth the trouble we spend on them. You have to renounce therapeutic aims in cases like this,' he said, 'and be content to learn what you can.' "

Kate became instantly alert. It sounded so like the Freud of the letter to Lou.

"I wasn't aware of this side of Freud," she said. "My grandfather, on the other hand, seemed to be interested in helping even seriously sick people, psychotics," her voice quivered – she hated the sound of the word, the sibilant hiss and harsh consonants. "But maybe that's not because he had a more compassionate character, maybe it's because he was one himself."

"I am very suspicious of diagnostic labels," Helene said carefully, "particularly when so little is known. If he was psychotic, of course, analysis would have been the wrong treatment for him. But when someone kills himself that way, you do have to wonder if the diagnosis is wrong. He certainly was more disturbed than I realized at the time. He never told me that he'd had periods of depression, or been in that sanatorium – but I don't think he was psychotic – troubled obviously, more fragile in hindsight than any of us realized – but not psychotic, and if he'd had help when he asked for it, I think he might have been saved. Freud's refusal was the last straw. But you won't find many analysts who are willing to admit that."

Exactly what Dr. Brinner had said. Kate sat very still, waiting.

Helene raised a hand to shield her eyes and Kate, noticing that the afternoon sun was shining right into Helene's face, went to adjust the blind.

"I told you that Freud offered Tausk other male analysts," Helene went on quietly. "Well, if we're speaking of honesty, that was a bit disingenuous. In fact, when Tausk refused the men, Freud offered a compromise solution – he suggested that I analyze Tausk. And I agreed. One didn't argue with Freud."

"You? Good heavens!" Kate sat for a moment astonished.

"I was Tausk's friend," she said quickly, "and I suppose Freud might have felt Tausk would have been more comfortable with me – with a woman."

"I don't know what to think . . . this is such a surprise . . . it's frankly unsettling." Kate pushed back her chair and stood up, walked a few paces, trying to calm her mind, looked towards the blinkered window then back at Helene. She could hardly begin to think what this might mean.

"I'd have thought that being a friend would make it harder," she began haltingly, after she sat down again, "less safe because you knew the same people, knew his family. And wasn't it . . . complicated? I mean, with you being in analysis with Freud at the same time? Or have I got that wrong?" Kate heard herself stammering. She felt slightly light-headed.

"No, that's exactly right." Helene said. "I often went straight from seeing Tausk to my hour with Freud." She was sitting stiffly erect. "I know how strange it must seem to you, but Freud respected me. He thought I could manage."

"But I wonder how Tausk felt about it," Kate asked hesitantly. "He must have been a member of the Society for years. You told me he was one of the most senior analysts, and you had just joined. I don't know how it was in the Society, but in the university nowadays, tenured professors aren't reviewed by beginners, and Tausk must have been one of your first analytic patients."

"He was the first," Helene said in a low voice.

"Your first patient? Kate asked, her stomach churning. "Mightn't he have experienced that as . . . well, as a put-down?" She didn't want to offend Helene but this seemed incredible. "Did Tausk talk about it, say how he felt?"

"I wasn't a beginner, really." Helene said. "True, I hadn't had any analytic patients but I'd worked in the hospital clinics for . . ."

"Please," Kate blurted out. "Maybe we shouldn't do this. It seems wrong for me to cross-examine you. Maybe you don't want to talk about this at all. Or at least not to me. I'd understand if you didn't. You're so much more involved than I'd imagined. . . ."

"Don't be afraid of offending me. Ask what you like – and I'll try to answer. Maybe I'm assuming too much, but I think you like me." Kate nodded assent. "I can't expect you'll feel quite the same now. That's all right too. But maybe you want to stop?"

"No," Kate shook her head vigorously.

"Well then?"

"I guess the first thing I'd like to know is how long his analysis was."

"It went on for a number of months," Helene said, "five days a week. In those days analyses were often much shorter you know. Mine was only a year."

Helene seemed slightly defensive, Kate thought. She made a note to come back to this later. Had Helene found him too difficult? Too resentful of being sent to a junior analyst? "I'm curious about his first sessions with you, whether he complained about being there in your office instead of with Freud."

"As soon as he stretched out on the analytic couch, he started to talk about Freud's refusal. After all his devotion to psychoanalysis and particularly to Freud, he'd presumed, he said, that Freud would undertake the 'burden' of his analysis. But as far as being discontent with me," her lips moved slightly upward in a half smile, "he was too gallant a man to express discontent to a woman. 'Freud having taken you himself is a mark of your excellence,' he said, 'I look forward to unburdening myself.'"

It seemed to Kate clear that he was being ironic. How could it fail to be insulting that Freud considered him a burden to be shuffled off. "If it was a mark of your excellence to be chosen by Freud, what did that make him?" she asked, her voice a little too loud. "Deficient?"

She suddenly remembered Helene telling her how she triumphed over her brother and sisters as her father's favorite. She could well have felt a similar triumph over Tausk – though being a decent person, she would have tried to banish it.

"In retrospect," Helene said, not losing her appearance of calm, "perhaps you're right. I was flattered by Freud's confidence. I probably didn't want to look into it too deeply. But I know when Freud terminated my own analysis prematurely a few months after

Tausk's death because he wanted to take back the Wolfman – I was depressed for a while, and I suppose if then he'd suggested I go to someone else, a younger beginner – yes, I can see I would have been upset."

Kate considered this statement for a moment. "But you said Tausk was too gallant to complain. Even if that meant breaking the analytic rule and suppressing his negative thoughts?"

"He was quite open about his negative feelings towards Freud," Helene said.

"If Tausk was angry at Freud, mightn't he have been angry at you for taking his place?"

"He thought of me as Freud's good daughter," Helene said with some satisfaction, "while he was the bad boy." She twisted her wedding ring on her finger. "His rebelliousness could sometimes be very compelling."

"You mean because even good daughters can have bad thoughts?" And Kate bet that he expressed them for her too. It would be sort of like having a problem child . . . defending him to Papa Freud, all the while showing off one's own devotion. She was beginning to be irritated by Helene's apparent sense that nothing was wrong here – a sort of smugness.

Helene shrugged. "No one is a saint."

"But wasn't it difficult for you to have a friend lying on your analytic couch relating his fantasies about you and your analyst? Wasn't it embarrassing? Wasn't there a conflict of loyalties?

"Tausk knew how completely devoted I was to Freud," Helene was saying "he never tried to interfere with that, but he wanted me to see his side too. He made his arguments with passion. Certainly he convinced me of his great talent. For a while I admit I had to struggle not to be too partial. He had a type of personality I was susceptible to, fiery, emotional, artistic – a poet. . . ." Helene tapered off.

Kate imagined that anger only heightened Tausk's seductive charm. She could imagine him wooing Helene the way he had Lou when she was drifting away from him toward Freud. Helene must have been still very attractive herself at thirty-five, with the maternal glow young mothers have. She had started her analysis with Freud when her son was one and a half, taken on Tausk three months later in January 1919, working from the apartment she shared with Felix not far from the Freuds'. Kate at first pictured her with a slight milky stain on her blouse, hurrying to Tausk after nursing her son – though, she reflected after a moment, Helene had probably weaned him to goat's milk by then.

Kate pictured her handsome grandfather stretching himself out, making sure his boots weren't dirty – Helene probably covered her couch with an oriental rug just the way Freud did – adjusting the pillow for his head. She saw him in a belted summer jacket with a pleated upper pocket sort of like F. Scott Fitzgerald. He couldn't help being aware as he talked that afterward – crammed full of his complaints – she would go on to her own session with Freud.

"He never had a real transference to me," Helene said quietly, as though guessing Kate's thought – he never fell in love with me the way patients usually do, perhaps because we knew each other well as real people."

"Wasn't there a rule by then – I know there is now – that you shouldn't analyze people you knew socially?"

"Freud officially cautioned against it, but the Professor never kept to his own rules – he wouldn't have been a great innovator if he had. I imagine he felt he was beyond them."

Like Nietzsche, Kate thought. Beyond good and evil. "Did you fall in love with Professor Freud?" she asked, knowing the answer, "despite the fact you knew him socially?"

"Oh, yes. If anything, having had a chance to know his wife made it stronger. It was obvious to me that I was younger and more attractive than Frau Freud. I was convinced he loved me, too. Once I caught myself standing in front of a shop window – filled with marvelous beaded handbags – wondering what poor Frau Professor would do in such a case. I think my analysis stirred up feelings I'd had for Lieberman, my wish that he would leave his wife."

"And Freud analyzed this?" Kate wondered if the sexually magnetic and rebellious Tausk had also reminded Helene of her grand passion.

"He saw it as a straightforward Oedipal triangle, hate for the mother, love for the father, and, as I told you, he didn't try to disabuse me of my father identification."

"You might say he became a surrogate father!" Or husband. Didn't he demand undivided devotion? Kate had the blasphemous thought that the ring Freud gave his favorite women analysts was a little like a mystic wedding ring. That might help to explain why women like Helene who loved their fathers did so well in the movement. Like the great abbesses in the Catholic church. But it might also mean that they – that Helene – couldn't openly endorse ideas about femininity that differed from Freud's. Her two-volume opus, *Psychology of Women,* was used as a text for training analysts. There Helene slipped her differences with Freud into her long and sometimes tedious case histories, the sly way a revered abbess might slip an occasional lover into the convent. In these cases, as in their earlier conversation about masochism, Kate had begun to see Helene's revisionist thinking. She had already noted the way Helene quietly re-defined female narcissism as positive self-esteem and rejected Freud's theory of penis envy as the basis of female development. But she was sure there was more.

"Freud treated me very much as an equal," Helene was saying. "Nowadays analysts won't let patients read any analytic literature while they are in treatment, with the unfortunate effect of turning patients into little children. Freud let me read everything. If he was a surrogate father, I was an informed daughter. Tausk, of course, knew much more than I and had spent years writing and thinking. One of my first papers – as I think I told you – was an extension of his paper 'On the Influencing Machine.'"

"But is that what Tausk talked about to you, his ideas?"

"I'm afraid so. I knew of course about his difficulties with women – and I was sympathetic. As you know, I'd had my own romantic troubles. I'd met several of his early lovers. I never thought much of Lou, I didn't think her relationships were genuine, and to my mind she was a kind of nymphomaniac. But Felix and I liked Lia, the actress he went out with after the break-up of his marriage. Tausk was extremely tender and loving with her. We both hoped he'd marry her, but no . . . it didn't work out. I knew he had trouble sustaining a relationship. He couldn't stand women being dependent on him. Even Lia's admiration seemed dangerous to him. He was afraid of being consumed." She sighed. "I would have liked to analyze that. I thought I could have helped him to make some necessary compromises.

"But that's not what he wanted. And you know . . . with free associations the analyst just waits for what emerges. What obsessed and tormented him was his relationship with Freud. I think he genuinely didn't understand why he was having such difficulties. After all – as you saw from his diary – he admired Freud tremendously, defended him at every opportunity. He wasn't angry, just enormously sad and distressed at what he felt was Freud's unwillingness to recognize the originality of his contributions."

"Did you think was there any basis to his feelings?"

Helene took a deep breath and Kate thought she saw her hand quiver. "At the time I thought there were remarkable similarities between their personalities. Both thought they were geniuses, Each thought the other was taking his ideas. And yes, Tausk cited instances where Freud had ignored him and then later expressed a similar idea or had cited him – but for the wrong paper."

"I'd love to hear some examples," Kate said.

"I'll try to think of some," Helene kneaded her right hand, pulling out the thumb, "but right now I think I need an aspirin."

Kate jumped up from the table. "Oh, did you hurt your hand?"

Helene smiled reassuringly. "Nothing serious, just my arthritis. I usually ignore it, but I don't want to be distracted right now."

"I'll be right back," Kate said heading towards the bathroom. Helene was so mentally alive, Kate kept forgetting her age until she saw that she needed a nap or had some ache or pain. She'd have to be more considerate, give her some time to rest. Especially since this work of remembering couldn't have been easy.

Kate rifled through the cluttered medicine cabinet. Diaphragm, jelly – which she had neglected to use one time too many – moisturizer, cleanser, light foundation, half-used lipsticks, Keith's razor, shaving cream, toothbrushes in various stages of broken bristles, vitamins of every size and description but no aspirin, bufferin, or any painkiller.

"It's ridiculous," she said when she came back, "but nothing. Why don't I run out and get a bottle. I can be back in five minutes."

"My legs don't hurt," Helene said, "just my hand and I think we're both getting weary. I know I am. A little fresh air might disperse the cobwebs."

"There's a pharmacy about two blocks down on Broadway . . . if you're up to it."

"Of course I am," Helene said with some impatience. She picked up her bag briskly with a 'see-I'm-just-fine' look and they headed out the door.

Despite Helene saying she had no trouble with her legs, she took the stairs leading with her right leg, the left obviously had trouble bending. Kate resisted offering her her arm. Just as they were going out the front door of the old brownstone, they ran into Kate's Romanian-Jewish landlady who greeted them in heavily accented English. When Helene returned the greeting in her own accented English, the landlady switched to Yiddish and asked if she was new to the neighborhood. Helene answered in English that she was just visiting. The exchange intrigued Kate.

"Your family didn't speak Yiddish?" she asked as they made their way past the row of dilapidated brownstones towards Broadway.

"No, but I understand a little. My family was thoroughly assimilated, we spoke Polish, thought of ourselves as Poles. I knew German of course, other languages as well, though a colleague once accused me of speaking them all in Polish."

She smiled and looked up at the house they were passing that stood out from its rundown neighbors.

"You can tell a German *hausfrau* by the clean window panes," she said pointing up "and the geraniums on the sill. Am I right?"

Helene was looking around as if she were in a picturesque village in the Alps instead of walking along a non-descript street between Broadway and West End. "I'm afraid to say I hadn't noticed," Kate said.

"There seem to be quite a few Spanish people on your block," Helene said, eyeing a group of young men sitting on a stoop further up.

"Puerto Ricans, I think," Kate said, looking at them, "and there are some Italians and Jews. It's not a great neighborhood in terms of being safe at night, but it has the advantage of being rent-controlled. And I like the mix."

Kate wondered if she would be so alert and interested in new things when she got old. She hoped so. It occurred to her she knew very few older people. Keith would say that was another failure of community.

"Was it hard for you to move away from your village in Poland to Vienna?" Kate asked as they turned the corner onto Broadway.

"What was hard was giving up Polish. I loved my language, still do. When we were first married, I tried to get Felix to learn it, but he wouldn't – when I went to visit my family, he would always tease me about returning to civilization. Vienna before the Great War was a paradise . . . a city of intellectuals and artists – most of them Jewish."

"Really? I always thought that the Viennese were the worst anti-semites."

"Not true. It was a marvelously open city, tolerant, a melting pot much as it is here."

Kate thought the anti-semitism was surely there, simmering just under the surface . . . look at Otto Weininger's self-hating rants – and the anti-semitic mayor of Vienna – but she let it go. If Helene wanted to clothe Vienna's past in a nostalgic glow, for the moment, well, let her. Kate was going to press her for hard truths soon enough.

When they came to a small grocery, its wares set out under a striped awning, Helene stopped and stood inhaling the scent of a cantaloupe she'd picked from the top of a sweet-smelling pyramid. Kate marveled at her look of rapture. The Italian grocer stepped outside, and Helene complimented him on the ripeness of his fruit. She seemed so relaxed now that they were off the difficult subject of Tausk.

They continued to stroll companionably, looking in the shop windows with their displays of blouses, handbags, skirts – serviceable but not exciting or chic. Kate lingered in front of a Chinese take-out place, but it wasn't exactly what she wanted. She discovered an inexplicable urge for a hot pretzel. Finally, a wagon appeared on the corner of ninety-third and Broadway laden with giant pretzels. Crisp, dry, and bland. Nothing she would ordinarily have taken a second look at. Helene insisted that they buy one and eat it while it was hot. The drugstore Kate was looking for was just a little further down, in the middle of the block. A nice looking Hispanic clerk in a white smock offered Helene a paper cup with water so she could take her aspirin and by the time they'd ambled back to Kate's brownstone, Helene said the painful tingling in her hand was hardly noticeable.

"So, you asked me for examples," she said when they were sitting back at the table again with a fresh supply of hot tea and the big bunch of purple grapes Helene had bought on the way back. "I was thinking about it as we strolled. It's complicated. . . . As I tried to explain, Freud ruminated sometimes for years before his formulations crystallized, whereas Tausk was more impulsive. You will have to figure out what you think.

"What seems certain is that they were interested in several things at the same time. One of them was melancholia. Tausk told me he had presented a paper on psychotic depression to the Society in 1914 – before I became a member. He complained that when Freud published his famous "Mourning and Melancholia," in 1917, Freud didn't cite his work on the subject, instead he cited him for something else, 'quite unimportant.' He was hurt, mystified. And there were other cases – of concepts, particularly in connection with the psychoses – where he felt he didn't receive his due. One of his truly original ideas was to suggest psychotic patients could be treated if the techniques were modified."

"That sounds as if it should have been important," Kate said.

"It was – it would be later . . . but it was something that Freud didn't take up – and if Freud wasn't interested . . . or just didn't think the time was ripe . . . well. He once remarked that he didn't like psychotic patients, they annoyed him. He felt them too distinct from him and everything human."

This observation clearly pained her, and she sighed heavily. "As for giving credit where credit was due – no doubt sometimes Freud could be arbitrary in his references. If you were in favor you'd be more likely to get a footnote. We joked about it among ourselves. Ernest Jones once remarked that the Professor distributed footnotes the way the emperor did decorations. . . . Ah, well," she ran a hand through her short white hair, "there was a certain innocence in those days."

Kate wasn't sure that was the way she'd describe it. This giddy acceptance of imperial rule. She determined to ask Helene if she could see her notes – but later, now she didn't want to interrupt the flow. "So when you went to Freud for your therapy with him, did you feel you had to tell him of Tausk's complaints?"

"Yes, I did. I became quite an advocate for him. It sometimes seemed as if he'd be content with so little, even a softening of Freud's attitude toward him, an acknowledgement of his value. And the tragedy was that Freud really did see his value. After Tausk's suicide, you know, Freud wrote a glowing obituary – he said he was a 'rarely gifted man.' It was published in the same issue of the journal as my paper corroborating some of Tausk's ideas about schizophrenia."

"Marius read me parts of it," Kate said, "though he seemed to see it as a sign of Freud's magnanimity rather than of Tausk's stature."

"Well, it was generous," Helene went on, looking pleased. "Freud described his career in a very positive way, speaking of his dedication and devotion, the sacrifices and difficulties he had overcome to enable him to be a psychoanalyst . He said it must have been terribly hard for Tausk to have been torn away from his growing practice by the war."

"Too bad that Freud didn't tell that to Tausk when he came back home," Kate said. Somehow all the praise made Freud's coldness seem even worse.

"Yes, it was too bad," Helene said, ignoring Kate's ironic tone." I cried when I read those things. I wished Freud could have brought himself to say them to him. He even admitted that Tausk had been right to rebel against the military authorities – something he might have been expected to view with suspicion. He said it was to Tausk's honor that he threw himself wholeheartedly into exposing the abuses which 'so many doctors observed in silence.'"

"Do you think it was genuine?" Kate asked abruptly. "I mean, here Freud is praising Tausk's conscience, his scrupulousness, his sense of responsibility. How does that fit with his calling him a barking dog, a biting dog? Even saying that Tausk was going to kill him."

"Oh, no," Helene made a violent rejecting motion with her hand.

"Yes, please listen," Kate leaned forward. "I've just found the man Freud said it to – a Dr. Brinner. Do you know him?"

"Very slightly. He was extremely partial to Freud. He must have felt very strongly for him to tell you that."

"I think he did. He felt Tausk had been treated badly and he didn't think he deserved to be forgotten. I'm not that naïve, I know there's a difference between a public statement and a private sentiment, but there's too big a gap here. Freud sounds positively paranoid."

Helene didn't respond, just sat there resting her cheek on her hand looking pained.

Kate wondered if she knew about Freud's brutal letter to Lou and Lou's response. She rummaged in her back pack and brought out the book of correspondence.

"I wonder whether you've seen this?" she asked, pushing the book across the table, open to the damning letter.

"No," Helene said, "no, I haven't." She read through the letter silently, then she took a big breath. Looking, Kate thought, as if she'd just come up from underwater. "It's . . . it's not the Freud I knew . . . or, certainly not all of him and . . ." she left the sentence hanging for a moment.

"I'm surprised," she finished. "Perhaps," she made an effort, "Freud felt somehow responsible for Tausk's death – not that he should have – and his guilt kept him from mourning properly."

"It's cruel whatever the reason. And what kind of danger could Tausk have posed to the movement?"

"I don't know, frankly," Helene's lips tightened. It was obviously difficult for her to have heard this.

"That's not all. According to Marius, the selected letters, a volume that's being prepared now, has this letter in another form with the nastiest comments absent." Kate leaned forward. "I think Anna Freud has probably censored them."

"It wouldn't be the first time." Helene said with a slight ironic inflection. She would do anything to protect his image. But how did Lou respond, I wonder?"

Kate motioned at the book, "Her letter's on the next page. She doesn't defend him at all . . . only says that he had a tender heart. I think it's shameful."

Helene read the letter quickly. "You know, I never liked Lou much, but frankly it's hard to criticize her for not coming strongly to Tausk's defense," Helene said, shifting in her chair. "It would have been impossible if she'd wanted to remain close to Freud. She probably felt she had to agree that she, too, saw Tausk as a threat

– albeit on the level of the unconscious – to Freud."

"Lou was a master of diplomacy," Kate said, "but that seems just dishonest. And anyway what does it mean?" Kate felt her face getting hot as she went on. "That while Tausk did everything he could to advance Freud and psychoanalysis, underneath his unconscious was plotting rebellion – like Oedipus. That way you can attack anyone. And there's no defense. It's diabolic. Really, Lou should have questioned that at least."

"You mustn't be too harsh," Helene said, earnestly. "It's hard to feel now the power Freud had over his group – some might even say the power of life or death.

Kate had a sudden image of a magnificent buck she had seen – she'd been hiking with Keith – cutting a younger animal out of the herd, driving him off.

"God knows what Lou's refusal to abandon Tausk might have led to," Kate said with an indignant toss of her head. "Questioning the dangers fathers face from their sons? Or maybe suggesting that a son might have something important to add."

"But you know she had abandoned Tausk even before he died," Helene said. "She told me once how badly she felt that she'd refused to answer his last letter, begging to see her. He'd written her soon after Freud refused to analyze him, that now no one would sit down at table with a wretch like him; not even her. She felt that she had deserted him." Helene rubbed her cheek.

"She had deserted him . . . awfully. I mean first Freud refused to analyze Tausk and passed him to you, and then his former lover refuses even to have a meal with him." Kate shook her head, "How I wish she were at the table with us right now. I have so many questions to ask her about what she didn't say."

Their interview session stopped very soon after. Helene was clearly exhausted, but Kate had a sense that she was also becoming more involved. That although she clearly didn't want to delve more deeply into her feelings about the letter, Freud's cruelty had shocked her and would make her think things over again.

Kate was intrigued by Helene's final suggestion that Lou felt more deeply about Freud's treatment of Tausk than her letter would suggest and wondered how she felt about her own betrayal. It would be so interesting to know how she felt about censoring herself . . . in a way it was emblematic of what happened to the other women in Freud's entourage, too.

Kate decided to go over to the Columbia Library again and see if Lou had written any story or play after hearing of Tausk's death. Lou – unlike Helene who tended to put unpleasant things behind her – tended to mull things over. She often reworked her life quite closely in her fictions.

Two hours later, Kate was at the Columbia University Library looking through articles on philosophy, psychology and literature, which she put aside. There was also a short story called *Geswistern* ("Siblings"), published in 1921 – just the right time, Kate thought – in an obscure German periodical.

After reading for a while, Kate could see that the basic configuration was the same as in Lou's earlier play, "Tor und Ur," which had two children – Lou and Tausk – and a revered headmaster, a stand-in for Freud.

In "Siblings," the headmaster becomes an equally beloved orthopedist, Trebor, and the two children in love re-appear as Jutta, a precocious eleven-year-old girl, and her elder brother, one of Trebor's apprentices. The boy is passionately in love with his sister, who wanders fetchingly around the house in blond braids and a nightie, but at the same time, each sibling wants to be preferred by the older man.

Though Kate recognized the basic triangle, this story had all sorts of complications that she didn't understand.

Toward the end of the story, the orthopedist Trebor is arrested and tried for "vice". Kate imagined this referred to the fact that Freud and his disciples spent their time discussing sex. But was it a joke – like making the great mind doctor into a specialist in skeletons – meant to suggest the ignorance of the general public? Their willingness to make a martyr of a great man? Or did it suggest a homosexual bond between Tausk and Freud? Or was it a disguised criticism of Freud himself? Kate wasn't sure. Like Tausk, Jutta's brother kills himself, stabbing himself in a jealous rage when Jutta visits Trebor in his room – just as Lou used to visit Freud.

This visit scene was especially puzzling to Kate. Instead of welcoming the young girl, Trebor violently repels her. Freud had never pushed Lou away in any sense. But he had certainly repulsed Tausk. Pushed him downstairs so to speak. In Lou's story, Jutta has a misshapen twin brother, Gottlieb, who assures her that Trebor "repulsed" her, not out of antipathy, but to protect her because he knew she was in danger. While Jutta weeps hysterically, Gottlieb insists that Trebor had repulsed her "for her own good." As a character, the twin didn't work for Kate, but the repeated word "repulse" kept nagging at her – it positively seethed with overheated emotion.

Equally bewildering was Jutta's subsequent dream. After her twin leaves, Jutta goes to bed and dreams that Trebor is on trial as a fraud or forger. If Trebor is Freud, in what sense could Freud be thought of as a forger or falsifier?

Kate's head was beginning to ache, and she thought she'd gone as far as she could for the moment. Of course, not everything had to correspond to a real event, maybe she was trying too hard. She wondered if she should ask Helene to help her. Kate would have liked to figure it all out herself, but if anyone could decipher more of Lou's overwrought drama, she thought it would be Freud's other darling, Helene.

Kate said she'd meet Keith for a drink at First Born, their favorite café in Morningside Heights, after his last class. He had been away for a few days at a conference at U.C. Berkeley, delivering a paper on how the civil rights struggle fed into the anti-war movement. Kate had been so busy she hadn't really missed him.

When she walked in she spotted him sitting in a back booth with a striking young black woman with a frizzy halo of hair around her head and dangling bronze earrings. They were leaning towards each other in easy intimacy, and Kate felt her stomach clench.

"I'm just going," the woman said as Kate came up. It was clear she'd been crying. She had a balled up Kleenex in her fist.

"No hurry, Steph," Keith said. "Maybe Kate will have a different perspective on your problem."

He moved over and Kate slipped in beside him.

"That's okay," Stephanie said, giving Kate an appraising look. "To tell the truth, I'm pretty much talked out."

Then she turned to Keith. "This may not be forever," she said, "things change – thank you for trying to help." She slid out of the booth. "This is for my coffee," she dropped some change on the table. "See you in class."

"It's really too bad that she had to get in a power struggle with Wally," Keith said after she left. "She's one of the few black women in the activist group, in the graduate program too. She was trying to speak on the need for more blacks in leadership roles, and Wally kept interrupting her, wouldn't let her finish."

"He probably wouldn't have done it if she were a man," Kate said.

"Maybe. But the upshot is she's leaving SDS. It's a nasty business."

"I'm sorry," Kate said. Then she called the waiter over and ordered a beer. Keith was still nursing his large ale.

When the beer came, she slipped it slowly, holding Keith's hand, then asked him how the conference had gone. "I was a little afraid of hostile questions, but it was really a friendly audience. Well, what do you expect at Berkeley?" He paused and studied her.

"You're a little pale. What is it? Have you gotten your period? It must be nearly three weeks late by now."

She hadn't planned to tell him yet, but somehow she blurted it out: "Actually, no. I've got my tests back – they're positive."

Keith's face lit up. Kate felt excitement exploding through him in a rush.

"That's wonderful, sweetheart," he wrapped his arm around her and pulled her as close as he could in the cramped space between bench and table. "We'll get married. We could get a license tomorrow. . . ." His words came out in eager bursts. "I want us to be a family. You can move into my apartment. It's bigger, and it's subsidized by the University." He held her back a little and looked into her face.

"It sounds so cozy, so sweet," she hid her face against his shoulder, "and I love you for wanting to plunge right in . . . but . . ."

"What is it then?" he asked.

"I'm not sure. Even if I decide to have the baby, I'm not sure about getting married. I've seen too many friends change afterwards. . . ."

"Are you sure it's for the worse?" he asked gently, releasing her and sitting back.

"Yes, maybe, if they give up things they're passionate about. One of my women's group moved to the suburbs when she married, gave up a job she loved. She's so depressed she can't even take care of her baby properly. I'd have to be sure that wasn't going to happen to me."

"Remember I was born in Brooklyn. I'm a city guy," he said in a heavy Brooklyn accent. "I ain't gonna take you to no suburb." He waited for her to laugh but she just managed a weak smile. "And," he went on more seriously, "I'm certainly not going to ask you to give up your work."

"You might not ask, but it might happen anyway," she said. Sometimes marriage and pregnancy seemed to her like mysterious illnesses – prognosis uncertain.

"It would be easier for me in a way if I'd fallen in love with someone who only wanted to stay home, make dinner and press my shirts, but I fell in love with you, Kate. We're both scared but . . ." he tried to put his arm around her again, "but don't worry, it will work out."

"How can you be so sure it will work out?" she said, her voice growing more shrill. "I don't even know if I want the baby. I've tried to tell you . . . but you can't seem to hear me, and I can't talk about it any more. Now, please, leave me alone." She stood up. "I'm going back to the apartment."

"Don't worry about it. I'll be back late," he said.

As soon as she got away from the café, she dissolved into tears. She was as angry at herself as she was at him. After all, she was just showing him that he was right to think of her as hysterical, needing a clear-thinking male to plan her future.

When she got back to her apartment, she heard the phone ringing before she opened the door but by the time she'd let herself in, it had stopped.

Kate went into the bathroom, threw some cold water on her face and blew her nose; when the phone rang again she picked it up.

"Hello" she said softly. She thought it might be Keith, but it wasn't, it was Rachel, the agent from Rivington's.

"Oh, good, I'm glad you're home." Rachel breathed. "I wanted to tell you how excited I am about your new idea. Structuring your material like a detective story is brilliant. I think this could have a big market. People love scandals."

"I wouldn't call it scandal exactly," Kate said. "But it does show a less appealing aspect of Freud's personality."

"And the triangles with the women, Lou and Helene. We could call it 'Lovers and Rivals' or 'Deadly Triangles.'"

"I haven't gotten that far," Kate said. She would have let her call it 'Love and Death in old Vienna,' she was so thrilled by the excitement she heard in Rachel's voice. "I want it to be my project, help you develop it."

"I'd love to work with you," Kate said.

"I'd like you to write up a proposal for the 'Freud and Women' too. It may take some time shopping it around, but I may be able to get you a two-book contract."

"That would be fantastic! Thank you."

Rachel told her not to thank her yet but she was hopeful. It sounded like she had some good contacts at places like Random House and Farrar Straus. When Kate hung up she sat for a few minutes just hugging herself.

The next morning she woke up feeling woozy. She'd meant to put some salt crackers next to the bed but with so much going on, had forgotten them. She sat up slowly, trying not to be overcome by nausea, then walked gingerly to the bathroom, getting there just in time to heave into the bowl.

After she threw up, she felt a little better and dragged herself to the kitchen where she made some weak tea and nibbled a saltine. A few minutes later Keith came in, rubbing his eyes.

"Hi Keith," she said.

"Hi." Kate could see the hurt in his eyes. "I'm baffled," he said after a minute. "I don't know what to do or say to you."

"I really am sorry," she said weakly, "but I can't just sweep the problem under the rug, and I can't solve it instantly either. Leaving aside the marriage question for the moment, I just don't know if I'll be able to keep on working if I have this baby. I just got another call from Rachel, that agent I told you about. I might be working on two books instead of one. . . ." Keith's look darkened.

"I do know I'd be missing something if I didn't have a child," she added, when he kept silent. "I wouldn't feel complete as a woman. She saw his eyes take on a slightly warmer shade of green. "But it doesn't need to be now. Not when I'm just getting started, and so many possibilities are opening up. And I'm still young, I'm only twenty-eight. We have lots of time to have a baby. Why should we have one now when . . ." she ground to a halt.

"Take a look at the research," Keith told her, "the best childbearing years are almost over for you. I read just last week in the *Times* that after thirty-two your eggs start going bad. So it's harder to conceive and there's a much greater chance of birth defects," he grimaced.

"But look at all the fertility work they're doing now. Lots of women are having babies when they're in their mid-thirties. I know someone who had a baby at thirty-eight."

"And we know someone who had a baby with Down's Syndrome – my cousin Lucy."

"She was young, Keith, not more than twenty-five, so that's really not relevant . . . and please . . . don't try to scare me, that won't work."

"All right," Keith said, just managing to suppress his frustration. "Let's say you manage to have a child in your mid-thirties, but what happens if you want more than one? I know I do. You try but you have trouble getting pregnant. All of a sudden you wake up one morning and you're nearly forty and you don't have a choice anymore. Is it that I won't help you? That you'll be left alone with a pile of dirty diapers? I'll help. . . ."

"How much? I won't need you just to put on a diaper once in a while or give a bottle, I'll need a real partner. I don't think you realize how much work is involved looking after another human being twenty-four hours a day. Besides, it doesn't seem right to go ahead and have a baby now just because of some vague fear I won't be able to later. It has to be something I want, want badly."

"But it's a fact already, don't you see? This isn't some hypothetical problem. There's a baby in there." He gestured towards her belly. "Do you want to get rid of it? Are you are just going to . . ."

Kate interrupted. "I need time to think . . . and I will, I promise . . . but give me some time . . . okay, Keith . . . I do love you, if that's any help."

"That just makes it worse." he said, "I'm going over to my place" and he strode out, slamming the door.

Two days later, Kate was no nearer to making a decision, and Helene was coming over to the apartment in five minutes. Kate had dropped off Lou's story for Helene to read before they met, and despite her worries, she was immensely curious to know what Helene made of it.

"What did you think?" she asked, as soon as she'd poured their tea.

"It's fascinating," Helene said, taking a bite of a proffered oatmeal cookie, "and of course you're right about the triangle."

"So you agree that Trebor is Freud, and Jutta is Lou? Though it's a something of a stretch to see her as an innocent girl in pigtails!"

Helene laughed. "Yes, she was far from that. But you are forgetting the hunchback twin Gottlieb. That's probably Lou's other half, her intellectual side."

"Why didn't I think of that," Kate said. "He is studious, his eyes are bloodshot from reading, and he has ink-stained fingers. I guess I took him more as a comic figure."

'No, I think he represents Lou's intellectual side, her twisted mind. And also, perhaps, a twisted part of Freud. The grossness of the charge against Trebor, that he is a sex criminal, convinces me that Lou was deeply shocked and repelled by Freud's letter after Tausk's death." Helene sat back with a satisfied look.

"If that's how she felt in private," Kate said, "It's hard to see how she managed to agree with Freud publicly. Moral repulsion. As feelings go, that's pretty strong."

"I think she tried hard to see Freud's frailties as part of his greatness."

"And how about you?" Kate asked, stung by a hint of agreement in Helene's voice. "Do you feel that way too? Did Freud's genius allow him license to act badly?"

"There are sins of omission and sins of commission," Helene said cryptically.

"A man was destroyed. . . ."

"Tausk took his own life. . . ."

Kate could see she was making Helene defensive. She tried another tack.

"When Tausk started analysis with you, you said that he seemed no more than ordinarily neurotic. Did that change?"

"Perhaps he became more fixated on Freud, I can't be sure. Freud mentioned to me in one of my sessions that Tausk had written him and asked him to analyze his son Marius. Apparently Marius had reported some troubling dreams – and Tausk thought that whatever Freud's reasons for not taking him into analysis, they wouldn't hold for his son."

"How humiliating for him to have to ask that, "Kate winced.

"It just made Freud more confident that he had made the right decision."

"Didn't he guess that sending Tausk to you when you were in analysis would encourage Tausk's obsession with him?"

"We didn't understand much about transference back then. After all, Freud analyzed his own daughter."

"Analyzed Anna! But I haven't read that anywhere."

"It was an open secret. He mentioned it in his letters. It was right after the First World War. No one would even think of such a thing now. He analyzed other relatives and favorite pupils as well. I think he had some doubts about Anna later. He worried that she had a father fixation."

"After his analysis had hardened it? How extraordinary." Whew. The analytic situation seemed to allow these first analysts to work without being aware of their cruelties.

"Freud asked Lou to help tear Anna loose – though of course he was as stuck on her as he was on his cigars. Lou refused; she thought Anna's incestuous relationship with Freud was more blissful than any alternative."

"That sounds like pandering to me . . . she's making him God. And he doesn't object. She's becoming a sort of wife to him – or daughter." The puzzle seemed to be falling into place.

"In his old age, he referred to her as his alter ego," Helene admitted grudgingly. "She once told me he said that he called the tune – mostly a simple one – and she supplied the higher octaves. He tore down, she made lovely order."

"A love duet! So he flattered her too." There was no way Tausk would have fit into Freud's fictive household.

"He could flatter, yes." Helene tilted her head, opening her green eyes wide, in an echo of what must have been once a fetching gesture.

"Do you think refusing Tausk and sending him to you could have been Freud's revenge for Tausk's temerity in loving Lou? It still seems like a devilish arrangement."

"I told you that Freud thought I could handle it – but it did put me in a difficult position. As for revenge, I don't know. I think Freud was very well aware of his advancing age and afraid of being overthrown. You know already that Freud told Dr. Brinner he was afraid that Tausk would kill him."

"What was really strange was that shortly after Tausk's suicide, Anna – who was completely identified with her father – dreamed that Tausk's fiancée had rented an apartment across from Freud's in Vienna with the intention of shooting him."

"By then it was too late for anyone to change Freud's mind. But earlier you said you became Tausk's advocate. Did you try to counteract Freud's negative view of him?"

"I did. I spent much of my own session with Freud talking about Tausk. I stressed his devotion, but also his yearning for more appreciation. Sometimes I gave Freud the particulars of Tausk's complaint – chapter and verse of what he felt had been appropriated or borrowed or not appreciated as an original contribution."

"How did Freud respond?"

"He was clearly annoyed. He said that Tausk was weaving a web of innuendo around me. Once he even suggested – during analysis of a dream of mine – that I was falling in love with him. He felt it sapped my own energy for analysis."

"And were you in love with him?"

"I was drawn to him, no doubt – perhaps he slid into my dreams. Freud told me Tausk was using me to attack him. He spoke of him as a wild boar and said I was in danger of being hollowed out by his tusks, that I wasn't the first woman he had tried to use that way, but that he, Freud, was the one he wanted to gouge."

Kate noted the animal metaphor. "It must have been difficult to keep defending Tausk in the face of that sort of pressure."

Helene looked at her gratefully. "It was . . ."

"But you kept on?"

There was silence for a moment. "I did what I could – but there came a point . . ." she stopped again.

"Yes?" Kate felt her heart beating faster.

"When it wasn't working. Freud said quite bluntly he'd given it a chance but that my fascination with Tausk was undermining my own analysis. I had to choose between breaking off my analysis with him or ending my analysis of Tausk." She paused, taking in Kate's horrified expression. "It never seemed like a choice to me. More like an order." Now she was rushing to get it over with. "I explained to Tausk the next day that it was the end of his analysis."

"Just like that?" Kate couldn't believe what she was hearing. "But that must have been awful for him. First to be refused by Freud and then you . . . though he must have known the order came from Freud."

"People terminated for all sorts of reasons back then on very short notice," Helene said stiffening. "It wasn't like now where it takes six months of preparation."

"And he didn't object or try to change your mind? No, I imagine he wouldn't have. And then a few months later . . ." Kate didn't need to say the words. They both knew what happened that July.

"I've always thought of Tausk as Freud's case, Freud's suicide," Helene said slowly. "I said to myself that if Freud had admitted responsibility for what he did, he would have gone off and killed himself. I did everything to avoid seeing my part in it. If you'd asked me how I felt about patients who took their lives in my care – I would have said I didn't have any suicides, never lost a patient. If you asked, but what about Tausk? I would have said, no, he was Freud's. But I was complicit. If I didn't quite realize it yet myself, your expression would convince me of it." She folded her hands and sat very still.

"Well," she asked softly after a moment, "where are we now? Do you want to keep talking to me?"

Kate had to admire the calmness with which she sat there waiting for judgment. Various answers came to her mind. The most visceral was negative. No, no I don't want to keep talking to you, that was a horrible thing to do. But she knew that she was hardly objective. In fact, she was close to tears just because she liked Helene so much. She didn't want to lose her vision of Helene as kind and, more important, wise. Yes, that was a horrible thing to do, but if Kate were being fair, she could see it was complicated.

Freud was not only the person Helene depended on for referrals but for her whole position in the movement. After her analysis, Freud made her head of the Vienna Psychoanalytic Society. A fantastic position of authority for a woman. She had a lifetime of work, of useful work, of important work ahead of her. If she'd left Freud then, how much of that could she have done?

But was that the point? How could you trust someone who sacrificed another human being to her own careerism? But Helene couldn't have known what was going to happen. Didn't know how strong a blow it was. And Kate still didn't know what else might have occurred in Tausk's last months. There was the whole relationship with her grandmother to consider. Kate knew already that he hadn't wanted her mother to be born, but she didn't know anything about their relationship. She'd known her grandmother only as an old woman.

"I'm grateful to you for telling me," she said finally. "You didn't have to. I think you wanted to help me."

"And myself . . . if I'm going to make an honest accounting of my life, I don't have much time left. So you see I'm selfish here, too . . ." she said, as if she knew what Kate had been thinking.

"Do you think," Kate finally asked, "that he might not have killed himself if you hadn't sent him away?"

"That was the first thing I thought of when Freud told me," Helene said her lips drawn into a thin line.

"So you did feel responsible!"

"But I didn't hold onto it, I carried my responsibility in my hands. I took it to Freud. I said, 'Perhaps if I hadn't sent Tausk away, he would have lived.'"

"How did he respond?"

"He said, very coldly, 'But you made the right choice, you chose yourself.'" Helene could still hear the disembodied voice floating up from behind her. "I was lying on the couch and I twisted my head to look at his face. It was perfectly calm, as though what he said was quite obvious. I can see now he didn't want me to feel too guilty. He was probably afraid it would paralyze me in my work." She sighed. "He was giving me permission not to blame myself. And I'm afraid I took it."

Kate imagined herself stretched out on Freud's couch. Wasn't the idea of analysis to induce regression, to make yourself dependent as a child? That would have made it harder to resist Freud's version of things, but Kate noticed Helene wasn't taking that defense.

"I had my own reasons for being willing to let Tausk go," she said in a low voice. "I was fascinated by him, obsessed with his genius. I didn't admit it to myself, not then, actually not until now. It could only have been disastrous. My marriage, my child, my career. . . ."

"So in some sense you may have felt as though Freud was rescuing you from an impossible situation, helping you keep your life together."

"It never crossed my mind that Freud had old scores to settle," Helene said with some bitterness.

"That he was getting back at you? But why?"

"Not at me – but it had all happened before," she explained, "with Lou and Tausk. Tausk's loving Lou. Freud didn't brook competitors. With Lou he had to go softly. She was nearly his age, she was a famous woman. I was a thirty-four-year-old beginner. . . ." Kate noticed a quickly suppressed smile flit over Helene's face.

"Having Freud act like a possessive lover must have been immensely flattering," Kate said dryly. "I know you broke with Warner-Jauregg for similar reasons and had nothing more to do with him. But how was it with Tausk? Were you able to keep up any contact with him? Or didn't you want to?"

"There was such a short time – from the end of March when analysis ended, to the beginning of July," Helene blushed slightly, "when he killed himself. But he did give a paper to the Society – so I saw him there." She hesitated, "he was cordial as always, didn't seem to hold a grudge."

"But you had no more intimate conversations."

"Just once. Somehow I mentioned that I had recently seen a small volume on war neuroses and was surprised he wasn't included since I knew he had written about them. Too late, I remembered that he had complained to me in our sessions about his work on war neurosis being ignored. I don't think he meant to say anything, but once he started he couldn't stop himself:

"'Were you?' he asked me angrily. 'Well, I expected to be asked to speak at the Budapest Congress, from which those papers are taken. But I've had expectations for a long while. The truth of the matter is that Herr Professor Freud wouldn't let me speak.'

"'Why not?' I stammered, wishing I hadn't brought up an obviously painful topic. 'Because,' Viktor said, 'he'd assigned the subject to a group of dignitaries – men from the international organization, who hadn't been in the war at all. Just because it looked good on the program.'

"I guess Tausk was embarrassed about his outburst because he sent me a note saying that relations with Freud had improved since he no longer sought them – having been cured of his desire for them. I was foolish enough to think that in my brief therapy, I had managed to help him overcome his dependency."

She shook her head. "Of course I was all wrong. I should have urged him to move away, go to Belgrade as his lady friend had wished, or, if he couldn't stomach that, move away from Vienna, away from Freud.

"I did remind Tausk that he'd done his best work when he was separated from him. I told Tausk to go to Berlin and be analyzed by Abraham.That's what I did myself a few years later. If Freud hadn't had such mixed motives he would have suggested that himself. I hate thinking about it. I wanted so much to help him. Such a waste, such a compelling, brilliant man . . ." she paused close to tears. "Soon afterward I heard that he had met a beautiful young woman – your grandmother. That he was thinking of marrying. I felt relieved that things seemed to be going well for him."

"But he'd had a history of failed relationships," Kate said, "Didn't you ever think that he might be reacting to your sending him away? Love on the re-bound."

"It passed through my mind, especially . . ." Helene stopped short.

Kate looked at her quizzically.

"I suppose I didn't want to face how much I'd hurt him," Helene finished. Kate had the impression that that wasn't what she had been going to say. That she was suppressing another thought. "I met Hilde once," she went on, "after a recital where she was playing, she was a talented young woman – perhaps too young.

She looked barely out of her teens. I didn't see her again until the funeral. There was some sort of quarrel about who should sit in the front at the service. Tausk's sisters thought Martha should have been there with her sons, but Martha had apparently said Hilde could be there too." She stopped abruptly, put her hand to her forehead.

"What is it?" Kate asked, "do you have a headache?"

"I just remembered the little note Tausk sent me saying he wouldn't be coming to our usual Wednesday meeting of the Psychoanalytic Society because he was busy solving the decisive affairs of his life and didn't want, by contact with Freud, to be tempted to ask him for help."

Kate observed a look of pain pass over Helene's face.

"Freud told me that Tausk had written him too, he showed the letter to me because he thought I'd be pleased at Tausk's saying that soon he'd be free to approach Freud, with a minimum of neuroses. Freud thought that I had helped him – that he was reining in his impulses. Tausk signed his letter graciously, saying that he remained cordial, respectful, and grateful."

"So Freud had set you to tame the beast," Kate said.

"I don't know about taming," Helene said sadly, "but he did think that I'd be good at imposing limits. I suppose because I'd so successfully imposed them on myself."

"I guess Freud took Tausk's expressions of gratitude as no more than his due," Kate said, "but they seem frightfully excessive to me." She reflected that Freud hadn't analyzed Helene's positive feelings towards him either. "They remind me of those footnotes in Tausk's paper, 'On the Influencing Machine.' It's as though he's struggling to remain loyal in spite of the way Freud is treating him. Tausk still desperately needed him," Kate concluded.

"Being a full grown human being is hard," Helene was saying. "Some succeed better than others." She sat with her hands in her lap. "Tausk had such a strong wish to be passive, to be loved; even when he was most rebellious, it was there underneath."

Kate suddenly remembered that in Lou's story, just before Jutta's brother killed himself, he stood outside Dr. Trebor's door and, unaware of what he was doing, frantically whispered 'come, come, come.' "Do you think he imagined Freud would appear suddenly and save him, forgive him?"

"I have no doubt Freud could have saved him, but I've told you that. All the rest, I know from Emil. The boy – he was a teenager then – came to me after the funeral and we talked. He was full of guilt for not being able to prevent it. Of course I told him it was in no way his fault.

"Tausk seemed preoccupied but not overly so. Then one morning, early, he was summoned to his father's house by the police. Tausk's body had been taken to the morgue. Emil said he was in shock and couldn't understand. He wanted to see his father's body. They told him he couldn't, he wouldn't recognize him – he was disfigured, the bullet had destroyed his head. Emil became suspicious that there was a mistake that it was someone else. He felt sure that someone had broken into the house, a thief, and murdered him – robbed and murdered him.

"Finally the officer had taken him into the woodshed and shown him how his father had done it, shown him the army pistol they'd found on the floor beneath the body – finger prints had already been taken – acted it out showing poor Emil how his father had put the curtain cord around his neck, then pressed the pistol to his temple and fired. It blew off the top of his head, the man had told him. He'd never seen a man so determined to die. As he fell, he strangled himself. The officer told Emil to take it like a man – he was seventeen, almost old enough for the army."

Helene noted Kate's look of amazement.

"It turned out the policeman had lost a son in the war – Emil found out later – he didn't sympathize with the son of this no doubt well-off doctor who had heedlessly taken his life. Besides it was a sin and he was a religious Catholic.

"When Emil calmed himself enough to be able to listen, the officer showed him the will with all his father's possessions noted down in a careful hand. Everything itemized down to the smallest detail. His nineteen boxes of books. You see, the officer said, he was quite determined. By that time Hilde had arrived and found the carefully prepared letter addressed to Freud, and the half-empty bottle of Slivovitz Tausk had sipped while he wrote."

"Yes," Kate said bitterly. "The letter saying how grateful he was to have been in Freud's movement, but I think he left another message," Kate said. "If we know how to read it. Otherwise why would he kill himself twice? One death was for himself, the other for Freud . . . he killed himself instead of killing Freud."

Kate felt she couldn't sit still another moment. She got up. "I have to go . . . walk, think . . . figure out where this leaves me. . . ."

Helene gave her a deeply sorrowful look, then sat still without saying a word. There was nothing more to say.

Two days later, when Kate came back from getting some groceries, she found a scribbled note from Keith that her mother had called and was having stomach trouble. She'd called back a second and third time and finally Keith suggested she'd better go to the Emergency Room at Mount Sinai and have it checked out. He would have taken her except he had a class. But she said she could manage, the doorman would get her a cab.

Kate wasn't unduly alarmed – there was a wicked stomach flu going around – she put her groceries away and phoned the ER. Her mother, the overworked attendant told her, had been taken somewhere. Maybe she should try intensive care. The ICU nurse who answered the phone asked if she was a relative. When Kate said she was, the nurse told her that Emily had had a heart attack.

"A heart attack!" Kate felt her own heart pounding wildly and sat down next to the phone. "Are you sure?" she asked when she had caught her breath.

"If you want to know more about her condition, you'll have to speak to the doctor," the nurse said huffily. Kate flushed but she couldn't rid herself of the thought that her mother was just having an anxiety attack, the way she had when she'd collapsed in a Japanese restaurant after an argument.

She grabbed her purse off the chair back, scrawled a note for Keith and ran over to Broadway. A cab was just coming along with its lights on. As it bumped and swerved its way through traffic, Kate wondered if she'd find Emily sitting up in bed perfectly fine. She imagined her making some lame joke about practically having to die to get Kate's attention.

But when Kate got to the hospital ten minutes later, her mother wasn't sitting up in bed, she was flat on her back hooked up to a respirator, a thick tube down her throat. Plastic bags hung from poles next to her bed and lines ran in and out of her body.

"Mom," Kate said, collapsing into the yellow plastic chair by the bed. She took Emily's limp hand, careful not to jostle the tube taped to her inner arm and tried again. "Mom. It's me, Kate."

A young doctor pushed aside the curtain and came in behind her.

"I don't think she can hear you," he offered. "She's deeply unconscious."

"What happened?" Kate asked. "Why all this . . ." she gestured at the whirring machines.

"She came in complaining of nausea and bad diarrhea. While she was waiting to be seen, she had a heart attack. Luckily for her, she was already in the hospital and we were able to resuscitate her."

Kate was having trouble grasping that this was real. "Resuscitate?"

"Her heart stopped. We had to apply paddles – electric shocks," he added, when she looked blank. "It's standard procedure in the ER. If she has another attack during the night, we'll do it again unless we have a living will stating categorically that she doesn't want it. Does your mother have a living will?"

"I don't think so. She's never mentioned it."

"Well, then . . ." he said, with a slight edge of impatience.

"But I think she wouldn't want to be kept alive by extreme means," Kate said. She'd seen her mother's horrified reaction when her friend Mary had been kept on a breathing machine and force-fed, like a stuffed goose. "Not if she's going to be badly damaged. But is she? Can she recover?"

"It's hard to say . . . we'll know more when she becomes conscious . . . if she does."

Kate noted that her own heart was beating faster.

"The thing I'm worried about right now is her lungs," his young face tightened.

"What's the matter with them?" Kate asked, wishing she'd retained more of her high school biology.

"They're filling with fluid . . . a lot depends on how she gets through the night. Tomorrow morning if she's still stable, we'll think about draining them. Don't worry," he added kindly, "we're doing all we can. She's otherwise healthy. I'm cautiously optimistic." He pulled back the curtain that separated her mother's bed from the nursing station, nodded at Kate and stepped outside.

In the sudden silence Kate heard the whoosh of the machine working her mother's lungs. She let go of Emily's hand for a minute and brought her plastic chair a little closer to her mother's head.

"Mom," she said touching her mother's face gently, "can you hear me? I know you can't talk with that thing down your throat but try to open your eyes."

There was no response.

Kate had often blamed Emily for having a face that expressed everything she thought – even when she tried to hide her feelings, you could see them in her eyes, or the slight pucker of her disapproving lips. Now with her eyes closed, and her mouth distended around a tube, her mother looked like someone else. Someone Kate didn't know. But still, the perfect oval of her mother's face with its clear high cheek bones was beautiful. Kate was surprised that she had never quite noticed that before.

She suddenly remembered that she'd read that people in comas can hear. Hesitantly, she started to talk. She told her mother about finding the diary and meeting her uncles.

"Marius is terribly repressed and up-tight" – she paused thinking of her last encounter with him at the library – "but I don't think he's a bad man, and Emil is delightful." As she was telling Emily what she liked about Emil, it struck Kate that the qualities she reacted to so positively – Emil's responsiveness and openness – were just the things that most annoyed her in her mother.

"I think you'd like each other," Kate said, meaning it.

"Emil's an artist too, Mom," she said, thinking that was something they both shared with her grandfather. "He does wonderful wooden statues that look like Egyptian Gods. You could show him your watercolors. You know that one of the blue bird or the dancing couple surrounded by jazz musicians. I love those. . . ."

She thought she saw her mother's eyelids flicker. She hardly ever told her mother that she liked her work. Now she imagined Emil kissing Emily on both cheeks, telling her how full of joy her watercolors were, or talking with her about Viktor, telling her that she had nothing to be ashamed of in her father. That in fact, in some ways, in her artistic talent, her magnetic personality and even in her looks, she resembled him.

"Maybe Emil could even help you get a gallery," Kate said. "But even if he can't, I think you've missed a lot by not having him in your life. He's your half-brother . . . he's family. I certainly want to have him in mine."

Kate talked on for hours until her throat got hoarse and she finally took a break to go down to the cafeteria for lunch. When she came back to the cubicle her mother gave no sign of consciousness. "I haven't talked to you much about my thesis," she said and stopped, realizing that she didn't really want to talk about it right now.

"I'm pregnant," she blurted out instead, "and I can't decide whether to have the baby . . . Keith really wants it."

As she repeated bits of their arguments to her mother, she suddenly remembered an incident she'd forgotten until now. When she was about three, she'd looked up from a doll she was rocking to see her father smiling at her. She'd asked him if he'd like to take her baby doll for a walk and he'd paced slowly beside her with a serious expression, helping her push her baby carriage. The next day he left home. His departure was one of the many things her mother wouldn't discuss.

"Dad loved me," Kate said now. "Whatever happened between you two, I think he really loved me."

That night Kate woke up after a couple of hours of exhausted sleep, tossing and turning, trying to find a comfortable position.

"Can't sleep?" Keith asked her softly. "Come lie close, put your head on my shoulder."

Kate hesitated, remembering their recent quarrel and the fact that nothing was settled – but his voice was tender and he had been very sympathetic when she told him that her mother was in the ICU. With a sigh, she moved closer, comforted by the heat of his body.

"I'm feeling bad," she said softly, "not just because Mom's so sick, but because I was so sure at first that she was exaggerating her symptoms. It seemed so unlikely at her age, and she'd never had any sort of trouble. I even thought maybe she was just having a fit of nerves. I refused to believe it when the nurse said she had had a heart attack. Am I a monster or what?"

He stroked her hair. "A bit set on your own view of things maybe, but definitely not a monster. Denial is a natural reaction to bad news. And even if you had some ungenerous thoughts, from what you told me when you came back from the ICU, you more than made up for them when you saw her. I think you were wonderful to keep talking to her the way you did."

"Do you? It's funny but once I started talking, there was suddenly so much I wanted to tell her, things I wanted to talk over with her . . . for the first time really . . . I can't have her die on me now . . . it's too soon."

Keith kissed her cheek. "I know, baby."

"I'm not ready," she went on, "I thought I'd have plenty of time to work on our relationship. I knew I needed to . . . I'm so irritable with her, and often she's not really doing anything wrong. It's not really her fault that she grates on my nerves."

She could feel Keith nodding his assent.

"I always thought that maybe later when I had children – she sensed Keith's body tense but kept on – "maybe I'd start seeing her as helpful instead of . . . oh, I don't know," She started to cry.

"People recover from heart attacks."

"But what if she wakes up and has to be in a wheel chair, what if she can't lift her spoon to feed herself? What if she can't talk?"

"I think she'd be able to cope with a lot, as long as her mind was working . . . as for the rest there's no point in torturing yourself until you see how things go."

"You're right. . . . Thanks," Kate said, trying not to think of the electric paddles.

"I've had some thoughts about us," Keith whispered, "but for now I just want to say . . . I'm sorry she's so ill."

"Me too," Kate said. She wanted to say something more but before she could form another sentence she fell asleep.

By morning the next day, Emily was propped up against some pillows, fading in and out of consciousness. They'd taken out the breathing tube but when she tried to speak her speech was slurred. Keith went right over and kissed her. Oddly, what struck Kate most, what brought her close to tears was that her mother's hair hadn't been combed; it was completely unkempt. Emily may have dressed eccentrically, but she never let her hair go – her hair and her nails were always impeccably groomed.

"How're you doing?" Kate asked her.

Emily just looked at them, flicked her tongue over her dry lips. Kate had a little collapsible brush in her purse and took it out and started to gently brush her mother's hair.

The nurse said Emily could eat some Jello, if Kate would like to feed her.

"Don't worry about me," Keith said, "I brought a book. There's a chair. I'll be out in the hall if you need me."

So Kate sat and spooned tiny bits of Jello into her mother's mouth.

When Kate had had her tonsils out as a child, she'd refused to feed herself for a few days after she came home from the hospital. Only ate when her mother had fed her. And only strawberry Jello.

"I know I've been difficult," Kate said, thinking she might not get another chance to say it. "A pain in the ass sometimes."

"You're good to me," her mother struggled with the words that all sounded blurred, barely understandable, "a good daughter."

Kate knew what her mother said was nonsense but she felt comforted all the same.

Her mother tried to say something more, though except for the words 'left' and 'gift,' it was unintelligible. Later, she realized her mother was trying to tell her where her will was.

At quarter past ten, the young doctor showed up – Keith followed him through the curtain.

As soon as she saw the doctor, Emily made a terrific effort. "Am I dying?" she asked him. He held her wrist. "Pulse isn't bad," he said, not answering. Then he turned to Kate.

"So we have to decide about draining the lungs," he said.

Emily shook her head vigorously – she no longer seemed able to speak.

"But she doesn't want it, "Kate said. "Let's go outside and talk."

"If it will help her breathe, I think you should do it, Kate," Keith said when they had left the room and gone down the hall.

"Won't it just draw things out? I feel as if we're torturing her."

"It's not like keeping her on permanent life support," the doctor said, "and by the way, I did try to speak to her about taking extreme measures. I got the impression that she's not ready to give up on life . . . but she's too confused and frightened to be consistent. If she seemed agitated just now, she probably doesn't understand that this is just a diuretic to flush out the lungs and see if they can start working better."

"Okay" Kate said. "I guess that's okay. Go ahead."

But it wasn't okay. The hospital called at 5 a.m. and told Kate her mother had had another attack in the night. They weren't able to save her.

Kate made arrangements for her mother's body to be taken to the undertakers, and for a small funeral, just family, then she told Keith she needed to be alone for a while. She walked the length of Manhattan before she was able to cry – all the way to the Brooklyn Bridge. Compromised as her mother was in the end Kate hadn't been willing to give up, to tell them not to try and save her – they tried but they couldn't. Kate hated most the waste . . . the waste of good years they might have had.

She found herself remembering a time – she must have been eight or nine – when a teacher had accused her of cheating and her mother had taken her by the hand and rushed to school to confront him, never for a minute doubting her. As Kate stood there, other memories came, small moments but fitting together like the squares of a patchwork quilt. Hadn't much of what Emily had done . . . even keeping those maddening secrets . . . been part of a fierce effort to nurture and protect her daughter?

Kate looked at the water. How many people had jumped off a bridge like this, she wondered, and what did they feel like when they did it? She tried to imagine what it felt like being so hopeless that it seemed like the only solution. She couldn't. She was repelled by it, didn't think she would do it even if she was terminally ill. A weight lifted from her mind . . . she wouldn't, she couldn't . . . she felt a vast relief.

But what about her brother? He might have said the same thing the year before he died. Tausk and her brother had became confused in her mind. Usually, she tried not to think about him, furious that he had left her the way he did . . . or sometimes, feeling that she should have known, should have talked to him somehow found the right words to help.

Looking over the edge at the gulls floating below, she realized that her brother hadn't actually planned to die. He had been miserable and angry over his girl's leaving him . . . wanted to hit or scream . . . needed the medicine of physical movement, the powerful catch of the wind in his sails. She saw him readying the boat, hoisting the sails, moving carefully out into the harbor. The medicine was working. As he moved past the headlands, the boat became part of his body, both of them triumphant against the wind that was tearing at him, buffeting his sail. He shouted back at it, held the jib firm, wrapping the rope around his arm – though he knew one should never do that.

The rules didn't seem to apply . . . the storm was outside him now, black waves, not misery but only water. . . . He shouted into it, water streaming over his face . . . challenged it. He could beat it, ride it out. He was too busy holding the tiller heading the boat slantwise into the waves, to feel any grief . . . or any caution. By the time he realized that the boat was foundering, it was too late . . . blackness, black waves black sky.

But even if he had killed himself, what did it matter really, Kate thought, to her and what she had in her belly? She was sure her mother had been afraid of tainted genes, but hardly anyone believed in them anymore. It occurred to her, now that she knew as much as she did about her grandfather, that it didn't make as much difference as she thought it would. Yes, he was a flawed man – tragically flawed even – but the others were flawed too. Lou and Freud and even Helene, whom she'd thought so perfect. Seeing how Lou and Helene had faced their choices, how they knuckled under to Freud or worse, in Lou's case, manipulated and deceived, Kate resolved she would try to do things differently.

Still, at least for Helene, it was an impossible situation. Kate felt a surge of compassion. How hard it must have been for Helene to live with the fact that she had dismissed her friend Viktor, with such devastating results, in order to secure her future with Freud. It was to her credit that she had dredged the whole story up again for Kate. Brave, really, when she must have known Kate would want to write about her grandfather – set the record straight. She would continue to work on it, but Kate knew that she didn't want to be so driven to succeed. Not now, not ever.

Wasn't it left up to her, to make her own model, to decide what she wanted to be . . . and then be it? But wasn't that being naïve? Helene hadn't imagined that she would betray her friend anymore than she had imagined neglecting her son. Certainly she hadn't wanted to be a bad mother.

There was no question, Kate thought, that she would make her own mistakes. Put too much energy into her work, or too little. Fail to find a balance in her life with Keith – even though she loved him more than ever after seeing him with Emily. She told herself not to think about how hurt he would be because she didn't want to marry right away. It would be time enough to worry when she was ready to tell him.

Kate decided then and there that she was going to call Helene. She would tell her that Emily had died – Helene had been fond of Emily – and explain that the funeral was just for family. It occurred to her that she hadn't told her mother whether she was going to have the baby. Maybe she would even tell Helene! She suddenly wanted very much to tell her.

She stood and stretched, tossing her hair. With love and luck, she wouldn't make too much of a mess of things.

A bird settled on the railing near her and fixed her with an intent yellow eye. She ran a hand over her stomach, assessing the slight fullness.

Afterword

Regarding the relationships among Viktor Tausk, Sigmund Freud, Lou Andreas-Salomé and Helene Deutsch, I have changed some details, including dates, locations, and, in one case, the provenance of an uncensored letter of Freud's. Freud's letter to Lou after Tausk's suicide is genuine, as are Lou's response, her plays and her account of Freud's cat. Tausk's long diary and the characters of Emily, Kate, Keith, Marius and Emil are fictional (though Tausk did have two sons with those names). Hilde never gave birth to a child. She apparently had an abortion after Tausk's death.

My interpretation of Helene Deutsch's relation to Freudian theory developed while writing my essay, "Helene Deutsch: A New Look" (*Signs: Journal of Women in Culture and Society,* Spring, 1985). Deutsch's memoir, *Confrontations with Myself,* gave helpful information about her childhood. Paul Roazen's book, *Brother Animal: The Story of Freud and Tausk,* was the main source of factual material for my novel, as was his biography *Helene Deutsch: A Psychoanalyst's Life.* I am greatly indebted to him for his generosity in numerous conversations and his enthusiasm for my project.

The Freud Journal of Lou Andreas-Salomé provided the scaffolding for my invention of Tausk's diary. Rudolph Binion's psychoanalytic biography, *Frau Lou: Nietzsche's Wayward Disciple,* was also useful in understanding her character. Many other books added to my understanding of the period.

Marius's character and his defense of Freud were inspired by Dr. Kurt Eissler's books defending Freud's treatment of Tausk: *Victor Tausk's Suicide* and *Talent and Genius.*

About the Author

Brenda Webster was born in New York City, educated at Swarthmore, Barnard, Columbia, and Berkeley, where she earned her Ph.D. She is a novelist, freelance writer, critic and translator who splits her time between Berkeley and Rome. Webster has written two controversial and oft-anthologized critical studies, *Yeats: A Psychoanalytic Study* (Stanford) and *Blake's Prophetic Psychology* (Macmillan), and translated poetry from the Italian for *The Other Voice* (Norton) and *The Penguin Book of Women Poets.* She is co-editor of the journals of the abstract expressionist painter (and Webster's mother) Ethel Schwabacher, *Hungry for Light: The Journal of Ethel Schwabacher* (Indiana 1993). She is the author of three previous novels, *Sins of the Mothers* (Baskerville 1993), *Paradise Farm* (SUNY, 1999), and *The Beheading Game* (Wings Press, 2006), which was a finalist for the Northern California Book Award. Her memoir, *The Last Good Freudian* (Holmes and Meier, 2000) received considerable critical praise. The Modern Language Association published Webster's translation of Edith Bruck's Holocaust novel, *Lettera alla Madre,* in 2007.

Wings Press was founded in 1975 by Joanie Whitebird and Joseph F. Lomax, both deceased, as "an informal association of artists and cultural mythologists dedicated to the preservation of the literature of the nation of Texas." Publisher, editor and designer since 1995, Bryce Milligan is honored to carry on and expand that mission to include the finest in American writing – meaning all of the Americas – without commercial considerations clouding the choice to publish or not to publish.

Wings Press attempts to produce multicultural books, chapbooks, CDs, DVDs and broadsides that, we hope, enlighten the human spirit and enliven the mind. Every person ever associated with Wings has been or is a writer, and we know well that writing is a transformational art form capable of changing the world, primarily by allowing us to glimpse something of each other's souls. Good writing is innovative, insightful, and interesting. But most of all it is honest.

Likewise, Wings Press is committed to treating the planet itself as a partner. Thus the press uses as much recycled material as possible, from the paper on which the books are printed to the boxes in which they are shipped.

Associate editor Robert Bonazzi is also an old hand in the small press world. Bonazzi was the editor and publisher of Latitudes Press (1966-2000). Bonazzi and Milligan share a commitment to independent publishing and have collaborated on numerous projects over the past 25 years.

As Robert Dana wrote in *Against the Grain,* "Small press publishing is personal publishing. In essence, it's a matter of personal vision, personal taste and courage, and personal friendships." Welcome to our world.

WINGS PRESS

Colophon

This first edition of *Vienna Triangle,* by Brenda Webster, has been printed on 70 pound paper containing fifty percent recycled fiber. Titles have been set in Papyrus type, the text is in Adobe Caslon type. All Wings Press books are designed and produced by Bryce Milligan.

On-line catalogue and ordering
available at
www.wingspress.com

Wings Press titles are distributed
to the trade by the
Independent Publishers Group
www.ipgbook.com